THE CHILD SHE LEFT BEHIND

Wren Avery

DISCLAIMER

This is a work of fiction. Names, characters, places, and incidents are the product of the author's imagination or are used fictitiously. Any resemblance to actual persons, living or dead, events, or locales is entirely coincidental.

The story references in vitro fertilization (IVF) and related medical procedures. These elements are part of the fictional narrative and should not be interpreted as a commentary on such procedures,' morality, ethics, or efficacy. The author does not intend to provide medical advice, endorse, or criticize any medical practices or technologies.

The views, actions, and decisions of the characters in this book are entirely their own and do not necessarily reflect the author's personal opinions, beliefs, or intentions.

CHAPTER 1

"Sir? Sir? Are you Jesus?"

The timid, quivering voice drifted into Crank's subconscious. The words took root, dragging him from a deep slumber to barely awake. It had been a hell of a week, and last night was his first uninterrupted sleep. He turned on his side and jammed the pillow over his ear.

"Sir?" the voice called again. "Are you Jesus, and is this Heaven?"

The voice was muffled now, floating eerily under the pillow and into his ear. Sighing, Crank turned on his back and tossed the pillow to the floor.

"No, kid, this is not Heaven. If it were Heaven, I'd be able to get a few more hours of sleep, and I can tell that's not going to happen." Still reluctant to open his eyes and destroy any hope of more rest, he lay there, hoping the kid would go away.

Slowly turning his head toward, the small boy standing by his bed, Crank took a deep breath and finally opened his eyes.

"Why would you think I was Jesus? You think Heaven looks like this dump?"

"You... you have long hair like Jesus, and you said you were taking me to a safe place... That could be Heaven. How did I get here? Mister? Mister. I lost two teeth. Where are they? I have to leave them for the tooth fairy. I've never had one come and leave me money—but it might happen—Sir? Sir? Can you tell me why..."?

Crank sat up and lowered his feet to the floor, and the boy stepped back, his newfound bravery quickly deserting him. Who could blame him? Crank thought as he stiffly hauled his six-foot four-inch frame out of bed, stretching and scratching his chest. *I probably look like hell*. He went to the bathroom for his first piss of the day and glanced at himself in the mirror: eyes bloodshot, a week's growth of beard on his face, his long hair standing out wildly from his head. Wincing, he thought, *Damn! I look like a savage.* The boy was hovering in the doorway, clad in striped cotton pajamas that swallowed his slight frame. Crank could tell he was too scared to stay but too curious to leave. Brave kid. He was a talker, though—some took months to start talking to anyone. Some of them never talked.

The toothbrush sticking out of his mouth was surrounded by white foam. When had he gotten so old and scary-looking? "Look, kid. I know you have some questions, but they'll have to wait until I get coffee. Sit down, and don't talk to me until I call you for breakfast." When he didn't get an answer, Crank stuck his head out of the bathroom in time to see Jeremy fleeing to the living room.

Good, he thought smugly, walking into the kitchen. The kid can take orders. That might come in handy later on.

The kitchen was well stocked with foods grown men and small children would need. The compact, clean, sparsely furnished apartment was in downtown Panama City. Panamanians, not known for their safe driving, could be heard honking their horns and slamming on their brakes. Crank stood at the kitchen window, sipping his coffee and looking down at the frenzied morning traffic. Colorful buses loaded with tourists darted in and out with a cheerful disregard for the absence of suitable space in the desired lane. Almost three million people lived in this country, and about a third lived in Panama City.

"Mister? Is it okay for me to—I need to—"

"What?"

"Mister, I need to—go—uh— go to the bathroom."

Crank set his cup down with a loud thunk on the tile counter.

"Look, kid, my name is Crank—so use it! For Christ's sake, you don't have to ask permission to use the bathroom!"

He can move fast too, he thought as the bathroom door slammed shut five seconds later.

He leaned casually against the kitchen doorway when the bathroom door slowly opened. All he could see was half of the boy's head and one eye looking carefully into the room.

"Come out. I'm not going to hurt you. The bacon's ready. So how do you want your eggs?"

Crank watched the kid come cautiously out of the bathroom.

"Uh, I don't know. I guess, all mixed up?" Sounding pleased that he had come up with an answer, he headed for the kitchen. His life gave him few choices.

Pushing away from the doorway, Crank returned to the kitchen to give him room. The new ones were always wary of human contact, and it helped to give them some space. This kid was no different. His eyes darted from place to place, never focusing long on any one thing, constantly scanning the area for danger and looking for a fast way out. Figuring the boy would be more comfortable in a larger space, Crank said, "We're eating outside. Grab your milk and go sit down." Almost before he finished his sentence, the kid was out the door onto the balcony, standing against the railing and watching Crank's every move.

Placing food on the table, Crank sat down. The kid's eyes darted from the food to the man, waiting for permission to eat. The kid had to be starving. Looking at his small, thin frame, Crank knew he didn't eat regularly.

Cutting into his eggs with gusto, Crank said impatiently, "C'mon, sit down and eat! You've got to be hungry!" Careful, he warned himself, remember you're dealing with a mistreated, scared animal; it'll take time for him to trust you. Unfortunately, he didn't have the luxury of time.

Several minutes passed. The kid hadn't moved. Putting down his fork, Crank crossed his arms across his chest. He caught and held the child's eyes. The kid didn't blink.

"I wish I had the time to go about this differently, but I don't,

4

so here's the deal: I came for you. You had no one else to turn to. I told you the choice was up to you—you made it—so set your ass in that chair and eat!"

The boy sat, unmoving, seemingly thinking it over. He acts like he has options or something, Crank thought. Just about the time Crank considered plan B, the boy slipped quietly into the chair. He started eating with slow, controlled movements as if he didn't want to give Crank the satisfaction of knowing how hungry he was. There was something about this kid that Crank admired even though he tried never to get emotionally involved. You never knew what was going to happen to them. The less he knew about them, the better. As it was, he always knew way too much. It was necessary to have all available information about a potential save before the snatch was made, but he didn't have to know things like how they liked their eggs or how brave they were under pressure. He always figured that if they were alive when he got to them, that was proof enough of their bravery.

"Eat up. We have a lot to do today. I have to take you to the hospital so they can check you over and—"

"Hospital! I'm not sick."

"Listen, I must get you checked out to see if you're okay. When I was putting your pajamas on last night, there were all sorts of bruises and bumps on you. Need to know if there are any broken bones or internal stuff messed up—" Crank's speech slowed as he watched what little color the boy had left his face.

Food was forgotten in the presence of a new danger; there was a slight tremble in the hand that held his fork.

"You said you would answer some questions, mister!"

"I said to call me Crank." My name isn't Mister, for God's sake. Can't you remember that one thing?"

"My name isn't kid or boy either. It's Jeremy"

Leaning back in his chair, Crank closed his eyes. He could feel the sun gently warming his skin. "Okay, Jeremy. *Ask* your questions, but I can't promise to answer them."

"That night—in the shed when you came to get me—" He was up and walking again, getting a distance away from his captor, waiting for an answer.

"That's not a question."

"I—don't remember what happened next—after that cold drink you gave me—I got real sleepy and..."

"If you're trying to ask if I put something in your drink to make you sleepy, the answer is yes."

Looking at the tropical trees sway in the wind, Jeremy turned to look at him.

"Where are we?"

"Next question," came the terse reply.

"Why—why did you come get me?"

"You had no one else—you needed saving—Didn't you?"

Slightly nodding his head, the next question forming on his lips.

"Where are we going?"

"To a safe place. I'd like to tell you more, but you'll have to wait. This is what I can tell you. Until we get to the safe place, you're in danger. What I did was against the law. I kidnapped you from your father. It doesn't matter that he was an abusive bastard. If the authorities find us, they will take you back to him. Do you understand?"

Dark eyes fastened on Crank's face, and Jeremy slowly nodded.

"Mister Crank?"

Wincing at the "Mister Crank," he sighed. "What."

"What happened to—to my two teeth?"

Crank studied the abnormally tense still body sitting across from him. Most boys his age vibrate with energy, exploding into action at a moment's notice. Not this one. With dark blue eyes focused on Crank's face, alert for any threatening movement, this kid's energy was brittle—and fragile. Without answering, Crank got up and started clearing the table. Walking into the kitchen, he yelled cheerfully over his shoulder to Jeremy, who, at his abrupt movement, had edged to the side of the balcony.

"Enough questions, for now, kid. We got stuff to do. You need a haircut and some new—"

The cell phone vibrated in his pocket, interrupting his sentence. Extracting the small silver object from his pocket and flipping it open smoothly, he stepped into the living room.

"Start talking."

"Guten tag, Freund," came a sultry greeting floating over the line. Crank smiled, thinking no one would ever connect that husky, sexy voice to a six-foot, leanly muscled female named Gretchen, his security chief. The 34-year-old German knew more about security and electronics than colleagues half her age.

"How are things on the island?" Staff cell phones were secure due to Gretchen's expertise and the security of their telecommunications systems.

"No incidents for the last 24 hours. How did your snatch go?"

"Without a hitch."

"And the 'save'?"

"He's doing okay. He's a strange one."

"What do you expect? I read his profile when I was creating the security plan. He has a bad time."

"Yeah, he isn't like our usual rescue. Sometimes I have to remind myself he is only seven. It's almost as if he has a secret—something that—"

"This does not sound like my big macho friend. What has you ghosted?"

"Spooked! You mean spooked, not ghosted. For God's sake, Gretch, you always butcher American slang when you try it. Anyway, I'm not 'ghosted,' as you put it. It's probably nothing, but here is a kid who has no one in his corner—at least that's what we know to be a fact—but when I say that to him, it's as if he knows it's not true. Still, he isn't going to correct me. He is

'allowing' me to think that, for whatever reason. I don't know...
I'm probably way off base."

"When will you bring the save here?"

"It depends. He still hasn't had his medical checkup or
psychiatric evaluation. If those check out, expect us in a few
days. I'll call when we're on our way."

Locking the apartment door an hour later, they stepped out into
bright sunlight, the warm, moist tropical air settling over them
like an invisible cloak. Without the narrow confines of the
apartment, Jeremy seemed to relax, swinging his arms as he
walked and looking around with little boy curiosity. Panama
City looked like any other big city with its high-rise apartments,
office complexes, and busy traffic. Crank was thankful for the
crowds of Panamanians as they walked to the bus stop, which
prevented Jeremy from reading any signs proclaiming,
"Welcome to Panama City."

"Where are we going now?"

"First, there is someone you need to see." Seeing the fearful
look on Jeremy's face, he said, "Relax, kid. She's a nice lady. She
is a doctor, but not the kind that gives shots. She just wants to
talk."

"Will you— I mean—will you stay with me?"

"Sure, if you want, but if you want to talk to her privately, I can sit in the waiting room."

After a life-threatening bus ride, which seemed to thrill Jeremy, they arrived at a tall glass and brick structure in the middle of the city. Entering the marble and glass air-conditioned lobby brought visible chill bumps to Jeremy's arms. Crank didn't care for air conditioning and avoided it when he could. Of course, shrinks and doctors seem to need it, so here he was.

"For God's sake, Jeremy, relax. The doctor's name is Ms. Smith. She'll talk to you and ask some questions. You'll like her. I know you can trust her. She is part of our network."

"But—but what if I don't want to answer her? Wha—what will happen to me?"

"Nothing. Have you ever had someone you could talk to and not be afraid?"

"The housekeeper, Maria, would let me in the top part of the house when no one was home. She would feed me and let me watch TV. She didn't talk like me; her words were different. She wore a cross all the time, and she told me about Jesus."

"Well, this lady does talk like you. She will understand you, and you can understand her. Okay, here's the elevator. She's on the twelfth floor; push that button."

"Hello, Jeremy; my name is Dr. Smith. I am glad to meet you today. Please come and sit down. Mr.—ah— Jones, you may sit in the waiting room."

Jeremy stood uncertainly in the doorway, staring at the beautiful woman. Her black hair was long and shiny, her brown eyes were warm and inviting, and she wore gold bracelets that made soft tinkling sounds whenever her arms moved. *It may be okay*, Jeremy thought. Crank said he didn't have to answer the questions if he didn't want to. It would be nice to talk to her and listen to her soft voice.

Crank stood in the doorway, watching Jeremy fall in love with the beautiful Spanish doctor. He could certainly understand that dopey look on the kid's face. He felt that way every time he saw her. She was stunning, all right. She was also married to a local politician, which put her out of his reach. He didn't mess with married women, especially those hitched to local government officials. Raising his voice so the love-struck kid could hear him, he said, "Glad to see you again, doctor. I'll be out in the waiting room if you need anything. You got the file?"

Smiling slightly, she answered," Yes, Mr. Jones. Your...staff is very organized. Thank you."

Watching Jeremy settle himself uneasily across from her, Alaina thought about the time she had first been approached two years ago about helping these "saves." Everything was anonymous, and she still knew little about the organization. She was glad to assist even though her role was very minimal. She was to evaluate the child to see if any diagnoses would make it impossible or dangerous for them to be around other abused children. Luckily, there had only been a couple of children so severely abused and damaged that they had become psychotic. She never asked what happened to them. It was hard having no one to talk to about her little clients. She had never told her husband, Miguel. How could she tell her politically-motivated husband that his wife was aiding and abetting kidnappers? He wouldn't understand—no matter how great the cause.

Smiling regretfully and leaning toward Jeremy, she said, "Now, Nino, we must talk a little. I know you are Jeremy and that you are seven years old. Can you tell me about your family?"

"I—only have the man I live with. My mother must be dead— at least, I think so. When the man is drunk, he talks about her and..."

"You say your father talks about her?"

"I think it's about her—he uses other words—bad words— his face looks mad... That's when he..."

"When he what Jeremy? Your father is mad and calling your mother bad names, and then he what?" Knowing he had to talk, Alaina gently pressed him for answers.

"He—he hits me—or kicks—me."

Alaina watched the little boy hang his head in shame. How many times had she seen this in mistreated children? They somehow thought it must be their fault. Resisting the urge to put her arms around him, she let him continue.

"When I was little, I used to cry and just stand there. Now, I run and hide. I can outrun him, and I am a good hider." Voice stronger now, Jeremy sat up straight in his chair, looking calmly at the doctor.

"Jeremy, did you go to school? You would be in the first grade this year."

"No, he wouldn't let me. He said I didn't need to know anything."

"I noticed you were looking at a magazine in the waiting room. Can you read, or were you looking at the pictures?"

"I can read good. Maria, the housekeeper, used to let me watch TV. She would bring some games her children had, and we would play them. She would bring me books and workbooks. I can add and subtract, too," Jeremy said proudly.

"Jeremy, did you have times with your father when he wasn't drinking or mad?"

"I lived under the house—in my room. It was locked unless Maria let me out when he wasn't home. He never knew about that. We would be really careful. I could shower, and Maria would cook me something good. Something with tortillas. Then, I would help her clean the house. We would watch TV and play games. I—I—never saw him—unless he was mad."

Leaning back in her chair, Alaina took a deep breath and gave Jeremy a minute to rest. He looked like he was taking this well.

His facial features were still. His whole body was held stiffly upright. There was little emotion showing. It had to be there. There had to be a lot of anger inside this little body. Sadly, she thought that it would be for his regular therapist to help him. For a minute, she wished that could be her. He was such a brave little boy.

"Jeremy, I'll ask you to take some tests in a minute. You just have to check some little boxes. There are no right or wrong answers. If you have any problems with the words, ask me."

Two hours later, Crank looked impatiently at his watch for the fourth time when the office door opened, and Dr. Smith and Jeremy walked into the waiting room.

"Jeremy? Could you wait out here while I talk to Mr. Jones? It won't be long. You did well today, and it was a pleasure to meet you."

Crank watched as Jeremy sat down in one of the soft waiting room chairs, the drugs still in his system helping to take the edge off. He yawned, put his head back on the chair, and closed his eyes. Crank followed the doctor into her office, not worried that Jeremy would escape. The office doors were electronically locked.

"Are you through with him, Doc? Do I need to be on the lookout for anything?"

Alaina smiled as she motioned for the big, impatient man to sit down.

"He did great. He is a wonderful little boy despite or maybe because of what he has been through. He will need some ongoing therapy to get him to open up more, but he is definitely not psychotic."

"Thanks, Doc. That's good to hear. We'll be on our way then. Just send the report as usual." He was halfway to the door when the doctor's voice stopped him.

"Mr. Jones, I have seen you several times in the last year. You are always in a hurry to get out of this office." He could detect a smile in her lovely voice. Alaina stood up behind her desk. "Do you have something against psychologists?"

"Don't take this personally, Doc. I know you are great at your job, but I think when bad things happen to you, talking about them doesn't help. You accept them, learn from them, and move on."

"So talking over your problems never helped you?"

Reaching for the door handle, Crank smiled and looked over his shoulder at the lovely, unavailable woman. "Don't know, Doc. Never tried it," he said, gently closing her office door.

"It's time to shake a leg!"

Crank stood at Jeremy's doorway, watching the sleeping child bolt upright with a dazed look. Giving the kid time to collect his thoughts, he headed for the kitchen, where his daily injection of strong coffee awaited. Grimacing at the thought of another day at a hospital, he raised his voice. "Jeremy! We got to get a bus across town. Let's get a move on!"

"I'm ready, Mister Crank." Said a small voice behind him.

"Jeeze, kid! Don't sneak up on someone that way!" Mopping up spilled coffee with one hand, he frowned at Jeremy. "I could've used someone like you when I was in the military. The only man able to sneak up on me like that was an Indian guy named Tonto, and he learned not—"

"Tonto? That was the Lone Ranger's friend. Do you know Tonto, Mister Crank? I watch their TV show all the time. So, if it is the same, could I meet him?"

Crank squinted a look down at the small boy trying to decide if he was being a smart ass. Crank could tell the kid was serious from the earnest, hopeful look on his upturned face. Not bothering to tell him that the Lone Ranger and Tonto were long gone, he said, "Nope, different guy. Remember I told you yesterday I needed to take you to the clinic so they could check you out?"

"Yeah, but I don't..."

"I know! You don't want to go! I got that—after you told me about twenty times yesterday. I told you we had three things to do before going to the safe place. What were they?" Thoroughly exasperated, Crank fixed the child with a stern look.

"Get new clothes—see the lady doctor who would see if I was "nuts" and go to the hospital...but ..."

"No buts! This is one of those things that is for your own good, so either you cooperate, or I'm going to drug you again. You want that?" He watched Jeremy's face grow pale as he stepped back about three feet, his eyes never leaving Crank's face.

"No! I'll go, but I don't like it." Head and shoulders straight, with a stubborn look on his face, Jeremy turned and walked to the apartment door, where he stood patiently while Crank grabbed his keys.

Crank was sitting in yet another anonymous doctor's office an hour later. After another death-defying bus ride, sitting beside a stonily silent seven-year-old had Crank needing a drink— badly. The kid had made him feel so guilty for using drugs as a threat he tried to make amends by explaining about his friend, Tonto. He told him how, in the military, everyone was given a nickname, and his friend, who was Native American, had been nicknamed Tonto. Jeremy asked why Crank was given his nickname. When Crank refused to tell him, he again turned away to study the passing traffic.

Do all doctor's offices have the same decorator? Crank thought hours later when he was ushered into the doctor's empty office.

Looking around at the opulent room with mahogany bookshelves, plush carpeting, and a water fountain hidden by fake ferns in the corner, Crank mentally kicked himself for not becoming a doctor—it would certainly beat what he was doing now. Arguing with smart-ass kids—when you're trying to help them. Of course, this doctor probably didn't make nearly the money he did. Slightly comforted, he settled his big frame in the tiny dark mahogany chair and watched the small Asian doctor sit behind his massive desk.

"Okay, doc, is he cleared?"

"Mister Jones, Jeremy is a lucky little…"

"Oh, yeah…that is our Jeremy…lucky. If we asked him— would he say he was 'lucky?'"

"Mister Jones. You did not let me finish. I meant to say that considering what he has been subjected to, he is a lucky little boy. We did all the usual testing and x-rays. He has a lot of bruising—at various stages of healing—some healed rib fractures. I don't believe there was any sexual abuse, and he has no sexually transmitted disease. However, not all sexual abuse results in injury, but his therapist can work with him on that. He was very cooperative and calm. Of course, there are still some traces of the drugs in his system, but they should be completely gone in about 48 hours. "

"He'll be relocated by that time. Be sure the DNA results are entered into a database anonymously somewhere—as usual— for the police to stumble across in their investigation."

"Mister Jones? I have always wondered. Is it permissible for you to tell me why we do this?"

Crank studied the doctor thoughtfully, wondering how little he could say. Crank only released information on a "need-to know" basis, and this doctor's question didn't fit that category.

"Doctor, I know you understand that anything I tell you is to be held in the strictest confidence—and any security leak could put the children at risk—"

"I know that, Mister Jones. You have my assurance."

"My organization intends to prevent the abusers from avoiding the consequences of their actions."

"I know that. It is one of the reasons I joined."

"That being said, I can tell you that to bring someone to justice, you need a body, a crime scene, and DNA. I'm sorry, but I can't tell you anymore except that there needs to be a record somewhere of the victim's DNA since the authorities won't have a body. Most of these kids have no registered birth, school, or medical records. That's where you come in."

Seeing understanding dawn on the little doctor's face, Crank stood up and walked to the door.

"Mr. Jones, I see what you mean about consequences. I know somewhere there is an Oriental philosopher with a saying that vengeance is best left to fate, but when I see what has happened to these children—"

Hand on the doorknob, Crank looked back at the doctor.

"I know what you mean, sir—Americans have a saying too."

"Ah! Of course, Mr. Jones. What is it?"

The doctor had to lean forward to catch the words floating toward him as the big man firmly closed the door.

"Payback's a bitch."

Crank leaned against the boat's railing, watching the early morning sun bleach all the color from the boy's pale blue shirt. Dressed like a native in a cotton shirt and shorts, he was all over the boat, going from one end to the other, following the fishermen as they pulled in their catches. Seeing the Mestizo fisherman pulling a two-hundred-pound yellowfin tuna on board, Jeremy ran down the fishing boat, yelling, "Mister Crank! Mister Crank! Did you see that? Look! It's still alive! It took them forever! But they got it! They said it's tuna! Like comes in those little cans and...."

Looking down at the breathless kid, Crank held up his hand to halt the boy's speech and approach, saying, "Whoa, slow down, kid! Remember, Captain Mike said, 'No running!' He's the Captain. He can make you walk the plank if you don't follow his orders."

"Plank? What's a plank? Why wouldn't I want to walk it? Where is it? I bet I could walk it if he said I had to because I'm..."

"I think I liked you better when you didn't talk so much." Crank grumbled as he stalked to the boat's bow just in time to hear the Captain yell, "Land Ho!" He watched the boat rapidly approaching a large island with dense green forests. The water passing under the boat turned from deep blue to lighter blue and then to pale clear turquoise. Crank took in a lungful of ocean air and smiled to himself. Isla Segura, the largest island in Central America, lies off the coast of Panama. A penal colony since the early 1900s, the island was dense with rainforests. It had species of plants and animals that had never been identified. Two years ago, the last prisoners had been cleared off the island. There had been some talk of making it a national park to protect its ecological balance, but the talk had stopped mysteriously. The Panamanian government had appeared to lose all interest in the island. Chuckling to himself, he motioned Jeremy to the bow of the boat. Money talks—always.

"Yes, sir, Mr. Crank! What did the captain mean? Land Ho?"

"I think he was just doing that for your benefit...so he would seem more like a pirate ship's captain." Usually, the gaunt, weather-beaten old captain was a man of few words. Still, for some reason, he had taken a liking to Jeremy. He had let him steer the boat during the three-hour trip with a grizzled bark of "Take the wheel, matey!" His bushy white beard, yellowed with tobacco stains from the unlit cigar held firmly in his mouth, would quiver with laughter when Jeremy would ask his numerous questions. Crank felt a little put out. After all their trips, the old so-and-so had never said more than a few words to him, even though Crank authorized thousands of dollars to the captain for his services. It costs a lot for a whole crew to suddenly not understand English and to develop memory loss if the authorities happened to ask questions. Come to think of it— the captain had never opened up like that with any of his other *saves*. There's something about this boy—he feels it, too. Too bad it hadn't softened up the kid's old man.

As they approached the island, pelicans swooped into the water, scooping wiggling fish into their droopy gullets. Endless white sand beaches laced the shore. Crank straightened up from the boat railing and took another deep breath. This was home to him. For now, anyway, and he was always glad to return.

Twenty minutes later, the anchor dropped, and all the crew was busy securing the lines. Jeremy, who surprisingly hadn't asked a question in at least thirty minutes, said, so quietly Crank had to lean down to hear him, "Mister Crank? Is this—uh—I mean—am I going to live here? Is the place where you said I would that no one would—"

Crank reached down and tipped Jeremy's face up so he could look him in the eye. "When I came to get you, what did I say?"

"You said—if I wanted a better life—to come with you."

"And?"

"That— it had to be my choice."

"And?"

"That you would take me to a safe place where—uh—no one would ever hurt me again."

Lifting him off the dock and setting Jeremy down on the warm white sand of the island beach five minutes later, Crank stood back, spreading his arms in a welcome gesture. "Jeremy, this is your island home now. Its name is Isla Sequra."

"Isla Segooora." Jeremy rolled the name around on his tongue, looking like a small wine connoisseur testing a new vintage. "What does it mean?"

Taking Jeremy's hand, Crank led him slowly inland toward the dense green forests teaming with exotic birds. The mestizos trailed slowly behind, carrying the supplies.

"Isla Segura means Safe Island."

CHAPTER 2

What a great thirty-fourth birthday, Sunny thought as she shifted in the overstuffed chintz chair. Sitting up and stretching, she took a deep breath and, with both hands, shook out the tangles from her long hair. One whole week… seven days to be exact…Sam had not had one of his bad dreams. Looking around the darkened bedroom with all its sports banners and posters, Sunny noticed that almost every team in the NFL was represented, thanks to her brother Matt. Sam could still not decide who his favorite team was. He cheered for the winners and felt bad for the losers, saying things like, "They put up a good fight" or "They'll do better next time." He had the soul of an optimist. Surprising, considering he had been wracked with horrible nightmares since infancy. Hours of testing and therapy had never shown Sam to be anything but a happy, well-adjusted child. The final diagnosis was "night terrors." The only hope given Sunny was that he would eventually outgrow them. She called the therapist when Sam quit having the dreams. The therapist happily assured her that the worst was over and she could look forward to getting plenty of uninterrupted sleep from now on.

A deep sigh and the rustle of sheets had Sunny quickly looking toward the twin bed, which held her beautiful dark-haired son. At times like this, she wished Sam had a father and her a partner. However, she chose to become a mother in a way that did not allow that option. She didn't regret it. How could she when she had given birth to this wonderful little person six years ago?

His teachers would brag about her son's good behavior and sweet nature. They didn't know what she and Sam went through nearly every night.

Always quick to fall asleep, within an hour, he would start tossing in bed, kicking off the covers, and mumbling to himself. He would jerk and twist as if trying to get away from something, crying out, "Don't—please—don't!" over and over until she would feel like screaming. Then he would lie still, breathing shallow and rapid as he turned back on his side and curled into a ball.

At first, she would try to wake him up, to bring him back to her and away from the terrible place his mind had taken him to. Eventually, he'd recognize her as she held his trembling, sweaty little body, rocking him back and forth, murmuring that he was safe and it was only a dream. When she asked him about the dream, he would only say, "It's the boy, Mom! It's the boy that looks like me but isn't me. He's hurting... he's so scared! Please help him!"

He was six years old now and usually had no difficulty finding the words to communicate. He said it was another boy who looked like him but wasn't him. The therapist finally decided that somehow, during these episodes, Sam would remove himself from what was happening and feel that it was another boy who was hurt or scared. He always adamantly denied that explanation. She finally quit talking to Sam about it since it upset and frustrated him when she didn't understand and couldn't help. A week ago, he had dreamed that a giant had kidnapped the boy. After that, nothing, no more dreams, just six blissful nights of uninterrupted sleep. Sunny got up and stretched. Maybe the therapist is right... he has outgrown the dreams.

Anticipating an undisturbed night and the unheard-of luxury of sleeping late on a Saturday, she slowly walked through the darkened house toward her bedroom. She loved this old house, with its warm woods and creamy white walls. Living here since early childhood, she didn't need a light to navigate her way to the bedroom. Her parents had moved their young family here before her baby sister had been born. Her neighbors, now elderly, had been faithful customers of every lemonade stand or puppet show located under the giant oak trees in the front yard.

After Sunny's father died of cancer, her mother rented the house to her and relocated twenty minutes away to a condo she shared with two friends. Her mother always said the house had a good aura, whatever that meant. Sunny smiled as she thought about her mother. The sixties and their dedication to "flower power" had left her mother open to any new ideas. She was in her "New Age" stage and changed her name every month according to some astrology guides' instructions. What made it even worse was she forced her children to use her new name by refusing to answer to anything else. Of course, her beloved grandson was allowed to call her "G" for grandma. This month, Nora Eugenia Day became Luna, or was it Celestial? Sunny shook her head in exasperation. The next time I called mother, she thought there'd be dead silence until I "open the spirit of communication" by saying the correct name of the month.

Reaching her bedroom, she checked the infant monitor on her nightstand to see if the power light was on. Just a precaution, she told herself, slipping between the clean cotton sheets and wiggling around to get in her favorite sleeping position, which she had named the "starfish" position: arms and legs spread out as far as they could get. Her brother Matt had called it the "Torture Rack Position," but Sunny shuddered at that mental image. The word starfish brought to mind balmy breezes blowing across ocean waves—much better. Her last thought before drifting into sleep was how happy she was at the prospect of seeing Matt tomorrow. They were taking Sam to a park for a picnic. He was looking forward to tossing a baseball to his Uncle Matt.

"Mom! Mom!" At Sam's cry, Sunny was out of bed and halfway to his room before becoming fully awake. She skidded to a stop in the bedroom doorway, prepared to watch her son go through another horror she could not prevent. She was shocked to see him sitting calmly upright in bed, looking at her with a huge smile. Sunny had never seen him look so peaceful and almost complacent. Sitting beside him, Sunny quickly flipped on his bedside lamp, getting a better look at him.

"Sam, you almost scared me to death. Why are you smiling like that? What is going on, for heaven's sake—?"

Leaning back against his pillow, sighing happily, he said, "Mom, we don't have to worry anymore about the boy! Eyes closed, her son whispered softly in the same voice of wonder he used when gazing at stars in the night sky, "It's so beautiful. There are big trees and beautiful birds—and waterfalls! The boy thinks it might be heaven!"

She is surrounded by beauty. Palm trees sway in the breeze as she walks on a deserted beach, waves gently caressing her feet. The air is fragrant with tropical flowers. She can't recall the island's name, but that doesn't seem important. She is waiting for someone—someone who excites her. Skin tingling in anticipation, she slows her steps, savoring the feeling. He's coming to her! She knows it—just as she knows he's not to be trusted.

There he is! Riding toward her on a large white stallion, his long hair glinting in the sun like pure silver. With the sun at his back, getting more than a sense of his size and powerful muscles is impossible.

Her heart is pounding, though with anticipation or fear, she's not sure. Squinting to get a better look, she stops and waits, fascinated by the fluid movement of man and horse pounding toward her. Her skin feels damp with cold sweat as she realizes something is wrong. Her survival instinct screams, Run! You can't trust him!

But she can't run. He took something valuable from her. He has something she wants.

Trembling, she stands, knowing she may not survive this meeting, but determined to get back what he stole from her. Suddenly, she hears a loud pounding that, at first, she thinks is the beating of her frightened heart. Sunny blinked and sat up, feeling a soft hand stroking her cheek and calling her name. The noise was no dream, and it was getting louder. Someone was at her front door. She shook her head and took a deep, cleansing breath. It had been a weird dream, but just a dream.

"Mom! Mom! It's Uncle Matt! Can't I let him in? Pleeeeze?"

Sam knew never to open the door to anyone, but hearing her older brother bellowing her name from the front porch, she nodded to Sam, saying, "Go ahead before he wakes up all the neighbors."

Hurriedly putting on her robe and bunny house shoes, she could hear Matt talking to his nephew about some baseball game and Sam's excited responses. Guy talk! Music to her ears! Sunny glanced at her bedside Mickey Mouse clock—a childhood leftover—ten o'clock. Sunny shook her head.

Her usual wake-up time during the week was six, but Sam had kept her up till after two, telling her all the good things he had dreamed about the boy—except she noticed he used the word *saw* instead of *dreamed*. At least he had pleasant dreams lately instead of nightmares. She padded to the bathroom to wash her face and brush her teeth, hoping these everyday routines would help her wake up. She had trouble leaving her dream in the night world where it belonged.

"Hey, sleepy head! Are you awake in there?"

She could hear Matt in her bedroom as she washed her face in the old pedestal sink. She loved her bathroom, with its white walls and yellow towels. The room's bright colors and natural light always put Sunny in a good mood. She was a morning person and usually bounded out of bed, ready to greet the day with a smile. She knew some people were grumps until they had at least two cups of coffee. Grateful she didn't have to live with someone like that, Sunny smiled. Her whole family, even Sam, was blessed with early morning energy and enthusiasm for the day.

"Boy, some people are really spoiled! You go out of your way to pick them up for a fun day, and they don't even have the courtesy to get up on time! Where are you, Sunshine?"

Unfortunately, Sunshine was not a pet name given to her as a child—it was her name. Born in the sixties, her hippie parents gave their daughters names they thought were beautiful, leaving their offspring slightly bitter. Her younger sister was Raine, and she was Sunshine. It didn't make them any happier that their older brother, named after a grandfather, had the normal-sounding name of Matthew. Since their last name was Day, Sunny and her sister had endured more than their share of teasing at school.

The light in her little bathroom dimmed as she thought about her younger sister, Raine. Her baby sister, a victim of a tragic accident almost seven years ago, was still missed.

Dragging the hairbrush hurriedly through her hair, Sunny muttered, "Oh, Raine. Why didn't you come home? If you had, you would be here with me and not burned up in some horrible explosion!" Angrily blinking the tears from her eyes, she finished putting her hair up in a ponytail. The family got even smaller when her father died a year later. Hearing her brother walking toward her bathroom, Sunny banished the dark thoughts from her mind and filled it with her love for her brother.

"Well, big brother, it is so nice of you to take time out of your busy career jet-setting all over the globe to visit your sister and nephew!"

Matthew was a newspaper journalist who worked in the field to report the news as it happened. Fluent in three languages, he had just returned after spending several months in Central America. She always missed him when he was gone. He was the typical tall, dark, and handsome adventurer at thirty-nine years old. Women fell in love with him everywhere he went, but no one held his attention long. When his mother and sister nagged him to settle down and quit roaming the earth, he would grin, saying he had never found any woman that could hold a candle to his two favorite ladies. Filling the doorway to her tiny bathroom, he leaned in to give her a peck on the cheek, grimacing at the taste.

"Yuck, you got stuff on your face, sis!"

"Well, I am thirty-four years old! Wrinkles on a man's face are *character*—not so on a female. Besides, I must keep myself beautiful for the day I meet my hero."

Since she had been old enough to say the word, Sunny had told her family she would never marry until she found her "hero." When she was five, he had to ride a white horse and be a magician who could make things invisible. Leaving the magic of childhood behind, she reluctantly decided her hero would only need to love and protect their family. This would be a full-time job since she wanted at least five children.

"By the way, how's work going? Is the business of making babies going well?"

Sunny was a registered nurse at a well-known fertility clinic in Austin. She loved helping couples achieve their dream of having a child. The many technological advancements occurring daily significantly affected a couple's chances, and Sunny was proud to be part of this miracle.

Her brother watched her face light up like always when discussing her work.

"Oh, Matt, my friend Diedre—You remember her? She was in my grade and had a tremendous crush on you."

"You will need to be more specific than that. A lot of girls had a crush on me. Was she that skinny redhead with braces?"

"She's not skinny anymore. She just delivered twins yesterday. She and her husband have been through so much. Her eggs would not fertilize and survive. Her vagina had a hostile environment and—"

"Hold it!—TMI!—Too much information!" Holding his stomach and making gagging noises, her brother pushed away from the door frame and walked back into her bedroom. "It was just a social question! Good grief! I don't want to hear about eggs and sperm—and vaginas—gross! What a word for such a beautiful instrument."

"Puleeeze!" Sunny said scornfully. "Some of the words you men come up with for it are better?" Finished with her morning toilette, Sunny walked back into her bedroom.

Offended, Matt turned around to argue, "There are a *lot* of beautiful words in different languages for that particular area! The Spanish call it—"

"Mom, are we ever going to leave?" came her son's plaintive wail. Grateful for the interruption of what she was sure would be a very embarrassing lesson in anatomy, she turned to see her son standing at the doorway, loaded with his baseball gear, picnic cooler, and blue gym bag that she was pretty sure held his swimsuit. Sam wanted to be ready for any opportunity to swim. He had taken lessons since he was four years old and was a strong swimmer for his age and weight. He had been looking forward to today all week. They were going to a private campground about thirty miles west of Austin. It was beautiful with natural spring-fed pools and shade trees, necessary in the Texas heat.

"Okay, sweetie. I'm ready. Let me check to see that you have everything in the cooler. Did you bring sunscreen, lotion, and towels?"

After quickly locating the needed items, Sunny stuffed her bathing suit and towel in her tote bag and shooed everyone out of the bedroom ahead of her. Keeping the momentum going, she grabbed her keys, locked the house, and steered them toward the driveway.

"Have you heard from Mom?" her brother asked as he lifted all their gear and stashed it in the back of his jeep. "I called last week and could hear the phone pick up, but no one answered."

"What name did you call her?"

"What do you mean? I called her Mom. What else would I— wait a minute! You don't mean she's—She's not still into that changing her name every month nonsense, is she?"

"Yep, " Sunny said cheerfully, ignoring her big brother's frown. "I am trying to remember if it is Luna or Celestial this month. I wish she would get me a calendar. You know, each month she could write with a new name. It'd be a lot easier to remember. Sometimes I have to guess two or three times before I can get her to …" Sunny's speech dwindled to a stop when she saw Matt's amazed look on her face.

"I don't believe this! You act like this is normal and only need a process for remembering the name, which would fix everything. Mom was always a little eccentric, but this spirit guide stuff is over the top even for her."

Walking around the passenger side after seeing Sam safely buckled in, she said, "Mom's had a hard time since Dad died. She is still trying to find her identity. She knows herself as a mother and wife but not as a widow. So even though it is irritating, I want to support her efforts. Remember when you wanted to be called the Lone Ranger and would not answer to anything else? This went on for months when you were six. Raine and I stopped talking to you, but Mother called you Lone Ranger. Can you imagine the laughter in the neighborhood when she would stand in the front yard and yell for the Lone Ranger?"

By the time she finished, Matt was chuckling, and Sam was rolling back and forth in the back seat, saying he would call Uncle Matt the Lone Ranger all day. After threatening Sam with dire consequences if that should happen and checking to see that all riders were safely buckled in, Matt accelerated onto the highway. "Okay! I get your point. We'll humor her. At least for now."

Hours later, after a wonderful picnic lunch, Sunny floated on her inflatable cushion in the pool. Fluffy white clouds moved slowly in front of the sun, giving some relief from the 100-degree temperature. This was a sheer luxury, allowing her thoughts to drift. She looked over at her tanned, healthy six-year-old son scooping up the ball, clutching the old hand-me-down mitt that had been her brother's. Cherished by Sam for its softness and pliability attained by countless applications of her brother's "secret recipe" glove oil. Her son was the center of her life. His vitality and enthusiasm for life forced her to live in the present, so sometimes, it was hard to remember her life before Sam.

"Sunny! Guess what! I have some great news—at least I think it is great—I hope you do too."

She could still hear her younger sister's voice over the phone eight years ago when she called with her "great idea." At the time, Raine lived in picturesque Savannah, Georgia, and was a hostess for one of the historic hotels. This job enabled her flighty sister to spend time with Savannah's eccentric and colorful characters.

"Raine! It's great to hear your voice! I keep calling and leaving messages, but you don't return my calls. I get worried when you don't call back. Did you get the family contact card I sent you?" Her breathless speech was interrupted by Raine's laughter.

"Once a big sister, always a big sister. Remember, you're only two years older than me. In answer to that last question, yes, I filled out a contact card with everyone's phone number in case something terrible happened to me. I carry it with me everywhere! Now, can I tell you my idea?"

"You know how I hate to be interrupted in the middle of a lecture," Sunny said with a dramatic sigh. Chuckling, she said, "I give up. What's your latest great idea? I sure hope it's better than the last one. Remember? You wanted us to have identical nose jobs and cheek implants to look like identical twins. Isn't it bad enough that most people can't tell us apart anyway? We're both five feet five inches, weigh one hundred and twenty-five pounds, and have red hair. The only difference is your eyes are that weird gray color, and mine are a beautiful baby blue."

"For the last time, they're slate gray! The color of storm clouds is sexy—so there! Anyway, I didn't call to argue who had the prettiest eyes. I have something important to say. Sis—I know—I mean, I'm not sure how to tell you. I know this is going to sound weird, but I want you to let me finish before you butt in. Just hear me out."

Sunny could hear an unusual hesitancy and insecurity in her sister's voice. Her stomach muscles tightened in anticipation of bad news. "No interruptions. I promise."

"I don't want anyone else to know about this. Promise me right now."

"I—I promise. I have kept a lot of your secrets! Mom still doesn't know about—"

"I know, I know," Raine's voice said softly. "You have always been a great big sister. That is why I want you to know about this just in case I—well—just in case. Anyway, it's actually good news—and exciting. You probably have already heard about this new egg-splitting technique. They take one fertilized egg and split it into four sections. The eggs can be frozen safely indefinitely in some cases and then—"

"Of course, I know about that procedure. Did you forget I work at a fertility clinic? We offer all the latest procedures—but I don't see—"

"I asked you not to interrupt."

"Oops! Sorry! But—please get to the point."

"The point is—I had the procedure done yesterday in Atlanta."

After this startling statement, there was quiet on both ends of the line. Raine held her breath, waiting for the explosion. Sunny was still trying to process the information, which was not unusual when speaking with her younger sister.

"Hello? Sunny? Are you still there?"

"Hmmm. Yep, I'm here. I was just wondering why would a twenty-six-year-old unmarried, unattached female do such a thing. What did you mean when you said you wanted to do this 'just in case'? Just in case of what?"

As usual, when she responded with less than enthusiasm to her sister's far-out schemes, Raine replied in an offended tone.

"I will attempt to answer your questions. I know I'm only twenty-six years old and unmarried, as you kindly mentioned, but I may never marry! I don't think I want to marry." Raine's voice got quieter and more subdued. Her words were almost a whisper. "I was thinking, what if I die young? Sunny, I have been having dreams where I know I'm dead. It's been more than once. It's always the same. I am walking through Savannah late at night. People pass me on the street without even seeing me. I reach out to touch them, but they don't feel it. Somehow, I know I'm dead. I can actually feel the cool night air passing through me. I'm not scared or sad. I'm just—dead—so I thought—"

"Wait a minute!" Sunny interrupted. "Dreams like that are common and could mean a lot of things. It could mean that you don't feel a connection with people. You know we have wanted you to move back home. You would be surrounded by people that know and love you..."

"Sunnneeeeee."

"Okay! Okay! Moving on! How are the dreams of an early death and your embryos connected? If you're dead, you can't use them."

"I want to leave something of myself on this earth! I've made no lasting contributions. When I'm gone, that's it."

"Let me see if I have this straight. You're leaving the possibility of multiple miniature Rainie's languishing in some freezer? Who is supposed to use these 'gifts to the world' you are so generously leaving? I mean, I could understand if you were a genius—but let's face it, girl—you barely made it through school." Laughing, Sunny was just getting wound up when the single word said softly over the phone interrupted her teasing.

"You"

"Me, what?"

"They aren't just eggs. They are fertilized embryos. I've already willed them to you."

"Well, that's certainly appreciated, but I had my eye on those pearl earrings Grandma Sheila left you. But I guess embryos are lovely, too—"

"Sunny, please take this seriously. I mean it! They are my gift to you in case something should happen to me. You know that doctor told you it might be difficult for you to get pregnant because your eggs weren't healthy or there weren't enough or something like that. If I'm still alive and you needed my eggs, I would gladly give them to you, but if I'm dead, you have to use a stranger's eggs. This way, it's all in the family."

Tears came to her eyes as she listened to her sister tell her how much she loved her and how important it was to be able to do this. Her heart felt so full that she couldn't breathe—her baby sister. This impulsive gesture was typical of her. Just when you thought she would never grow up and commit to anything long-term, she would give you a "love offering," as she called it, and you would forget all the frustrations and disappointments.

Three years ago, Sunny's gynecologist had told her that she didn't produce enough healthy eggs to ensure getting pregnant. She had not worried about it since many other options were available today. Her soft-hearted sister had devised her own solution.

"Oh, Raine! I'm so sorry." Remorse filled her voice. "I didn't mean to make light of this loving gesture. Even though you will live another fifty or so years. I want to thank you for your gift."

"You're very welcome! Now, get a pen and write down the name of the embryo bank and my code number. You won't even need the will to get the embryos. I signed a paper allowing you to get them if I died, but you must have the code. You can have the embryo implanted at any fertility clinic, so that wouldn't be a problem. You haven't asked but I want to reassure you that the sperm donor is an amazing person. I made sure he was a good candidate."

Letting go of the poignant memory, Sunny felt the sun drying her tears as she trailed her fingers in the cold spring water. A year later, her sister was dead, killed in a car accident. It had been over seven months since she had seen her sister, and even though they had talked weekly over the phone, the embryos were never mentioned again.

Sunny took a deep, cleansing breath and slowly paddled to the pool steps. Three months after her sister's funeral, she had flown to Savannah, walked into the embryo bank, and presented her code to the white-uniformed receptionist. Ten minutes later, she walked out with a metal cylinder filled with a solution to keep the embryo frozen during transport. Tears streaming down her face, she boarded an airplane, clutching the cylinder as she headed back to Austin. Two hours after landing, she was lying in a stainless steel and white room, having the embryo implanted in a relatively painless procedure, surrounded by cheerful, anonymous people wishing her good luck. That night, she dreamed her sister handed her a beautiful gift box wrapped in shiny white paper and blue ribbons. With huge, excited smiles, they tore off the paper together. They lifted the lid. A beautiful dark-haired baby boy was lying there, nestled in the tissue paper, smiling and cooing up at them. Sunny woke that morning with dried tears and a smile on her lips. Her baby would be a boy! She would give him a manly-sounding name.

After four hours of labor, Sam Allen Day was born nine months later.

She never had a moment's regret about her decision. She loved being a mother; one day, she would find her hero, and together, they could make more beautiful babies. Watching as the sun descended, she walked up the steps to the pool, anchoring her towel on her shoulders. Smiling, she thought, "And if my hero never finds me—-there *are* more embryos."

"Matt, tell me what you have been up to for the last few months. You never tell us much about your assignments. All we knew is you were somewhere in Central America." They were heading home in the gathering twilight. Sam was sprawled out in the backseat, gently snoring in a deep sleep only little boys and puppies could do after a hard day's play. The jeep windows were down, and the early evening wind played throughout the jeep. Tossing plastic bags and papers in a silent dance, remnants of a wonderful day.

"I have to be careful what I tell you and Mom," Matt replied as he drove. "You know women can't keep a secret." He glanced over at her. "What? What is that look for? You know it's—" Her brother's teasing sideways glance was the only thing that kept him from getting jabbed in the ribs with her elbow.

"Very funny! Yes, Mother and I do like to dish with our friends—but if we knew that leaking any information could endanger your undercover assignment or get you hurt, well, they could torture us, but we wouldn't talk! I mean, I like to think I could hold out—of course, I do have a low tolerance for pain, and after all, you *are* only a brother! Sunny said as she extricated her long red strands from her brother's tightening grip.

"OK, What do you want to know?"

"Everything! Start at the beginning, and don't leave anything out!" Sunny said, settling comfortably in the car seat. Her body turned slightly toward her brother so that she could look at his handsome profile. *Chiseled and manly, such a lovely man,* she thought fondly.

"As you know, I was in Central America, specifically Panama. There were some reports that a military installation was being set up on one of the islands on the Pacific side."

"Why would that be a cause for concern? Is the United States worried that the Panamanian government is going to use nuclear weapons against us? I thought everything had been relatively peaceful there since the early nineties."

Turning slightly toward her, Matt replied, "The rumored installation wasn't Panamanian."

"Hmmmm—A foreign power setting up on one of Panama's islands? I can see where they wouldn't be happy with that. What did you find out? That is—if you can tell me. If it isn't classified, I don't want to know anything I'm not supposed to know. "

"I'm not CIA! I'm a journalist." Sighing unhappily, he continued, "Anyway, I didn't find out much. I stayed in Panama for two months pretending to be a tourist. Trying to get information from the officials is impossible. Even though it's improving, the government still needs help with corruption. I got more information from the Mestizo laborers than anyone else. It helped that I could speak their language and—"

"Mestizos are—?"

"They are a mixture of European and Indigenous descent, making up about sixty-five percent of the population in Panama. They are friendly, slightly superstitious people eager to talk about the 'mysterious happenings' on the island."

"What makes the locals think anything is going on? They must have a reason?"

"Lights twinkling on and off throughout the island. A loud humming sound is heard at night. The dock workers have unloaded huge shipments of what they think are building supplies and weapons. During the night, the supplies vanish, and no one seems to know where they go. What bothers me is they have reported all this to government officials, and they're just ignored."

"Well," Sunny said, now thoroughly engrossed in the mystery, "What did you come up with? Did you find out anything?"

"Nothing"

"Nothing? That doesn't sound like the investigative journalist I know and love!" exclaimed Sunny, more than a little annoyed that her curiosity would not be satisfied.

"Nothing conclusive, anyway. I saw lights! I heard the humming. It sounded like a huge generator going all night long. No supplies came to the docks in the two months I was there. I tried to get someone to take me to the island. None of the local captains would even land on the beach. They said they were afraid of the spirits. I did fly over it a few times, and—" Matt paused and seemed hesitant to continue.

"And what? Don't stop now!" Sunny pleaded. "I'm fascinated by this story. It's scary. All we need is a moonless night and a campfire—"

"Well, I didn't find anything concrete, but there was something odd about the place. There were paths."

"Paths? Where did they go?"

"To clearings"

Abruptly throwing up her arms, Sunny let out an exasperated sigh. "Paths! Paths and clearings! Is that what you found odd? Why would that be odd? They would have to clear the land and build paths to the military buildings. I don't see why you would think that was so weird. You had me thinking there was some kind of never-before-discovered monster on the island, like in Jurassic Park!

"You're right! Ordinarily, I wouldn't have given it a second thought. Still, the missing supplies had disappeared from the dock at least a year ago. Supposing they were for the island— there was enough wood and shingles delivered to make a hundred buildings—but there were no signs of any buildings or building materials. There was no sign of habitation. Nothing but flowers, trees, paths, and clearings."   \

Realizing her brother was genuinely perplexed, Sunny said, "Maybe supplies were hidden in the trees, making it difficult to see from the air."

"I don't know. It just gave me a strange feeling when I looked down from the plane." After a lengthy silence, Matt turned his head and smiled ruefully. "So that's it! For two months of investigative work, all I found were paths and clearings. I need more to impress my editor, that's for sure. He told me to drop the whole story and come back home."

Matt turned back to the road, lost in thought. Sunny could tell he was back in Panama and reliving the last two months, so she sat quietly watching the scenery pass until the jeep pulled into her driveway just ahead of the setting sun.

"Easy slugger," Matt said as he gently pulled the half-awake child from the back seat. "We're home. It's time to get you in bed." Sam groped blindly behind him on the seat, finding his favorite baseball cap and setting it backward on his head. "Uncle Matt, will you be here when I wake up?"

"Can't, kid, but I'm not going on assignment for a while, so I'll be around."

Leading through the darkened house to her son's bedroom, Sunny smiled at her guys' murmured conversation about possible adventures they could enjoy this summer.

"Mom, can I sleep in my clothes tonight and not brush my teeth either? It's summer, and I don't have to go to school."

"Cavities don't take a summer vacation, buster, and the dentist found two new ones on your last check-up, so no to skipping the teeth brushing and yes to sleeping in your clothes."

Still half asleep, Sam stumbled into the bathroom with a satisfied smile. One out of two wasn't so bad.

After a few minutes of quiet conversation, Sunny locked the front door behind her brother and started for the kitchen to get a glass of water. Grabbing an apple to take to her room, she noticed the message light on the wall phone blinking. She pushed the button. In the quiet house, a cheerful female voice echoed loudly in the kitchen.

"Ms. Day, this is Mrs. Schneider from the Savannah Embryo Center. Please call us back and enter your code number. I have an important private message for you!"

Thoughts churning furiously, she quickly dialed the number and entered her private code. After a moment, the same cheerful voice rang out: "Thank you, Ms. Day, for retrieving this message! Remember that your remaining embryos are now almost eight years old. We hope that the two previous implantations worked out well. If your plans have changed we would be glad to work with you concerning possible adoptions. If you need to hear this message again, please press the star key! Thank you!"

Midway through the message, Sunny froze with the apple halfway to her mouth. Her hand trembled. Sunny carefully set the half-eaten apple on the counter. *Two* previous implantations?

Sunny lowered the machine's volume and played the message again, hoping she had misunderstood.

"Mom, I'm through brushing my teeth! Wanna come look?"

Sunny and Sam played this game every night. She always made him open his mouth and smile real big so she could pronounce the job done satisfactorily. But not tonight.

"Sam, go—go get in bed, and I'll check them in a minute. You can read one book and then lights out." She heard him mumble, "Okay," and saw the light from his small lamp shine into the hall.

Sunny paced up and down the darkened den, furiously twirling a strand of her hair. There must be some mistake. They must have her mixed up with someone else.

Raine had told her she only had two viable eggs successfully harvested, fertilized, and split into four pieces each. That would make eight embryos. Sunny had one implanted because she couldn't take the chance of having more than one child. Being a single parent was tough enough.

Her pacing stopped. More than six years ago, she had withdrawn a single embryo. There should be seven left, not six, as the message stated. Her feet and hands were beginning to grow cold like they always did when she was anxious. Her pacing resumed, and she rubbed her hands together, more for something to do than to help chase away the cold.

Stopping again in the middle of the room, a new thought burst into her mind. Had her sister used one of the embryos before her death? Could her sister have gotten pregnant and had a child? She went over the timeline in her mind while the cold feeling spread from her hands and feet throughout her body. It was possible! But when the family attended the funeral in Savannah, none of Raine's friends or coworkers had mentioned a child. No child's body had been found in the burned car—only her sister's.

Her heart was racing as she sat down hard on the couch. The embryos were all she had left of her precious baby sister. If they were implanted and delivered successfully, they would be Sam's brothers or sisters and her nieces or nephews. Six potential family members are under lock and key in the embryo bank. Number seven is safely in his bedroom reading a book, and number eight is unaccounted for.

She picked up the phone, and seconds later, she heard a beep, "If you're bleeding, call 911. If not, leave a message!"

"Matt, quit screening and pick up the damn phone! One of Raine's kids is missing!"

CHAPTER 3

"Sunny girl, you have to turn around here and look at this! You won't believe it!"

Sunny looked up from contemplating her first cup of coffee to see a slim brown column of energy standing by her desk, waving the daily newspaper. She had arrived at the clinic early, taking time to get her thoughts in order, sipping her coffee, and looking out the windows. The fertility clinic was on the top floor, overlooking a wooded park.

"I don't know what this world is coming to! I know this has to be a mistake! My mama would say this is a bad omen for sure! Why, the other day, we were walking into the supermarket, and a black feather blew across our path. I wouldn't have thought anything about it, but she knew—she tells me it's a bad omen, that it means your life will be swept away. We went straight home and didn't leave the house all day."

Listening to her friend rattle on about omens, Sunny smiled and shook her head. Everything about Jackie was exaggerated. Speech, clothing, emotions. She didn't *walk* into a room—she *exploded* into it. Entered talking and left talking. Dressed in beautiful, brightly colored clothing and heavy gold jewelry, she was undeniably a stunning example of her African heritage.

Sunny felt very blessed to have Jacqueline Bu Font as her closest friend—usually.

"It amazes me how a person with a master's degree in nursing can spout this sort of nonsense," Sunny said, slightly put out that the quiet start to her morning was being interrupted. "Ever since your mother came to visit, all you can talk about is good and bad omens. We've talked about this before. You don't believe this stuff anyway!"

Sunny was usually more diplomatic with her excitable friend. Still, she'd had a rough Sunday, talking on the phone to Matt until nearly 3 am. She had never told him about Raine's embryos. Of course, he knew Sunny had in vitro fertilization to have Sam. Still, he had respected her wishes not to discuss her decision. He had no idea that Sam was Raine's biological child. The explanations took awhile as she gave him a very simplified explanation of the techniques involved in egg splitting and embryo implantation. It got so late they decided to talk this evening after work.

"You're right," Jackie hastily assured her friend. "I don't usually believe this stuff, but this is so odd—"

"Okay, okay! I'm guessing there's something in the newspaper that has you rattled, so why don't you tell me about it an—" Sunny jerked her coffee cup out of harm's way just as the whole edition of the morning paper was plopped on her desk.

"It's in this morning's paper. Do you remember that little

boy in Savannah? The one that was killed in that horrible explosion?"

"I remember—what a terrible tragedy. That poor baby—people should watch their children better—they're so precious. That happened on Tybee Island, a few miles from Savannah."

"Yes—yes. That's the one. It happened last Friday night. The boy was in the lower part of a condo on the beach—it exploded. The only one home was the child."

"See, that's my point. It happened around 10 pm. Why was that seven-year-old boy alone at his house? Boys that age are so accident-prone. Some people shouldn't—" Sunny stopped as she watched her agitated friend pace up and down in front of her desk, running her scarlet-tipped nails through her hair.

"That's what I'm trying to tell you. The police don't think it *was* an accident! A neighbor came forward and told them they suspected the father of being neglectful. They think he got drunk that night—killed him and set the fire to cover it up!"

As her friend continued, Sunny spread the paper. In bold print, the headlines exclaimed, "FATHER INDICTED IN GEORGIA BOY'S SLAYING!" An informant had come forward and said they had first-hand information regarding the abuse. Since the police were not releasing many details of the crime scene, the column was not very informative. It did say that the district attorney's office was going for premeditated murder. The father, James Ashton, was indicted yesterday and held in the county jail without bail. Flipping pages to find page four for the rest of the story, a warm brown hand grabbed her arm tightly.

"Sunny, before you turn the page, there's something. I know it looks bad, but it has to be some odd mix-up."

Looking at the concern in her friend's eyes, Sunny felt a chill starting in the pit of her stomach. Glancing at the page, she briefly read the remainder of the story, noticing a few pictures at the bottom. One was a picture of what was left of the condo on the beach—charred timbers and black sand. Tears welled in her eyes as she imagined how scared the little boy must have been. Underneath the picture of the condo were two more pictures. A studio portrait of a fair-haired portly man with light eyes and what looked like an amateur's Polaroid of a small, dark-haired boy. Her first thought was that the father and son looked nothing alike. She studied the little boy's picture, thinking he was close to her son's age. She smiled slightly, looking at his slicked-down hair and stiff smile. It was as if curving his lips up to form a smile was a new thing for his face to do. A brave smile all the same. Gazing at his small face, she felt her hands grow cold as her pulse started a slow, heavy beat she could feel in her temples. She had felt this way before. The night a Savannah detective had called, saying her sister was dead. Her body was trying to tell her something her mind had not registered. What was it? Why couldn't she comprehend what her eyes were seeing?

"Sunny? Sunny? Say something. Don't worry—it's just a mistake."

Something about the boy...

Ignoring Jackie, Sunny's eyes narrowed, looking closer at the grainy image. Her brain suddenly accepted the message her eyes had sent. It had been there all along! How could she have missed it? The dark-haired little boy was her son! No! That's not right! It couldn't be Sam. But he was an identical image to her son. Same eyes, same hair—the same cleft in the middle of his chin!

"Jackie? This child looks exactly like Sam! Even down to that dimple in his chin! I don't understand how this could happen."

"It couldn't be. That's what I've been trying to tell you! How would that even be possible? I've heard of a person having a doppelganger—someone who looks exactly like you, but..."

As Jackie spoke, Sunny mind churned. This was too much—first Raine's missing embryo, and now this. The ringing of her office phone interrupted her thoughts. It was the front desk alerting them that the first patient had arrived.

"We got to get busy," Sunny said. "We have four procedures today and some follow-up appointments. Let's not talk about it anymore right now. There's a rational explanation. There has to be. Mom and Matt are coming over tonight to discuss another family matter. Matt has contacts and can get more information about the little boy. I'll fill you in tomorrow."

Minutes later, both women were escorting patients to exam rooms and getting them prepped for in vitro procedures. The goal was to create beautiful, healthy babies. I'm so blessed, Sunny thought. I have a great job and wonderful, caring friends and family. Finishing the thought, she felt a cold chill run down her spine. Refusing to identify it as anything other than a chill, she happily went about her day.

"Hi, Mom! Guess what G and I did today? I bet—I bet you'll never guess in a gazillion years! Go ahead and—"

Trying to enter the door that evening loaded with grocery sacks, Sunny responded with wary enthusiasm, anxiously sweeping her eyes over her son. His hair's not a different color— that's good. Nails not painted. No extra holes in his ears. Okay, so far. She never knew what to expect when her mother and son got together. Mom was the designated babysitter when needed. She loved doing it and loved her grandson. The problem was that her mom's ideas on suitable activities for a six-year-old boy could be unorthodox. When Sam was four, the two spent the day at the spa. She came home to a son who had been the proud recipient of his first facial, manicure, and massage. He'd also added several new words to his four-year-old vocabulary, such as cellulite, exfoliate, and Botox. Sunny laughed as she recalled

THE CHILD SHE LEFT BEHIND

her brother's look when his nephew walked in that day with glowing skin and scarlet nails.

"Where's G, honey?"

"She's sleeping," he smiled sheepishly. "I'm supposed to be— but gee, Mom. I'm too old to take naps. You know that—but G won't listen. So I pretend to go to sleep and then watch TV— but I keep it real low."

Her little diplomat, who never wants to hurt anyone's feelings, is amazingly resourceful at avoiding doing just that.

"You can tell me about your day while you help with the groceries. What exciting things did you and G do today? Oh! By the way. Did she mention what her name was for this month? I think it's Luna, but I'm not sure, and you know how she—"

"Well, the sicko she took me to called her Celeste something."

"Celeste! She must have said Celestial—great! That was my other choice. I knew it was one of those. Wait a minute! Sicko? She took you to a sicko?" Pulling Sam over to the kitchen table, they sat down. Sitting across from him, filled with dread for the answer but knowing she had to ask the question, she said, "Okay, take it from the start. What did you and G do today? Don't leave anything out. What's this about her taking you to a sicko?"

"You know, mom. A lady who knows things."

"Knows things?"

"Yeah. We went to her house. It was smelly and dark in there."

"Where was this house?"

"I dunno. We had to drive a long time to get there."

"The house was smelly?" she asked, now thoroughly confused.

"Yeah, like that stuff you use when you go out—but a lot more smelly."

"Well, thanks... I didn't know you thought my perfume was 'smelly,' but go on."

"She wore a lot of clothes that you could see right through and something on her head—like a towel."

"See-through clothes! What could you see?" Sunny was beginning to get a picture here, and it was one she didn't like.

"More clothes. G called them scarves or something. Anyway, she knew stuff, Mom. She really did!"

Understanding finally dawning, Sunny breathed a huge sigh of relief. A psychic—mother had taken him to one of her offbeat friends for an afternoon of palm reading and glass ball gazing.

"Mom, she told me you were going to get married, and I would have a bunch of brothers and sisters!"

Looking at her son's hopeful face, she felt like she had to do some damage control. "Sam, the lady was just one of G's friends. I'm sure she was nice, but no one can tell the future, sweetie. I hope to get married someday and have other children, but."

"Yeah, mom. I guess you're right. She didn't get some of the stuff right."

What stuff?"

"The stuff about the brothers and sisters—"

"Go ahead—what about the brothers and sisters."

"She said I already have a brother. I don't—do I, mom?"

"Well, here everyone is. Hello darling! Welcome home! Did I interrupt a deep philosophical conversation between mother and son?" Sunny's mother beamed into the kitchen like a ray of sunshine. Her trim figure was clad in bright yellow sweats, making her look younger than sixty. Calm blue eyes looked from mother to son, waiting for an answer so she could either stay or make herself scarce until the discussion was over. Her tentative smile gave Sunny a good indication that her mother knew very well what they were talking about.

"Hi, Celestial! Sam told me what a wonderful day he had had. Nothing boring, like swimming, skating, or playing video games. He got to have his fortune told! He will have a lot to tell his class when school starts this fall."

"Sweetie, sarcasm is so unattractive in a female. Besides, I'm over all that silliness about changing names each month. So you can call me mom or mother like you used to. I'm looking into the Native American religion now. I'll let you know my new Indian name when—"

"Great, Mom—using your name will make it much easier. However, I wouldn't mention that you will be getting an Indian name to Matt just yet. Let's just let him enjoy the return to normal for a while."

"Okay, dear. Whatever you say."

Getting up to put the groceries away, Sunny returned to the more important subject of the psychic.

"I would like to talk about this psychic Sam saw today. He—"

"Oh, dear. That was just Vivian. She's not been a psychic long but is amazingly good at it! She's the one who told me I had an Indian heritage and to look into that religion—of course, she's not right all the time. The things she told Sam were just nonsense and didn't make any sense at all! I told her I wasn't going to pay her!

What nonsense!"

"Hold it! Things—as in more than one thing? Sam told me she said he had a brother. What else did she say?"

"Really, dear. It was just drivel! "

Sam looked up from dunking his cookie in his milk and smiled at his grandmother. "We didn't really believe her—did we G? It was just for fun—like a game."

"Mom? I'm waiting."

"Well, first, she told him he already had a brother. Then she said the strangest thing—It was so bizarre—I mean, if you want people to believe you—you should say something more believable."

"Please, Mom, get to the point."

"Vivian said, 'Sam has many other brothers and sisters, but they have not yet begun their life passage. Sunny! Honey? What's wrong? You're as white as a sheet. Are you sick—"

Sunny felt dizzy. Her mother's voice sounded like it came from another room, and she felt like she was going to faint. Looking at her mother and son's worried faces, Sunny took a deep breath and smiled.

"Uh—uh, it's okay, mom. I just felt a little dizzy for a second. I skipped lunch today. The clinic was a madhouse. I'm fine. I'll get a cracker."

"You sit right there, honey. I'll get it."

Still shaky, Sunny patted her son's hand and smiled at him. "Okay, Buster, I have a treat for you today!"

Still searching her face for signs that she was alright, Sam responded slowly. "What treat? Is it swimming? Are we going swimming at the park?"

"Yep! You're going swimming but not to the park. Casey's mother invited you over to swim with Casey after supper."

Sunny watched the conflicting emotions play across her son's face. The joy of doing the one thing he loved most in the world but unsure about leaving his mother. From an early age, her son appointed himself her protector. It was a position she had tried to discourage. But it was difficult when it seemed he could always sense her sadness or anxiety. She would joke and call him her little mind reader. But as the "man of the house," Sam felt he had to watch out for his mother sometimes. This was one of them.

"She has a neat pool, mom. It's got a diving board and a waterfall, but—"

"No buts, my man! You're going. I already told her mother you would be there. G and I are going to be home. So if you need us, you can call or come home. Casey only lives two houses down and—."

"Hey, where's everyone? What's for supper? I could eat a horse!"

"It's Uncle Matt!"

Sunny watched as her son turned and ran out of the kitchen to greet her brother, who had just let himself in the front door. All concerns for his mother had been forgotten. Getting up to help her mother set the table for supper, she thought about how good it felt to have all her little family in one place for a change.

"Mattie! Come here and hug your mother! I've missed you so much!"

Watching mother and son embrace brought tears to her eyes. There was so much love between them.

Sam was a lucky little boy to be included in this family. All children should be so blessed. Tagging at the end of these thoughts were other thoughts. Would Sam's other frozen brothers and sisters have loving families?

If it were in her power, they would.

❖

Supper was over, and Sam was safely occupied. Sunny joined her mother and brother in the living room. Perched on the arm of the couch, she took a deep breath and said, "Matt! I haven't told mother everything yet—haven't had time—"

"What's going on?" her mother interrupted. "Is it Sam? Is there something wrong with Sam?"

Before she could reassure her mother, Matt said, "Sam's okay. Sunny has some information about Raine."

"Raine? Did something turn up on the investigation? You know, I never did think her death was an accident. It hurts my heart to even talk about it—"

"There *is* something we need to talk about. The last few days, there have been some—I guess you could call them 'revelations.' I haven't pieced them all together yet. Yes, Mom, before you ask. Some of it involves Raine—but not her accident. You remember? The police closed the investigation about four years ago because they couldn't find any evidence of foul play. It was ruled an accidental death."

Seeing her mother nodding, Sunny continued. Since Matt knew most of this, she addressed her mother.

"Mom, you knew about Raine's embryos but didn't know I had one implanted. Sam is Raine's child. "

Ignoring her mother's shocked silence, she briefly recapped the information she had received last night on the voicemail left by the embryo bank staff. She verified the information this morning when the clinic opened. There *were* only six fertilized embryos left of the original eight. One had been removed by

Raine a few days after it had been frozen. So, the missing embryo was no longer missing.

"Honey? I'm trying to understand this, but why—I mean— why didn't you tell me this years ago? As my friend said, 'Sam has siblings who have yet to start their life journey.'"

"You knew that Sam was not my biological child and that I had artificial insemination to have him. I—"

"Yes—yes. I know. I wish I'd known Sam was Raine's child. Maybe it would have made losing her a little easier."

Seeing the tears trickling down her mother's face, Sunny kneeled on the floor before her mother. "I'm sorry, Mom. I guess I could have handled that better."

"It was a tough time for all of us, Mom. I'm sure Sunny was trying to do the right thing," said Matt. "Sunny? You have something else to tell us?"

Squeezing Sunny's shoulder, her mother stood up and walked toward the kitchen. "It's just been a shock. Let's have some hot tea. Keep talking, Sunny. I want to hear all of it."

Taking a deep breath Sunny began, "After learning about the missing egg Sunday night, the newspaper gave me another shock this morning. Matt, do you remember Saturday when we drove home from the park, and I switched on the radio?"

"Yeah, the oldies station you always listen to when you know I like country!" he said teasingly. This response was his heavy-handed attempt to give tonight a lighter tone. He didn't like to see his mother upset and was always at a loss on how to handle it.

"That's the one. The news came on and mentioned a little boy dying in that explosion in Georgia," said Sunny

"Sad story, but what about him?"

"This morning's edition of the newspaper says the father has been charged with first-degree murder. They say he'd been abusing the child and ended up killing him." Hearing her mother's distressed sounds from the kitchen doorway, she moved past the abuse and got to the photographs. "On the fourth page, there were pictures of the father and the dead child." Walking to her purse as she spoke, Sunny extracted the newspaper page from her bag. She handed it first to Matt, watching him scan the pictures. She watched him frown as his gaze lingered on the poor-quality portrait of the child. When he looked up at her and started to speak, Sunny shook her head to silence him.

"Matt, give the page to Mom so she can look."

"Oh, Sunny," her mother moaned. "I don't want to look at any bad pictures of that poor little—"

"No, mom. They aren't bad pictures. I promise."

Her mother relented and took the news clipping. The tension mounted as she studied the photos until her brother finally erupted.

"Sunny, what the hell is going on here? That kid in that picture looks exactly like—" Matt stopped mid-sentence as he watched his mother put on her bifocals to get a better look.

In a silence thick with tension, they watched as their mother held the picture up to the lamp. She looked at it for several minutes and quietly removed her glasses, folding her hands on her lap.

"That child looks like Sam. Identical to Sam. He was living on Tybee Island, ten minutes from Savannah. Sunny. Did that man kill my grandchild?"

Leave it to her mother to put into words what everyone else was afraid to think. Sighing, Sunny responded.

"I—I don't know—there's got to be an explanation. People do have look-alikes, but—this child even had Sam's cleft in his chin. You don't see that everywhere. The paper says he's seven years old, which would be the right age. It breaks my heart to think that he could be Raine's missing child. That he had been in Georgia all these years, abused, alone, scared, with no none to turn to." Sunny stopped, tears now rolling down her face.

Sunny wiped the tears from her cheeks, straightened up, and said firmly,

"There is only one way to find out for sure. We have to go to Savannah and talk to the detective in charge of the crime scene. The victims always leave DNA, even in an explosion. We can match it to Sam's." She paused, and everyone stared at her like she had lost her mind.

"Well, I do work in a fertility clinic. We use DNA all the time." She finished defensively.

"We're not doubting your knowledge, Sunny," said Matt." I have been in enough active investigations to doubt you would ever be given access to DNA reports on a hunch."

Holding up his hand to halt his sister's objections, he continued, "Though I am sure you have a plan. You always have a plan.

Let's hear it."

"Get your suitcase packed, Matt," said Sunny. "We're heading to Savannah!"

CHAPTER 4

"Hey, are you alone?"

"Uh—yeah—I guess. G is asleep. I guess I'm asleep, too. Why can't we talk when I'm awake? Why do I have to be sleeping? *You're* not asleep."

"I dunno. I've never—I've never had to be asleep to talk to you. I don't even know how we do this! Where's your mom?"

"She and Uncle Matt have gone to someplace with a girl's name—in Georgia.

"Savannah?"

"My aunt Raine used to live there before she died. It's something about her, I guess. They were all serious last night. My mom was crying after she went to bed. She tries to be quiet, but I always know. It makes my stomach hurt. I feel bad that she doesn't know about you. I—I don't like to keep secrets from her."

"Yeah—I know. I had a mother, but I don't remember her. Sometimes, I think I remember the way she smelled, but then— anyway, your mother seems nice."

"She's a great mom! She knows about the bad dreams. She didn't understand when I told her they weren't about me, so I guess she wouldn't understand now. The bad dreams

were terrible. You know—when you lived in that place—with your dad. I never had a dad. Do you miss him?"

"He's not my father! I know they said he is, but he's not!"

"Don't yell! It makes my head hurt! Anyway, I'm glad you're away from him. I could feel it—you know. Every time he—"

"I know—that's when I first knew you were there. I could feel you screaming with me.

"Yeah—but he's gone, and you're somewhere better! It's been three days. I saw in my dream that you left the boat and walked on a beach toward some trees. How will I come to get you if you don't know where you are? I know my mom will help you! You could live with us!"

"I'd like that, but there's so much stuff I don't get. Why do I look like you? How do I know we look alike? How can we talk this way just by thinking something? How can you feel if something bad happens to me—but I can't tell if something bad happens to you?"

"Don't forget—I can feel if something good happens to you—at least sometimes."

"Weird"

"Yeah. You told me you're on an island, but that's all I know."

"I know the people here call it Isla Seguro. I found out that means Safe Island in Spanish. They speak Spanish here too—like

Maria, the housekeeper at the beach where I lived before. It rains
a lot here—every day. There are lots of trees and flowers, big, huge
ones. Millions of birds and animals, too! There are poisonous
snakes, so we stay on the paths."

"Isla Seguro? Yeah! I forgot! You told me the name the day
you arrived on the island. I tried to look it up on my big globe. I
couldn't find it. I got on the computer, and G helped me look—"

"You told G? Are you nuts? You can't tell anyone anything until
we have a plan!"

"I didn't tell her why I wanted to look up stuff. I just asked
her to teach me to do it. But—"

"What! What did you find?"

"Nothing! There isn't an island with that name! I tried and
tried—nothing."

"It's okay—I have an idea. Are you a good drawer like me?"

"My mom and my teacher say I'm really good. I like to draw.
Why?"

"Where I used to live, Maria would let me watch this channel
on TV with all sorts of animals on it—from all over the world, but
I never saw anything like some of the animals here! Maybe you
could draw them and then look them up to see—"

"Where they live! I could do that! Wait a minute! G's awake!
She wants to go to the store, and she won't let me stay—"

"It's okay. I'll look around for some really weird animals.
They're all over the place. I will send them to you tonight when you
sleep, so keep your colored pencils and paper by the bed."

"Draw when I'm asleep? I don't know—I've never done that before—there must be—"

"Don't worry about it. We'll figure out a way. Wake up and go with G—hurry!"

"Sammy! Where are you? There you are, you rascal! I've been calling, and you were asleep on the couch! I thought you didn't like naps!"

Sam looked into his beloved grandmother's eyes. Throwing his arms around her, he hugged her so tight she drew back with a frown.

"Sweetie, is something wrong? Did you...did you have a bad dream?"

"G? "

"Yes, doll boy. What is it?"

"Do you wish you had another grandson to love, G?"

Surprised at the sad look on her face, she quickly replaced it with a smile when G saw his frown.

"Hmmmm...Let me think. He would have to have a smile just like you. He would have to be as sweet as you are!" She laughed. "He would have to be just like you or—What? Why are you grinning? Get off that couch, lazy bones, and come on! We're having your favorite thing for dinner—pizza! We need to go buy the stuff to make it!"

❖

Early the following day, Sam looked happily at the brightly colored drawings spread across his bed. Bending over to pick up the one he liked best, he smiled as his finger traced the outline of a beautiful red feathered parrot with blue-tipped wings, admiring the colors. After a dream-filled night, he had awakened and began to draw feverishly. He remembered three animals— one was a beautiful parrot. The other two, though not as colorful, were different from anything he had seen in books or on TV, but then he was only six.

He picked up a picture of a monkey. The black, shiny eyes looked out from a face surrounded by thick, fluffy fur. The third animal looked like a giant rat holding food with his hands while standing on his back legs.

Thoughts flashed furiously back and forth all night as the boys tried to find a way to get help identifying the animals. Sam knew he wasn't good enough yet on the Internet, even though he would try. Finally, he knew—he knew a way for sure!

"I got it! I know someone who can help us!"

"You do! Who? Can we trust him?"

"It's Professor Berger! He used to be an explorer. He's been everywhere and tells me neat stories of the places he's been! He even had a run-in with pirates! Besides—I'll tell him I saw them on TV and just wanted to know where they come from."

"Aw—he's lyin'! There ain't no pirates anymore."

"There is, too! He told me and even showed me a picture of their ship. I can take them to him after breakfast!"

"Well—I guess it's okay. Just be careful. If we're lucky, the animals live only on this island!"

"I'm getting tired of all this thinking. I need to sleep for real now. My mom will be home tomorrow. I'll get up early and talk to Professor Berger before she gets home."

"I know. The people here get us up early. G'night, Sam."

"G'night, Jeremy"2

CHAPTER 5

Sunny sat in an uncomfortable metal chair, clenching her hands, wondering what was taking the detective so long. She glanced at Matt and admired his air of calm detachment. They had only been on Tybee Island, where the alleged murder occurred, for less than an hour, but it was already too long. Tybee was only twenty minutes from Savannah, Georgia, where her sister lived before her death. The historic, picturesque town was a big tourist attraction for thousands yearly. To her, it was a place of grief and mourning.

Relieved when the dispatcher told them the detective assigned to the boy's case was at the station, they were placed in this tiny, gray, sterile office. Twenty minutes had passed, and there was still no sign of the detective. The long flight into Savannah that morning, combined with the stress of the last few days, had left her temper a good match for her red hair. Unable to stand the suspense any longer, she turned to her brother.

"What is taking them so long? I mean, this isn't a huge building. How long would it take anyone to walk the length of it? What if they won't—"

Her brother leaned over and took her hands.

"You've got to calm down. We'll get what we come for. Relax."

"How do you know that? It's such a weird story—he's going to think I am an escapee from the *Jerry Springer Show* or something!"

Laughing gently, her brother lightly rubbed her back.

"Sit up and let me do the talking," he said, hearing voices from the hallway. "Just look fragile and helpless. I've had dealings with a lot of law enforcement, and they're suckers for a damsel in distress."

Sitting straighter in her chair, Sunny watched as two men entered the room. The shorter man crossed the room and offered his hand, first to her brother and then to her, before sitting at his desk. He was nice-looking, stocky, and muscular, with an open, friendly face and shiny black hair almost to his shoulders.

"Mr. and Mrs. Day, my name is Detective Lambrusco. My dispatcher said you came to talk about the murder investigation concerning the young boy. If you have some information, you think we need to hear—"

"Detective Lambrusco," interrupted Matt. "Could I clarify some things right up front?" Noting the detective's nod, he continued. "We're not husband and wife. We're sister and brother. So please feel free to call us by our first names, Matt and Sunny. Also, we didn't come to give *you* information. We are hoping that you'll be able to supply *us* with some information."

Still sitting silently in her chair, Sunny noticed that the other detective had stationed himself in the doorway. She realized it was his utter stillness that drew her attention. Light grey eyes moved slowly from Matt to her. Well, she thought. Whoever he is—we're certainly getting his full attention. His lean, rangy build, clothed in an expensive dark grey suit and tie, contrasted oddly with the rumpled casual clothes of his partner. Strange, she thought, watching Detective Lambrusco glancing toward the door as he spoke to Matt like he was getting some unspoken guidance from this enigmatic man.

"Folks, I don't know how much help the department can be. This is still an open investigation, so the public record statute doesn't apply."

Still looking toward the door, Sunny spoke for the first time.

"Detective, I don't believe you introduced your—"

"Oh, yeah. Sorry." Vaguely waving his hand toward the man, he introduced them. "This is—uh—Ables. Now, back to the information you want. Why don't you tell me what this is about?"

Matt slowly turned from his silent contemplation of the man standing in the doorway, now known as Ables. He had been around a lot of law enforcement, and if this guy were an island detective, he'd eat his hat. His clothing and attitude shouted federal government, likely FBI. Not surprising. They were into everything now. Still, it would make it harder to get any information. Turning back to the detective, Matt said, "Detective Lambrusco? We do have a story to tell. It may or may not directly relate to the incident on your Island. That's why we're hoping you can help.

I'm going to let my sister tell you about it. Sunny?"

At the sound of her name, Sunny jumped. She had been going over the story for the last few minutes. How much to tell? What could she leave out and still get the help? So much was riding on the police department's help.

"Ms. Day?" the detective said briskly. "I've got limited time today, so if you could—"

"Of course, I'm sorry. It's a rather long story, but I'll try to condense it down. My sister, Raine, died in Savannah over seven years ago. Months before she died, she had some of her eggs fertilized and split into four sections each. They were then frozen for her use at a later date. There were eight sections. She willed them to me, and I used one to have my son, and one is missing. We think she might have had one implanted. We don't know for sure. No child was found in the car after the accident. We think the murdered Tybee boy might have been my sister's child." Satisfied that she had provided enough information, she leaned back in her chair and smiled hopefully at the detective.

"Why?" The dry, one-word question floated over to her from the doorway.

.

77

Glancing toward the still-standing detective, Sunny watched as he pushed himself away from the doorframe and walked over to perch on the front edge of the desk.

"Uh, what do you mean why?" Sunny glanced at her brother for help.

"Why do *you* think the murdered child might be your nephew?"

Sunny had wanted to keep her son out of this. She should have seen this coming. Of course, they would like to know how she made the connection.

Matt abruptly stood up and moved behind his sister's chair, putting his hands on her shoulders while addressing the welldressed man. "We have more information, but first, I want to know who we're talking to. Detective Ables? I doubt you're a detective. I'd guess the FBI. I'd like to see your identification before we go any further."

Smiling slightly, the man reached into his jacket pocket for his identification. He passed it slowly in front of Sunny and Matt.

"You're right, Matt. Good call. I am FBI. Sorry I didn't clarify that earlier, but this case has been a problem since day one. Kooks come here claiming they have information, especially since the local newspaper reported our involvement. This particular crime is part of a larger investigation I can't discuss now. I hope you understand." Settling back onto the edge of the desk, he turned to Sunny. "I gather you have information that enables you to arrive at an educated guess that this murdered child might be your nephew. I need to know what that information is. I can assure you it will be kept confidential."

Sunny realized she had been holding her breath. Feeling the reassuring pressure of her brother's hands on her shoulders, she continued with her story. "The day after I found out an embryo was missing, there was an article in the Austin newspaper about the incident on Tybee Island. It was a long article and went into great detail about the boy. There was a picture of him. It wasn't a perfect picture, but it was good enough to see that he looked identical to my son, Sam." Sunny stopped and looked at both men, waiting for it to sink in before she went further.

The agent and detective exchanged looks. Impatiently, Sunny shifted in her chair, awaiting some indication that it was time for her to proceed. Finally, the agent nodded to Sunny.

"Well, I know what you're thinking! It's a long shot—a wild guess on my part—but there's more. When fertilized eggs are split into the four sections, each section will be identical to the other sections—same sex, same coloring, same genetic makeup—identical. After my sister's death, I had one of her embryos implanted."

Seeing the surprised looks on both men's faces, she continued, "She wanted me to have them. She knew I might have trouble conceiving, and she wanted me to be able to have babies. She left them to me in her will." Sunny's voice dwindled to a stop as she realized how crazy all this must sound to the two men who, before today, probably thought they had heard it all.

Defensive now, she continued. "I know. It was a crazy but also an extremely loving, generous thing to do, and that was my sister. I felt by having her baby, I was—was able to keep a part of her living and grant my wish for a child."

Seeing the tears in her eyes, the agent leaned over to give her the tissue box on the desk. Sunny looked at the half-empty box, wondering about everyone sitting in this chair before her, pouring their hearts out in despair in this tiny, sterile room. She suddenly felt a kinship with the whole human race. Knowing she was not the only one to use these tissues gave her strength to continue.

Matt sat beside her and took her hands. "Do you need to take a break or get a drink of water?"

"No. I'm okay. If Raine *did* have one of the sections implanted, the child would be an identical twin to my son. So, Agent Ables, here are the reasons why I think this murdered child might be my sister's son. Number one is the age of the child. He was about ten months older than my son, Sam. Number two was Tybee's proximity to Savannah, where my sister lived. Number three, his startling resemblance to my son. Number four, the missing embryo."

Emotionally spent, Sunny leaned back in her chair without breaking eye contact with the agent and silently willing him to see what she saw, to go along at least with the possibility of it. When the silence continued, she said, "We have to rule it out—I pray it isn't him. I—I have to know."

Still mindful of her damsel-in-distress role, she put a tremulous smile on her face and opened her eyes wide in what she hoped was an innocent look. Detective Lambrusco abruptly stood up, pushing his chair back from the desk, and walked toward the door.

"Folks, I understand what you're going through, but as I said, the investigation is still open, so the Tybee Police Department can't divulge anything that has not already been made public." He walked through the door and continued, "However, the FBI operates under different regulations. They can divulge anything they feel necessary, so...it was great meeting you both, and I will make myself scarce."

Turning to give Sunny a warm smile and a wink, he gently closed the door.

Silence hung in the room after Lambrusco's exit. It was Matt who finally spoke up. "Okay, Ables, what's it going to be? Are you going to help or not? You can trust us to keep anything we find out confidential. This won't be the first time I've had access to information but couldn't use it."

The agent stood up and walked to the only window in the room. Looking out at the sunlit street, he said, "You understand this is all off the record?"

"Not a problem. You have my word on that. Right? Sunny?"

"Yes. As long as we're given the same courtesy, Agent Ables."

Turning from the window, the agent sat in the detective's chair. His manner suddenly became more open and approachable.

"Ken," he said. At their confused looks, he explained, "My first name is Ken. Please feel free to use it. As I understand it, you want to know if the boy in question could be genetically identical to your son, Sam. Can you get a DNA sample from your son and send it to me quickly? This incident is part of a more extensive investigation, and I never know when I'll have to leave town. "

"You were able to get some DNA samples?" asked Sunny. "We were afraid the explosion would leave nothing. The newspaper picture was pretty—graphic."

"It was a devastating explosion, but it's almost impossible for a fire to get hot enough to destroy all DNA. There were some blood smears and—" Seeing Sunny wince, the detective didn't complete his sentence.

"There was also a lot of DNA in the parts of the shed that weren't destroyed. The kid lived there, under this expensive beach condo. He lived there like some animal you put out in—" He stopped, mouth grim.

Sunny watched the agent tamp down the emotions.

"The DNA from my son is no problem. I can download it from the embryo bank files and send it to your cell."

"That should do it. DNA will establish the genetic relationship if there is one. You know, Sunny, this is such a long shot. Don't get our hopes up too high. I hate to wrap this up, but I have a conference call scheduled in the next thirty minutes."

Sunny watched while the two men stood and shook hands, exchanging contact information. Something else was floating around in her brain, triggered by the agent's words. How could we find out if her sister ever had a baby? Even if this poor dead boy was not her nephew, she had to know if her sister had given birth to a live infant. Raine was dead. How could she tell her?

Sunny jumped out of her chair, startling the men into stopping their conversation.

"I got it! I know a way we can find out for sure if Raine had ever been pregnant!" Her brother and the agent exchanged looks as she stepped between them, turning to face the agent.

"I need one more thing. I might not need your help to get it—I don't know, but I need a copy of my sister's autopsy report!"

"What good is that going to do?" asked Matt. "Those things are filled with gory stuff you don't need to see," Matt said as he tried to pull her away from the agent and toward the door. "It's been a rough day. Let's go back to Savannah and have something to ea—"

"Matt! Let go of me! I have a perfectly good reason for wanting to see the report!" Turning back to the agent, she continued, "The report talks about the state of the deceased's organs. That's how we'll know! If she had a baby, it would have been a couple of months before her death. A pathologist would note that she bore signs of a recent pregnancy! Stretch marks, the shape of the uterus! That information would be in the report."

Pleading now, she continued, "Please! It's the only way I'll know there was a birth. You said the chance that this dead child will be my sister's child is a long shot. I agree! That's why I have to know if she actually gave birth. It will mean I have a nephew somewhere out there who needs his aunt, and I intend to find him. Please, please help me!"

She waited impatiently as the two men exchanged looks of resignation. Finally, the agent spoke, his tone serious again. "You promise to keep me informed of any developments? Even if you don't think they're important? No secrets?" "You have my word," Sunny replied.

"Okay. Leave me the name of your hotel, and you'll have your sister's autopsy report by this evening."

Several hours later, Sunny sat on a park bench surrounded by tall oak trees in downtown Savannah. Before Raine's death, it had always been her favorite city, built around twenty-two parks with statues, fountains, and beautifully manicured landscaping. As she took in the historic buildings and slow-moving pedestrians, her thoughts turned to her visits to Raine when the two sisters would explore the antebellum mansions. Raine loved walking through the town at night and even took a weekend job as a guide for one of the walking ghost tours that started at dusk and took visitors through a cemetery, telling ghost stories and watching eyes widen. She was a great storyteller— which had gotten her into trouble more than once, mused Sunny.

In the gathering dusk, Sunny watched her brother lope down the steps of their hotel and scan the area until he spotted her on the bench. After shamefully stuffing himself with worldfamous fried catfish and pecan pie, Matt declared he needed a nap and returned to their hotel. Sunny strolled to the park, enjoying the calm green peacefulness. Her phone call to Sam earlier had left her feeling homesick for him. He said he had been drawing some "neat stuff" but wouldn't elaborate. He sounded happy, and that always made her glad. She hung up, reassuring him that she and Uncle Matt would be on the plane by 8 am tomorrow and home a few hours later.

Feeling relaxed and beginning to get a little sleepy, she watched her long-legged brother lope across the park. Watching him run was always a pleasure. He had been a track star in high school and moved with the loping, lazy grace of a giraffe.

Plopping down next to her and only slightly out of breath, Matt pulled out a manilla envelope lodged under his armpit.

"It's just arrived! I was getting out of the shower when I saw it shoved under the door." Seeing Sunny's puzzled look, he continued, "The autopsy report!"

"Already? I didn't expect it until much later in the evening. Those FBI people are fast!" she exclaimed, grabbing the folder.

"Hold on a second! Are you sure you don't want me to look at it first, Sunny? There is going to be some gruesome stuff in here."

She looked up at her brother and said thoughtfully, "I know it's going to be bad—to read what my sister's body went through at the time of her death, but—you know, Matt? She's in heaven now, and she'll never have any more pain or disappointment again. I can deal with this. I know Raine would want and expect me to care for her child if there was one. I'm going through this, so hand it over!"

Looking at his little sister's determined expression, he knew better than to argue with her, so he slowly opened the folder and gave her the report.

Sunny looked at the official-looking document labeled with her sister's name and felt like she had been socked in the stomach. This document declared her sister to be officially dead. She was so dead that they could cut her open and examine every organ of her body without fear of hurting her. Tears welled up in her eyes as the acceptance of this new and somehow more painful loss lodged in her heart. Bending over her knees and cradling the report, Sunny looked up at her brother, who had tears in his eyes, watching her. They sat on the bench in silence, sharing this new phase of their grief, wondering if this would be the last.

An hour later, they sat in the hotel bar, the report lying unread on the table. She sipped her coffee and felt the life-giving caffeine sliding down every nerve ending, bracing herself for the task ahead. Looking around, Sunny thought about what a lovely, peaceful place this was. Thick carpeting, soft background piano music, and candlelight tables were all soothing to her soul—and badly needed. She smiled at her brother, who sat sipping a bourbon on the rocks, declaring earlier coffee wouldn't cut it for him tonight.

"Are you sure you don't want me to look at that report?" he asked, smiling gently at her.

"Nope! I can do it! I'm better now, and I have medical training."

Finally, she picked up the report and opened it. She quickly scanned the pages while Matt waited impatiently.

After several minutes of watching Sunny flip pages forward and backward, muttering under her breath, his hand hit the table, exclaiming, "What! What—have you found? I'm going nuts just sitting here. Tell me something!"

Hands shaking, she closed the folder and carefully placed it on the table. Her face chalk white.

"How much do you want to know, and how detailed do you want it?"

"Well, uh—what do you mean? How much do I want to know? I want to know—Dammit! Did Raine have a baby? What the hell else were we trying to find out?

"Yes"

"Yes? You mean, yes, she had a baby? It says that? In the report? I need more—give it to me slowly and as nonmedical as you can make it."

She grabbed his clenched hands and held them tightly. "Raine had an episiotomy scar, and her breasts were full of milk at the time of death.

Taking advantage of her brother's shocked silence, she took a big drink from Matt's glass and felt the warmth of the bourbon as it went down. Now they knew. Raine did have a baby, but what happened to it?

Later that night, Sunny stretched out under the cool cotton sheets in her hotel room. Her mind shifted through the facts. Her sister had been pregnant and delivered a child. And the child had been alive at the time of Raine's death.

She turned on her side and stared into the darkened room. Why hadn't the investigation turned up a child? Surely, if the infant were in the car, they would have found remains. She should call Raine's former roommate, Lisa! The last time Sunny had seen the heavily made-up, curvy brunette was at Raine's funeral. Both had been too distraught to say much. Lisa and Raine had roomed together for two years and were very close. She would know about a baby. Sunny couldn't fathom why she hadn't said something about a child at the funeral.

As usual, she felt more relaxed with a plan to follow. Finally getting drowsy, her thoughts drifted in and out from all directions—no control, no order. Catching one as it came by, she would acknowledge it, release it, and put it back in line with the others. Mostly, her thoughts were questions—questions she didn't have the answer to.

In the morning, she would be back in Austin with her son. She smiled sleepily, imagining his soundly sleeping form safely in his bedroom. As she settled into a deep sleep, she made a mental note to call Lisa as soon as she got up.

"Whoever this is better be bleeding! It's 6 o'clock in the damn morning!"

Sunny winced at the outraged, sleep-filled voice.

"Oh, Lisa! It's Sunny—Raine's sister! I'm so sorry to call you this early, but—Lisa? Are you there?" Sunny asked when no response was forthcoming.

"Uh, yeah. I'm here. How's it going with you? It's been a while."

Her less-than-enthusiastic words put Sunny on guard. She had always been so outgoing and friendly, but now Lisa acted like she was talking to a bill collector.

"I know it's been over six years since Raine's death. I'm sure you have gone on with your life and never expected to hear from me. I was surprised you still had the same phone number, but—" "I can't help you," came the flat response. "I have to go now. I already gave you the box. I shouldn't have done *that*, but I thought you would want her stuff—"

"Wait a minute, Lisa! What box? I never got a box from you. Ever!"

"Oh—I—uh—I meant to. Damn! It must still be in that storage place. Oh well! You know what they say about good intentions and all that. Look. I really got to go now so—"

"Wait! Don't you dare hang up on me! I need that box. There are questions I have to have answered. I'll meet you at the storage garage. Where is it? I need to do it now. My plane leaves in two hours."

"Sunny, please!" came the pleading voice. "I just can't meet you! I can give you the lock code and the address. That's it!" Giving up on the hope that her sister's ex-roommate would help solve some mysteries, she hurriedly wrote down the information.

"I got it. Lisa, I don't know what's going on, but something is wrong. Do you need help? Is someone threatening you? Is it about my sister's death?"

"No! No! Nothing's wrong! I'm just busy, and you woke me up—and it's been so long. I wasn't expecting to hear from you, that's all."

Determined to get some information before the line was disconnected, she asked, "Did Raine have a baby?"

"Sunny, I can't talk. I got to go! Please don't call me again!"

She heard the buzzing that identified the end of the call. Replaying the strange conversation repeatedly in her mind, she ran to the connecting door, yelling for her brother to get up.

Two hours later, safely in her airplane seat, Sunny braced herself for take-off, her least favorite part of flying. They had barely made it to the airport in time. Naturally, the storage facility was on the other side of town. A cheap, run-down place with separate wooden garages. Grateful the combination for the lock worked, she was dismayed to see the shed's interior. Not climate-controlled or pest-controlled. The cardboard box was right where Lisa had said it was. Running out of time, Matt loaded the three-foot square box in the trunk of their rental and raced to the airport. It was safely logged in as baggage, and Sunny could not wait to open it.

Leaning over to speak quietly in her ear, Matt said, "I wonder what was up with Lisa? She was Raine's best friend. Something about this makes my reporter's nose start twitching. After we find our *nephew*, I might return to Savannah and poke around a little."

"Something definitely was bothering her. It sounded like she was strung out on drugs or something. Right now, I can't worry about Lisa—unless," she said, smiling at her older brother. "If I don't get what I need from Raine's box, I'll return and shake the truth out of her."

Smiling at the determined glint in his little sister's eyes, he pushed the recline button on her seat.

"It's good you've been taking Pilates classes and lifting weights. You may need all those muscles! Lisa's got about six inches on you. Get some rest! We'll be home in a few hours, and you know we'll have to listen to Sam's exciting news before anything else gets done."

Reclining his seat, Matt closed his eyes and squirmed his long body into a semi-comfortable position. Minutes later, Sunny drifted into a light sleep, lulled by the drone of the airplane engines. Her brother's sleepy chuckle drifted to her.

"That is some kid. Asking when you called earlier if you would like another son."

CHAPTER 6

"I can't believe you did it! After we discussed it and agreed it was too dangerous right now, you snatched that politician's kid! You are only one member of this team! It's just like you, going off alone and doing what you please, no matter the risk! Plus, I had to wait until your return from this last mission to yell at you!"

Crank watched the older man pacing back and forth in front of him. Red-faced, he would stop frequently to glare at Crank before resuming his pace, his anger gathering steam with each step. Giving his old friend time to calm down, Crank remembered the first time he met Lawrence Plankton, or "Chief," as he was affectionately called.

It was December 17, 1989, during the Panama Invasion. Two days earlier, the Panamanian dictator Noriega declared war on the United States. A big mistake was made even more significant when his soldiers killed a U.S. Marine. President George H. W. Bush ordered the invasion to capture Noriega and bring him back to face drug charges in the United States. Crank was a member of an elite Army ranger team named "snake eaters" because of their unconventional survival training and remote operation locations where food sources were scarce. His squad had orders to locate and release Noriega's political prisoners held on an island off the coast of Panama. Arriving on the island in the middle of the night, his squad silently infiltrated their holding area and found the prisoners or what was left of them. The camp was like a scene out of a horror movie—charred, dismembered bodies lying around— giving testimony to the Panamanian dictator's brutal methods of leadership. On his knees, puking up his guts minutes later, Crank felt a heavy hand on his shoulder and a cigarette-roughened voice yelling in his ear.

"Get your ass back to the beach, soldier! We've got to get out and get out now!"

Stumbling back to the beach with a heavy hand pushing at his back, yelling and cussing in his ear, Crank wondered who in the hell this man was. Two years ago, while off duty, he was attacked by a gang of thugs and nearly beaten to death. At least that's what he was told. He had lost all memory. He didn't even know his name. While recovering in the hospital, he was approached by this mystery soldier. He suddenly remembered the mission and the man but so far little else. Chief explained the organization's goal and asked Crank to join. Since he was medically discharged from the military, he agreed. He still wasn't sure what the Chief's status in the military was, but he sure as hell knew who the boss was in this setup. Military to the core, he was their group's admired and respected leader.

"Chief, if you let me get a word in—"

Rubbing his hand over the top of his iron-grey crew cut, the Chief stopped and glared at him. The sight of Crank lying back in his cushioned leather office chair with his feet on the desk brought a fresh wave of anger.

"What 'word' could you offer to make this political nightmare disappear? I told you we would try to help the little girl another way. I promised you that. It might take a little longer, but it—"

"She didn't have a little longer!" Crank dropped his feet to the floor, tired of being yelled at. With his hands on the desk, he growled, "Why don't you ask me where she is? This little girl who *could wait for rescue!*"

The Chief's anger slowly disappeared and was replaced by a look of dread. Sitting down heavily without a glance at Crank, he said, "Where is she?"

"She's in the hospital in Panama. They don't know if she'll make it. Dammit!" Crank exploded. "If I hadn't waited those extra few days and snatched her when we first located her—"

Long minutes of silence filled the room as frustration, anger, and sadness passed between the two men without a single word being spoken. Their discord was gone; they were united once again. The Chief rose slowly. A trim and muscular six-footer, no one would have guessed his age at sixty-two. Calmer now, he said, "I'll need your full report tomorrow to start some damage control. We'll get the team together around 3 p.m. to plan our strategy."

Walking toward the door after catching Crank's tired nod of agreement, Chief said, "Shake it off, son. We can't save everyone. Get some sleep."

Later that morning, Crank lay in his rope hassock. Located among the Cecropia trees with leaves as tall as a man. It provided a screen from the children playing in the water. Their healthy, tanned bodies flashed in and out of the natural pool. They dived under the waterfall, surfacing seconds later like dolphins exploding from the water. Some of the newer saves were still guarded in their movements, testing the limits of freedom and questioning how far they could go without being hurt.

Crank focused on a scene being played out at the pool's far end. There was a small boy, one of the new saves, still stiff from his injuries, trying to stay afloat, while a bigger boy kept his face above water. Watching the kind gestures and assistance, it dawned on him that the helper was Jeremy. Crank had not seen Jeremy since he brought him to the island two weeks ago. Watching the powerful strokes as Jeremy showed the smaller boy how it was done had him silently congratulating the kid. Usually locked in a shed, how did he learn to swim like that? Remembering the adult composure and stubbornness the kid had displayed—it would figure he found a way. Crank's real reward was seeing the kids play and knowing no one would ever abuse them again. He let people think it was the money, which he had to admit was damn good. He also wanted the staff to believe he was a hard-ass mercenary. As a kid, he remembered praying daily for a safe place to stay. He only started feeling safe at fifteen when he beat the crap out of that son of a—. He stopped himself, not wanting to delve into his past. He had a team meeting in an hour and was getting hungry.

Regretfully extricating himself from the hammock, he stood up and stretched, breathing in the heavy perfume of the rainforest. Huge hibiscus flowers in brilliant yellows, oranges, and reds hung over the edge of the shallow pool, lovingly guarding their charges as they frolicked in the water. Lush greenery hugged the sides of the waterfall. Scarlet macaws hopped around the pool's edges, hoping for a handout. Shaking bad memories from his head with practiced ease, he followed the path to his hut, stomach growling, anticipating lunch.

"Jefe! You are late! Food is ready!"

Crank stepped onto the lanai, taking a tall glass of chilled fruit juice from his frowning houseboy, Angel. He thought back to the night when he first encountered this jungle native.

Wrapping up a long night of visiting the local nightclubs in Santa Catalina, he was standing outside a local bar when he noticed the Panama National Police scouring the sidewalks and alleys, looking for someone. He wouldn't wish his worst enemy a stay in one of their jails. Substandard housing-overcrowding-

nonexistent medical care. Not to mention the beatings and torture that went on daily.

Settling his large frame into the front seat of the rented Chevy, he felt the car shift and settle. Furtive movements from the back seat, and he knew—he had a passenger. Not relishing a knife in his back, he slowly started the car and pulled away from the curb.

"Do you speak English?" Eyes on the road, Crank spoke slowly, hoping like hell he did. His Spanish wasn't good enough to converse with an excited, frightened fugitive.

"Yes," came the soft reply.

"What do you want me to do?"

"Drive, please."

After twenty minutes and total silence, Crank pulled onto a deserted part of the beach. His boat was waiting to take him back to the island. Without turning around, he said, "Okay, this is the end of the line. I got to catch a boat. There are plenty of places you can hide so—" The back door clicking shut stopped Crank cold.

Thirty minutes into the one-hour trip to the island, Crank leaned on the boat rail, cradling his beer, still thinking about his anonymous passenger. He didn't blame the guy for running. Panamanian law puts an accused in jail pending a trial, which could take years. Many innocent people stayed there for years before even being arraigned. But what if he had just helped a murderer or child molester escape?

Hearing a commotion on deck, he turned away from the railing. The deckhands were chasing a small, half-naked man all over the boat; the air was thick with Spanish curses. Seeing the fugitive leap off a barrel and run down the boat toward him, Crank prepared to catch the little guy. Bending down to scoop him up. He froze in place as the native slid to a stop directly in front of him, breathing hard.

"Jefe. You must save me again."

"Well, son of a...! It's you. My criminal from the car! Well, I'll be damned!" He looked over as the ship's captain approached. "Ah, hello, Captain Mike. How's everything?"

"Funny, you should ask that Crank. Everything's not too damn good! I have a stowaway on my boat—an unpaid passenger—and you seem to know him. Is he with you?"

Crank looked from the angry captain to the four-foot native standing calmly by his side. Words so strange tumbled out of his mouth that he felt like he was in a ventriloquist act, except this small teak-colored man was the ventriloquist, and he was the dummy.

"Uh...Oh, yeah! Captain! You weren't on deck when we came on. I was going to settle up with you before we departed. He's with me!"

The bowlegged captain stomped away, chewing furiously on his unlit pipe, mumbling about passenger lists and needing to know who was on his ship. There was more, but Crank had other fish to fry, albeit a small one. He devoted the rest of the trip to listening to the little man's story revealed in surprisingly good English.

"My name is Angel. I come from a village near the upper Chagres River. I am Embera. We live in a rainforest. I learned English at school and was working in Santa Catalina at restaurant. I am great cook! The owner accused me of stealing from him. I did not do this! Embera, do not steal! But I run. If I go to prison, I do not get out. My family will starve! I wish to work for you—on your island. I will be your tribesman, and you will be my jefe— my Chief."

Crank had been in Panama long enough to know he was right. If he went to prison, his size alone would likely ensure his death. The Embera, indigenous to Panama, were hard workers and generally happy people who lived off the forest. Due to the steady destruction of the rain forest, the coffee-colored skin and brightly clothed people could be found working in service areas around Panama City.

"I've seen your people working in the city. They're not usually as small as you. You're barely four f—"

"I have same size heart as you, Jefe."

Angel cooked for him, cared for the house and his clothes, and taught him about the wonders of the rainforest and the importance of preserving its delicate ecological balance. Crank wasn't sure how, but Angel had quietly and persistently transported his entire family to the island. No one seemed to mind.

Good help was hard to find.

Pulling his chair up to the wooden table one of Angel's relatives made, he took in the delicious lunch of fresh tropical fruits and a sizzling piece of grouper wrapped in plantain leaves. A typical fish found in the waters around the island and prized for its taste. The little man could definitely cook.

"Okay, I'm ready. What's happening around here?" he said, diving with relish into his lunch.

Angel knew everything that was happening in their paradise. No detail was too small, and no incident was too insignificant that the native gossip mill didn't know about and repeat. It was amazing that in the absence of telecommunications, his little tribe of relatives could quickly and accurately transfer information. There were no embellishments—just the facts.

"Jefe, the brains are unhappy with you."

He grimaced as he made an educated guess as to why. The "brains" were a group of people that made up the core committee on the island. Nicknamed the "brains" by the Embera, who stood in awe of their knowledge, they were all highly skilled professionals, hand-selected because of their expertise in a specific area. The committee made policies for every aspect of island life. They interpreted policies as laws. To Crank, policies were "guidelines" he could use or ignore. This fundamental difference in point of view gave the "brains" heartburn some days. It looked like this would be one of them.

A little before three, Crank walked down the path toward the island's administration building. He was in no hurry to face what he was sure would be a lengthy discussion of his most recent operation. It was essential for the island to keep a low profile, and they worried about unnecessary exposure. Patting his shirt pocket to be sure he brought what he needed for this "meeting," he found the marker for the building and located the door. Leaving the humidity behind, he entered the tastefully furnished, temperature-controlled interior, which reminded him again what unlimited money could do. Plush chairs grouped around a long conference table of beautifully polished mahogany and soft ambient lighting made the room feel cozy and welcoming to Crank. Usually.

Walking toward the two committee members already present, he gave a big smile to the beautiful Italian lady seated next to the Chief. Mona Leesa, which she assured everyone was her legal name, was the island's "Director of Animal Preservation and Identification." Her lush, sensual body and outgoing, friendly, if somewhat eccentric manner hid a tremendously intelligent brain. There was nothing about the animal world- mainly tropical animals that she did not know. She had been with the Smithsonian in their tropical studies division for seven years before joining the group. Crank really liked her and would have moved on that feeling, but he only wanted a "no strings" relationship and respected her too much.

"Ciao, my friend! You are in trouble again. You naughty boy!" said Mona, flashing him a wide smile. "Come sit by me. I will protect you!"

"Mona, this is no joke!" came the stern rejoinder from the Chief. "We have policies for a reason! They keep the children and the island safe. Crank knows this."

Crank strode around the table and sat next to Mona. At least he had one ally. Turning to look into her sparkling brown eyes, he took her hand and kissed the soft palm, saying, "Ciao! La Bella signora!"

Hearing sounds from the end of the room; Crank turned to see Jack Grayson walking to the table with four slim brown bottles of imported beer that made Crank's mouth water in anticipation. Chilled rivulets of water were sliding down the cold bottles. Getting an imported beer on the island was a treat since it had to be purchased at a certain bar in Panama. The Texan, nicknamed Bubba, *was* the purchasing agent for the island. The man could get anything. It was amazing. No one delved too deeply into how he got what was needed. Especially if it was imported beer, you could tell by the beer belly on his five-footeleven-inch frame that he liked beer, too. He didn't drink off the island. He took island security seriously and didn't want his loose lips to sink any ship. Bubba was responsible for procurement, running the maintenance departments, and keeping the island vehicles going. All the island inhabitants appreciated his jovial, easygoing manner. Sliding the cold, wet bottles to each member present, he smiled and sat across from Crank.

"Ya'll drink up! There isn't enough for the rest of the group. My next shipment will arrive tomorrow." Taking a deep, satisfying swig of the cold amber liquid, he swallowed noisily and wiped the back of his mouth with his hand.

"There is no beer for me?" said Gretchen, chief of island security, as she entered the building. Gracefully folding her long, toned frame into a chair beside Bubba, the platinum-haired director of security smoothly lifted the almost full bottle of beer and took a long swallow.

They had just finished their beers in silence when the last members entered the room. Twin sisters Ruth and Sophie smiled and took their places. The Jewish sisters represented the island's medical and psychiatric areas. Both were 69 years old, identical in looks but different in temperament. Their looks and conversation reminded Crank of a pair of twittering house wrens. Sharing brown hair, large, soft brown eyes, and matronly bodies, they were impossible to tell apart until they started speaking or walking. They loved to wear bush clothes and sensible walking boots even though they were rarely out in the rainforest.

The school children loved Dr. Ruth, the staff psychiatrist, who was firm and no-nonsense, and Dr. Sophie, the medical director, who was soft and gentle.

The sisters grew up in New York City. They worked with the child welfare division of the Health and Human Services Department on a national level. After losing both their husbands and being thoroughly disillusioned with the federal and state's answers to abandoned and abused children, the opportunity to try an alternate solution, even though it put them on the wrong side of the law, was something they couldn't pass up.

Everyone greeted the last two members as they took their seats. Nelson, the team's ethnobotanist and protector of all plants and vegetation on the island, sat next to Mona. Samantha Rutledge, the director of education for the children, sat at the end of the table.

Nelson Marnee was probably the closest thing to a male friend Crank had on the island. Nelson was the type of guy who could blend into the jungle and become one with nature. In part because he always dressed in camouflage gear. He was a brilliant kid and had been one of the top researchers in the field. His shy, quiet nature made it easy to tease him, and the team did— about almost everything. His shyness around women. His diet. He only ate raw foods, nothing cooked. Bubba never missed an opportunity to rag Nelson about his raw food diet. However, once he saw Nelson give an exhibition in Judo and Jiu-Jitsu for his students, a lot of the jokes stopped. The organization wanted the students to learn to be confident and protect themselves in the future, so Crank and Nelson trained them.

Samantha was a strikingly unusual woman. She had fair, almost white skin and silky white hair. Her eyes were a transparent light green. If she weren't wearing makeup, her green contacts would have produced the only color on her face. To see her tall, athletic frame walk into a room wearing brightly colored tropical prints with her snow-white hair and lashes was breathtaking. She was responsible for the school system on the island and loved her charges. Her curriculum followed most states' recommendations, but she could provide excellent teachers and supplies with unlimited money. It was an educator's dream come true. Her easygoing and calm manner was appreciated by her colleagues, whose passions and convictions could make meetings tense, to say the least.

While waiting for everyone to get refreshments and settle back into their chairs, Chief addressed the group.

"Okay, everyone. We're not on island time! We're ten minutes late in starting!" Seeing everyone finally get settled, he continued, "We all know why we're here since we have a very efficient native communication system." He paused as everyone nodded slightly and gave smiles of support or furtive glances in Crank's direction.

"As you know, Crank made a snatch this morning at 0100 hours. The 'save' was the three-year-old girl of a Federal Judge in Washington, DC. A few days before, we sat in this same room and, as a committee, voted to proceed differently with this child. Due to the intense media exposure, I decided to pull some strings and try another way. Well, our senior operative decided to take the matter into his own hands and take the girl and, as usual, set up the crime scene so the judge would be accused of murder. We are going to need a lot of damage control and fast!"

Crank watched the members' faces as the Chief spoke. He knew they could vote him off the island. They had the power, but he knew no one was more qualified to train the other operatives. He patted his shirt pocket to ensure his trump cards were safe. He knew Mona and Nelson would not vote against him. He wasn't sure about the Chief. He was a stickler for the rules. Sophie would vote the way Ruth told her.

"Chief?"

"Yes, go ahead, Ruth."

"You know I'm not as up on the security issues as some might be, but why would this particular operation be such a problem for us? The FBI is always called in any way since it is a kidnapping. Crank does a thorough job of creating the crime scene, so I guess I don't see the problem."

Watching Gretchen smirk at the naiveté of the little psychiatrist, Crank winced, waiting for her to strike.

"In my country, the higher you are in government, the less you are held accountable," said Gretchen." They will find a way to get him free of the murder charge. There will be much coverage in the newspapers and for longer."

Looking at Crank from across the table, her unsmiling gaze fixed on him, she continued.

"If the mission is to succeed, all members must work for the good of the whole island and not just one child. One child is dispensable."

After Gretchen's statement, total silence filled the room. Sophie and Mona looked distressed and kept shooting him sympathetic glances as if he had already been discharged. The rest of the members' faces were impassive, but none looked Crank in the eye. The Chief stood up and faced the members, sighing heavily, and said, "It looks like we have two issues to decide on. I agree with Ruth. Our security measures are excellent; we'll just lay low until this blows over. The second issue is your actions, Crank. You acted outside the committee's decisions and risked our operation. If everyone went around doing that, we'd have to close up shop. You've been in this from the beginning, and I know there's no one more dedicated to our ideals than you are, so do you have anything to say for yourself before we decide?"

Everyone watched as Crank slowly got up from his chair, carefully pushed it into place, and pulled something out of his shirt pocket.

"Thanks, Chief. I would like to say something to the group. I admire and respect all of you and the work you do to keep this island a paradise of safety for the kids. I understand the need for rules. I'm used to rules. The military had plenty of them, and I've tried to follow the island rules." He paused and looked each member in the eye. He wanted them to know he respected them and realized their work was essential. He wanted it to sink in because now it was reality time.

"Most of you don't know much about my area. I think it's time you did. Even though committees and rules are needed, they don't count for shit in the field. I'm the one who sits day after day and watches internet videos of kids being violated, hurt, and even killed. Real live kids. Not actors."

Crank leaned forward on the table, bracing his hands before continuing.

"I sit there, knowing the clock is ticking and that the abuse is continuing every minute *I* take to decide which child can be safely snatched and which one to leave. I'm the one who walks in the room, never knowing in what condition I'll find the child. Have they been hurt so often that their faces are frozen in a perpetual scream? Am I too late? Will they even be alive?"

The committee sat frozen, giving him their full attention. Taking the pictures out of his shirt pocket, he walked around the table, gently placing one image in front of each member. Hearing the soft gasps behind him as he walked toward the door, he added, "Sometimes, it's just me and the child. No committee. There are no rules, and the clock is ticking. You'll have to excuse me. Another kid is running out of time tonight in New Mexico. I'm not going to be too late for this one."

CHAPTER 7

"Ms. Day, this is Agent Ables from the FBI. I know it's early, but I thought you would want to know that the DNA results are back."

Awakened from a beautiful dream she couldn't quite remember, Sunny's sleep-filled brain registered that she was holding the phone to her ear.

"Uh, what—? I mean, hello?"

Even in her half-awake state, she could hear impatience in the agent's voice.

"Ms. Day! Did you hear me? I have the DNA results!"

DNA! Results! DNA! Those keywords ratcheting through her brain caused her to snap awake. Her heart racing, she threw back the sheets, pushing the tangled hair from her eyes.

"Agent Ables? Do you have the results? So—so soon? Oh, thank you for hurrying... I'm so grate—"

"Sunny," the agent interrupted. "I will be in Austin this afternoon and can bring the results to you then. There is another case involved and—"

"This afternoon!" Sunny's heart sank. "I can't wait that long. Just tell me. Please! You don't know how hard it has been for us—my mother—my brother, all of us."

Sunny listened as the agent explained that he couldn't discuss this with her over the phone and that he would see her at three. Seconds later, he hung up, and Sunny sat on the edge of the bed, staring at the phone. She felt anger wash over her at his cold professionalism.

Since their return from Savannah yesterday, she had no time to think about the DNA test that would either prove or disprove her suspicion that the dead boy in Georgia could be her sister's child and Sam's identical twin brother.

Later that afternoon, with her son safely out of the way on his trip to Lake Travis with his best friend, she paced the length of the living room anxiously, Matt watching from the couch. Her Mom burst into the room, already talking.

"Sam is out of the way now. What did you find out in Savannah? And Sunny, I want the truth. Don't leave anything out. This concerns Raine. I have a right to know."

Smiling wearily, Sunny patted her mother's arm.

"I know you do, Mom, but it's a long story. Let's go in the kitchen and have some iced tea while Matt and I bring you up to speed. Mr. Ables, the FBI agent will be here at 3 with the DNA results."

Earlier, in downtown Austin, Sunny would have been surprised to find out she and Sam were the main topics of conversation between two FBI agents—and not just regular agents but special agents assigned to the Crimes Against Children unit.

"What makes you think the Jeremy Day case should be included in this investigation?"

Resting comfortably at the desk with his feet up, Ken Ables watched as his partner, Jaxson Creed, walked in. Not a stranger to Ken, he was surprised two years ago when the agent requested an assignment for this task force. Blond crewcut, ruddy angular face, thick muscular body, the agency tended to underestimate him as all brawn and no brains. A man of few words and little emotion, he kept to himself. Their investigation had taken them all over the United States and overseas. When a meeting was needed, they commandeered a local bureau office. It beat meetings in restaurants where security was always an issue. So far, this investigation has been a ballbuster. It was times like this when he missed his old partner, who had disappeared during a mission in Thailand three years ago. *Come on, Rand, you old bastard! Where are you? FBI agents don't disappear without a trace. Of course, if anyone could do it. It would be you. I'm not giving up on you, old friend.*

"Have you read the file?" Ken asked, pushing the file across the desk toward Jax. He watched silently as the other agent quickly scanned the contents before replying.

"I remember reading this earlier but didn't realize it was to be included with the others. It fits, though. No body recovered but plenty of DNA, alleged murderer a player on the porn sites."

Frowning, he held a sheet of paper up. "This DNA report must have been misfiled. It's for a Samuel Day. This wasn't in the report earlier, but it's a match for the missing boy. They're twins? Is this kid dead, too?"

Ken sat back in his office chair, watching the other agent's expressions as he processed the new information. It might take him a while, but there was no better field agent than Jax at combining two and two and coming up with four, except for me and Rand. Well, it's time to fill him in.

Jax settled his bulk into a chair while listening to Ken's report on Sunny and Matt's visit to Tybee Island and the subsequent DNA testing.

"So we have a live kid that is an identical twin to the dead one. We also know the female who supplied the embryos for both kids is dead, too. A strange coincidence. Or is it? Anyway, how does this help us in our investigation?"

Taking a deep breath, Ken dropped his feet on the floor and said, "I think the best thing is to recap the whole thread, start to finish. About two years ago, the FBI's trend-tracking division noticed similarities between several child murders that occurred nationwide. The kids were all victims of sexual or physical abuse that was shown on the internet. The suspects weren't always guardians or adoptive parents. Just random people who somehow had these kids. How did they get them, and from where?

Why hadn't someone reported them as missing? The CSU teams never found any actual bodies. There was always plenty of DNA scattered around the crime scene. We found DNA from hair, blood, tissue, and teeth. Posted videos pointed clearly to the abuser, allowing for easy convictions. They refused to say how they got the kids."

He paused for a minute, lost in thought, and then continued.

"We organized a task force and began investigating the unknown kids. Little information has been forthcoming in our two years on this. In the meantime, we have added eighty more kids to the database—thousands of investigative hours and nothing. No one has seen anything. We feel these kids may not be dead but are being kidnapped and used for God knows what reason. Jeremy is an exception so far because allegedly his father killed him.

"Last week in Tybee, when this brother and sister brought me this fantastic and unlikely story which, unfortunately for them, turns out to be true? Jeremy and Sam Day are genetically identical. The DNA report bears that out. Ms. Day has found and lost her nephew all at once. So, this afternoon, I must tell this nice family the news. I am following a hunch on this and including this case in our investigation." Ken sat down and tipped his head back, closing his eyes. For a moment, both men sat in silence. Finally, Jax said, "There's been another one."

Snapping his head forward, he frowned at his partner. "When?"

"Last night. In Washington, DC," came the careful reply.

"Last night?" he exclaimed angrily. "Why the hell didn't you call me?"

Holding up his hand, Jax said defensively, "Whoa! Hold on! I just found out about two hours ago! It happened around 0300. The FBI wasn't even called in until around 0800, so—"

"Five hours! They waited five hours to notify the FBI. The DC police know better than that—they know how important time is on something li—"

"They weren't told either." Jax waited for this information to sink in, knowing his partner's next words.

"A government official's kid," Ken said softly. "It would have to be. They're the only ones who would take the time for a coverup—to protect one of their own, guilty or not. Who was it? Senator, Congressman or—"

"Federal Judge Wharton Hennessey," said Jax.

"Hennessey? That old son of a bitch? Does he have young children? He must be at least 70 years old?"

"Don't you remember about three or four years ago? It was in all the papers. His wife of thirty years found out there was another woman and kid and divorced him. No one is sure where the kid came from. They heard it was a scam the woman pulled to get him to marry her. He eventually married her. The judge eventually found out about the deception and kept them out of the limelight. They were never seen at official functions. Now I guess we know why."

"The crime scene the same as the others?"

"Almost identical. If this was a setup and the kids were being kidnapped, the abductors were getting more creative. CSU team found skin this time. Skin and blood, a lot of blood. On knives, all over the place." Wanting to get this part over with, he continued. "The knives were lying beside a vat of acid."

"Could they estimate how much blood was at the scene? Was it—?" He stopped, dreading the answer.

"Yeah," Jax nodded. "It was more than a three-year-old girl could lose—and live."

Hours later, Jax left the building and stepped into the dry heat, feeling the sweat evaporate as quickly as it formed. When Bolo's guy approached him several years ago, it had seemed straightforward: monitor the investigation and report back. A half million dollars to relay information and make a few calls? He knew they were traffickers, but after Thailand, he realized it went a lot deeper than that. By that time, he was in too deep.

Pulling the dusty cardboard box toward her, Sunny felt excitement and dread. The box held the last of her sister's worldly possessions. What she would find inside could be her last hope of knowing for sure if Raine's child was born alive unless the DNA test was positive. So why didn't she just open the damn box?

She knew the answer. She was scared. If Raine had given birth to a child, then that child was now likely dead.

Taking a deep breath, she quickly pulled the tape off the top and flipped open the flaps. She pulled out a small plastic box filled with two tiny blue tennis shoes. Hands shaking, she took out the little items. They looked brand new. Next, she lifted out a blue vinyl photo album. She slowly opened it with hands suddenly so stiff and cold that they felt like the hands of an old woman, rusty tools stuck on the end of her arms. Her breath catching in her throat, she gazed at the lovely young pregnant girl smiling at the camera, surrounded by flowers. Her features were slightly in shadow, but it was definitely her sister.

Hot tears splashed the pictures as she turned the pages, each showing the advancing pregnancy. Finally, a photo of a newborn with spiky black hair and fair skin. He looked just like Sam as a newborn. There were few pictures of the mother and infant together, but Sunny wasn't surprised. He couldn't have been very old when Raine was killed.

Twenty minutes later, she came to the bottom of the box. Sitting back on her heels, she brushed the hair out of her eyes, suddenly drained. She was emotionally exhausted and a little disappointed. She needed more information. Sighing, she carefully gathered the contents off the floor—the album, baby clothes, and one light blue fleece blanket that still had a powdery baby smell. Clutching the blanket tightly, she heard a crackling sound. She turned it over and found an envelope. From inside, she pulled out pages of notebook paper filled with her sister's childish, almost illegible scrawl. Standing up, she took the pages to the table by the window, moving carefully and slowly, afraid it would be just a shopping list or a bill. She smoothed out the sheets and sucked in her breath when she saw her name on the first sheet.

My dearest sister,

If you are reading this, it means I'm no longer in this world. There are some things I need to tell you—but—first, I want to tell you how much I have always loved you. My earliest memories are of running on wobbly legs after my sister. I worshipped and admired you. I want to say you are the best!

That was the easy part—now for the hard part. You have always accused me of writing like I talk, so this letter may need to be more organized. In addition to being a letter of love—it is also a letter of confession. I have done some things I'm not proud of. I know I have hurt people with my selfishness and immaturity. I want you to tell Mom and Matt I'm sorry for any hurt or disappointments I've caused. It goes without saying that I apologize to you. That being said—I have a story to tell you. It's a beautiful story, and every word in it is entirely true, no matter how unbelievable.

I know this—because it is my story. Sit back and get comfortable, sis! It's a long one.

One rainy spring night, I left work and went upstairs to the bar. I can hear your question now. No! This was not a routine practice. I don't even like the taste of alcohol. I was feeling a little lonely that night—missing all of you. I had just ended a bad relationship—not the first for me. Well, anyway—I didn't want to go home to an empty apartment.

The hotel lounge is on the top floor, surrounded by glass walls looking out over Savannah. Remember, Sunny? I was going to take you there on your next visit. On this night, the rain streamed down the walls, and flashes of lightning lit up the sky, so my candlelit table in the corner was welcoming and cozy.

Sis? You know, sometimes you will be in a public place, but you're so absorbed in your thoughts that it's as if you're alone and insulated from people. That's the way I felt that night. Do you remember what I told you about the dreams? The ones where I was walking on the street at night? No one could see me, and I could feel the cool night air going through me. That's the way I was feeling. But something happened, and this is where it gets a little weird—okay—a lot weird.

Remember I told you I was sitting in a corner? Suddenly, I could feel the presence of the outside world pressing in on me—as if to say—Hello? Come back to the real world! I looked up and glanced around the room. The bar was dark, but all the customers' faces were highlighted by candlelight. It was a busy night for the bar—every table was full of laughing people. Behind the laughter floating to every corner of the bar were the soft sounds of the piano. Suddenly, I felt great! It felt wonderful to be in that room—with all those lovely people! I didn't feel alone anymore, and I could feel a huge grin spreading across my face. I remember thinking how silly I must look—sitting at a table—all by myself—grinning like a fool— but it felt so peaceful!

Sis, have you ever felt the pressure of someone's stare? You might be in a market, and you feel someone watching you. You turn around, and

119

sure enough—someone is staring at you! It happened to me that night! Sitting there—smiling— feeling so in the moment. I felt this feeling and looked at the other far corner of the room. I noticed a man sitting alone at a table. He was looking right at me! Smiling! With the same kind of look I had on my face. We were suddenly so glad to be in that bar at that very moment, but he was not the sort of man that usually attracted me. It's not that he was ugly—far from it. But he didn't have the flashing good looks or the dangerous sophistication of the guys I usually like. Okay! I'm shallow! I admit it. At least, I used to be.

As we smiled at each other that night, I became aware of him in every way. His beautiful silver-blue eyes seemed to beam acceptance and love! I remember sitting there in total awe, knowing it was ridiculous. He didn't even know me! All I can tell you, sis, is that I knew without a shadow of a doubt that I could trust this man. To me, that felt like love. I got up and walked to his table. I sat down without saying a word or even taking my eyes off him. I never believed in love at first sight, but— anyway—back to the story. I want to stay on track.

As the thunderstorm continued to assault our glass cage, we talked for over three hours! I can't remember one detail about our conversation! I just knew things about him—not factual things like where he lived or where he grew up. I knew he was kind—and gentle—and trustworthy. I knew he would do great things with his life. He looked about my age— but when you looked into his eyes—you felt he had an ancient, knowing soul. I can hear you now—your little sister is usually not so spiritual. I was as shocked then as you are now.

All I knew was that I was attracted to him sexually. I have always been picky, but not that night. I wanted him and could not wait to take him back to my apartment. As we waited by the street for a taxi, he gently placed his arm around my waist and drew me close. I felt this delicious warmth spread over me from just that contact. I felt so treasured—so safe.

Do you remember I mentioned that I'd just gotten out of a destructive relationship? It's funny, but sometimes, negative relationships are almost impossible to leave. I had been struggling with this one. He was a bad person. I'd left him a couple of times before, only to go back—each time losing a little bit more of my soul. Well, I saw him that night as we got into the taxi! He was walking along the street when our eyes met. We looked at each other, and all the warmth left my body. Rubbing my arms—trying to get warm—my skin had that cold, rubbery feel that dead people get. Remember how Gram's skin felt when she died? He smiled a cold, dark smile, and I felt I had to go to him. I had to—or I would die— right there on the spot! It was like we were the only two people on earth. Dark promises were being sent to me—if I would only return to him. I guess this is what all the self-help books would call withdrawal feelings from the "love object." It sure didn't feel like love. All I felt was fear and darkness.

Sis, you know I'm not a strong person. I am easily swayed, which hasn't helped me make the best decisions in my life. But I knew— somehow, I knew—I had to reject him. I jerked my eyes from him and leaned against my new man's warm body. As the taxi pulled away from the curb, I could feel his rage, but it didn't matter! I felt so strong! Would the feeling last? I didn't know, and I didn't care at that moment.

Our relationship lasted a few weeks before he had to go away the first time. Surprisingly, and certainly not because of me—we didn't have sex that first night at my apartment. We spent the rest of the night getting to know each other. He said he couldn't tell me much about himself—not even his real name. He could tell me he was not married. He was on a dangerous mission and didn't know how long he would be in Savannah. He held me in his arms and promised that if he had to leave without telling me—not to worry—he would be back. I know! I can hear you now, sis, but I believed him. He's been gone for months, and I still believe him.

As unlikely as it seems after reading the first part of this letter, now comes the hard part. Remember when I called to tell you about the embryos? Of course—what am I thinking? How could you forget that conversation? I think you naturally assumed that I had used a sperm bank specimen to fertilize my eggs. I also think you assumed I hadn't used any of the embryos. Wrong on both counts, sis.

In my last relationship—you know—with the dark lord? I had wanted a baby at some point and had been nagging him about it. He said he didn't think he even wanted children, but when I said I could guarantee a boy, his colossal ego made him agree. So I had my eggs harvested, and he was going to provide the sperm. Then, as you know— the lab could separate the little girls from the little boys. We could have them in the order we wanted! I know, sis, you're shaking your head at my stupidity. All I can say is that he had me hooked—but good. I just knew children would make our relationship better. Anyway, I need to continue before I lose my courage.

The last night, my angel and I were together—somehow, I knew he wouldn't be back. It was just a feeling of sadness that hung over the whole evening. Both of us felt it. We made love for the last time that morning

before he left. It was beautiful, gentle, and sensual. I stayed in bed after
he left, listening to the gentle spring rain. I could hear every sound in the
apartment. The clock ticking. The humming of the refrigerator. I glanced
at my dresser and saw he had left his watch. Tears welled in my eyes as I
realized it was the only proof I had that he had ever been there. Right
next to them sat the sperm specimen kit my old lover was going to use.
Suddenly, my thoughts started taking off on their own. I did have
something else of his. He did leave evidence of his being in my life!

This next part is gross, but you can take it since you're a nurse. We
were always careful, so there was a condom full of his warm, fresh sperm
in the wastebasket. I'm sure you can guess the rest.

It was wrong! It was wrong of me to steal something from him,
especially from someone like him, who I knew would take fatherhood
very seriously. Please understand that I would only use the embryos once
he returned and gave me permission. But he didn't come back.

After he was gone for a while, I accepted that something terrible had
happened to him and that he wasn't returning. I know he would have
returned if he had been physically able— I know it! I was beside myself
with grief at first, but after a month of grieving, it got a little easier. I
could start looking toward the future again. I was planning to move back
home.

He still felt so much a part of me that I wanted to have his child. I
knew it would not be easy being a single parent. I also knew my family
would be there to love and help us. I had only one of the boy embryos
implanted. I had to be careful. Twins or triplets were out of the question.
It took, and that is why I am sitting here tonight to write this letter. I am
pregnant! I just found out today! I am so excited and happy I can't sleep!

I'm including this letter in my will so that if something happens to me, you will know my story and that I'm entrusting my son and the rest of "my children" to you. Don't let them go to waste, sis. They were conceived in love. I know you can't have seven children, so please give them to good couples who can't have their own.

Well, that is all there is to tell. Quite a story, huh? I am packed and will leave at the end of the week to come home to my family. I want my son to know his excellent aunt, manly uncle, and eccentric but loving grandmother. You may never see this letter since I intend to sit down with you late one night and tell you the whole story in person, but—I have grown up a lot in the last few months, and we never know what fate has in store for us.

Yours truly and forever,
Raine

Sunny sat stunned; the letter still flattened out on the table. Why hadn't Raine told her? She had to have known her sister would support her, no matter what.

Sunny jumped when the phone rang. Professor Berger had returned and would drop by when Sam returned to answer his questions. Too distracted to ask the professor about Sam's questions, she thanked the professor and returned to the porch and replaced all the precious items in Raine's box.

❖

That afternoon, Sunny found herself pacing back and forth in front of the couch where her brother was sitting. After filling Matt in, they decided to wait until they had the test results to tell her mother about the agent's visit. It was almost three o'clock. Between waiting for the agent to arrive with the DNA results and Raine's letter, it had been the longest day in Sunny's life.

"For God's sake, light somewhere, will you? You're making me dizzy," exclaimed her brother. Patting the couch beside him, he added, "C'mon, it's almost three, and his type is always on time."

Plopping down on the couch, she faced her brother and said, "I don't know if I can stand this! I need to know—one way or the other!" Taking a deep breath, she leaned back and crossed her arms over her stomach. "Let's change the subject. Talk about something else. How's your love life? Got anyone spec—"

"Saved by the bell," said Matt, smiling, as he walked to answer the door chime."

Temporarily diverted, Sunny rushed to the door with Matt.

"I thought you would never get here! Please, come in!" she said, dragging the unsmiling agent into the living room. "I should offer you something to drink, but that will have to wait. Tell us— what did the DNA test show? No! Wait a minute! I've got to sit down for this!"

Both men watched as Sunny sat down hard in the armchair. Matt smiled grimly at the agent and said, "Sorry, Ken, but you can see how anxious we are. Please, take a seat."

The agent sat. Speaking for the first time, he cleared his throat and said flatly, "The results were a match."

It took a second for his statement to sink in. Agent Ables watched as Matt went to sit on the edge of his sister's chair. She sat hunched over, arms wrapped around her knees, rocking gently back and forth. Ables cleared his throat again and said, "Sunny? Matt?" He paused, waiting until he had their attention before continuing. Seeing Sunny's dazed, tear-stained face, he spoke slowly and softly. The regret in his voice was authentic. He didn't have much to offer except more questions. He took a deep breath and said,

"I'm sorry to make you both wait, but the line wasn't secured, and my information needs to be kept confidential. You both hoped the results would prove that the boys were not identical twins. Unfortunately, they are.

"We appreciate your help on this, Ken," said Matt. "We know our story is unbelievable, and it says something about you and the FBI: that you're willing to help us and give us a little hope."

"How much hope do you need?"

Hearing the agent's question, Sunny abruptly straightened, locking the agent's gaze on her own.

"What do you mean?"

"This information, not the DNA results, needed to be shared in person. I have a story as farfetched as the one you came to Tybee Island to tell me."

Feeling the need for space, he abruptly got up from the sofa, continuing as he walked further into the room, pacing for a minute before returning. Neither sister nor brother moved a muscle. The shadows grew long in the living room as the agent told them about the task force he was leading and how the FBI had become involved in the children's cases. How they had noted certain similarities that led them to believe the children were being kidnapped. Especially the crime scene leading back to the abusers as the killers.

"The reason I'm telling you this is—"

"Jeremy's crime scene is like the others! That's why you told us, isn't it?" Sunny walked to where the agent stood. "So now our options are either my nephew was murdered or kidnapped and taken to God knows where— or," voice shaking, she continued, "he might be alive and in the hands of some other abuser."

Holding her hand up to ward off her brother as he came to comfort her, she paced furiously. So many questions flashed through her mind that she didn't know which one to ask first.

"Let's go into the kitchen, get some iced tea, and talk. We'll be more comfortable at the table." Heading into the kitchen without watching to see they followed, she continued, "I'd like to know everything you—"

"Mom, Uncle Matt, I'm home! Did you miss me? We had a blast! Randy's dad got a new boat and pulled us on a giant inner tube around the lake! Can we get a boat?"

As always impressed at her son's sense of timing, Sunny felt the impact as his sun-warmed, sticky body ran to her. Sam was a great believer in hugs and dispensed them freely. Landing a quick kiss on his mother's cheek, he launched into his uncle's waiting arms. Sunny noticed the agent staring at Sam. *He knows he's looking at a replica of the missing child.*

"Sam, let go of your uncle and say hello to Mr. Ables. Then, go in and get cleaned up. You need to shower that lake water off of you, sweetie."

Always polite, Sam promptly offered his hand to the bemused agent, saying, "How do you do? I'm Sam."

"Hi, Sam," he said. "I'm glad to meet you. It sounds like you had a good time!"

"I did, sir! The best!" Sam responded, glancing hopefully at his mother. "They're going back next week, and Randy's dad said I could—"

Seeing where this was heading, Matt intervened, "Okay, sport. You can talk that over later with your mom. The grownups must discuss some things, so why don't you get cleaned up."

"That's right, honey," said Sunny. "Get your stuff and take it to your room. We're almost done here, and then we want to hear about your trip." Turning to the still-silent agent, she continued, "Ken, sit down at the table while I fix some iced tea."

The agent stood by the kitchen table, still staring after the boy. The resemblance was uncanny. But there was something else about him that reminded Ken of someone, but... Shaking his head, he slowly turned back to the table, stopping when he saw both brother and sister staring at him.

"See?" Sunny said. "I told you they looked exactly alike. I knew they had to be twins! Now you believe, don't you?"

"Okay! You win! Even after the DNA test, it still didn't seem real, but after seeing Sam—" He smiled ruefully, holding up his hands in surrender.

"I know," Matt responded. It hit us the same way: They're carbon copies of each other."

After handing the men their tall, cold glasses of tea, Sunny joined them at the table. It was quiet as the three silently sipped the cold liquid.

Matt said, "Ken, I think it's time I told you what I do for a living. I am a freelance invest—"

"Investigative reporter for the last six years," interrupted Ken. "We know all about you. I've read your reports on Columbia. Good stuff. Dangerous work." Turning to Sunny, he continued, "Your brother is one of the best in the business. He has helped the FBI out several times."

Matt hastily interrupted, seeing a worried frown on his sister's face, "I appreciate the compliments. I knew you guys would have already checked us out, but you don't have to share it all with my sister."

Ignoring the men's chuckles, Sunny decided it was time to get back on track. After all, she had a job to do and needed information.

"Ken, have you told us everything you know about the task force? Or at least everything you're at liberty to tell us?"

"Yeah, like I said before, we have a lot of information, but it all leads to a dead end. We know when the kids are snatched, but we don't know by who or why. Nor where they're taken. The bastard is good. He doesn't leave any evidence of his presence. He has to be a professional, probably ex-military."

The metallic sound of his cell phone sounded loud in the kitchen. The agent smoothly palmed the small silver instrument, responding quietly to the caller. Flipping it shut, he smiled his apology.

"I'm sorry, but I have to leave. There was another snatch last night, and the FBI was invited late to the party, so we're trying to catch up before evidence is lost. I could get in a lot of trouble sharing this information, so keep it to yourself.

The agent was out the door within a few minutes, promising to contact them in a few days.

Silence filled the kitchen as they listened to the agent's car drive away. The faint sound of Sam singing in the shower could be heard floating down the hall. Brother and sister sat lost in thought. Slapping the table with his hand, Matt said, "I guess we play the waiting game now. What are we going to tell Mom...?"

"I have no intention of sitting around here waiting for that FBI man to remember us!" Said Sunny emphatically.

"I don't see what choice we have—"

"You're an investigative reporter! She interrupted." We can do this, Matt! We can find Jeremy! I—"

"Whoa, wait a minute! How in the hell do you expect us to find one missing child when the FBI can't find dozens? No! Absolutely not! This is not some Nancy Drew mystery, for God's sake." Looking at his beloved sister's determined face, he played his one trump card. "I'll tell Mom!"

"No, you won't," his sister said dismissively. "You don't want to worry her any more than I do."

Seeing her brother's frustrated look, Sunny put her hands on each side of his face and looked him in the eye. She couldn't do this without her brother's help. She knew he was very good at finding out things, and that was a skill she needed.

"Mattie, please! Listen to me! Jeremy has already been missing too long—every second counts. I know we can do this! We'll tell the FBI if we find anything out. I'm not saying we go this alone, but I can't sit here and do nothing!" Seeing him wavering but still unconvinced, she added, "Mattie. What if it was Sam missing?"

"Okay," he said impatiently. "You've made your point. I can put out some feelers, but I'm not—"

Knocking at the back door kept Matt from finishing his sentence. Feeling incredibly grateful for the interruption, Sunny hopped up from the table, saying, "I bet that's Professor Berger! Matt, get Sam, please!

Minutes later, they were all sitting at the kitchen table. Sam was so excited he couldn't sit in his chair. The Professor carefully laid a manila envelope on the table, turning to Sam with a huge smile. The burly Scotsman was pleased to help out his young neighbor.

"Well, laddie. I have to say you are an artist. You did a great job capturing the colors and features of these animals. Mira told me you needed help identifying where these animals lived and—"

Beside himself, Sam interrupted, "Professor, did you find out? Do you know where they come from? It's really important. I have a friend, and he needs some—"

"Sam! His mother said gently. "You're interrupting the professor. Smiling at their guest, she said, "I'm so sorry, Professor Berger, but as you can see. My *normally* polite child is about to go into cardiac arrest here. Matt and I are in the dark. Are these some pictures Sam got off the television?"

Interestingly, her son suddenly became quiet and very still. Mother's intuition alerted her, and she glanced across the table at Matt. He looked at the drawings being pulled out of the envelope, a puzzled frown on his face as he leaned forward for a better look.

Spreading the pictures on the table, the professor continued as Matt and Sunny looked at Sam's drawings. "Sam, where did you see these animals? Was it on a TV special or the internet?"

"Uh. Yes, yes, sir! It was on the internet. I just came across them, but it didn't say where they lived. Do you know?"

Watching her suddenly squirmy son, Sunny knew he was not telling the whole truth. But why? Why would he lie about something so insignificant?

"Ahh! Well, that explains it." Holding up one of the pictures so all could see, he continued, "This parrot is not just your everyday parrot. It is a scarlet macaw. This bird has almost disappeared and is now found primarily in one place." Carefully laying down the bird picture, he held up the next one. "This monkey is not just your everyday monkey either. Its official name is *Alouatta coibensis,* or the howler monkey. It can also be found in just one place. This giant rat or agouti is endemic to only one area."

"Where? Where is it, Captain? Can you find it on a map for me? Please? I need to know!" pleaded Sam.

"They live on Coiba Island, son, off the Pacific Coast of Panama. The island was a penal colony. It is very remote and unexplored. It's loaded with species that have never been identified. The whole island is covered in virgin rainforests— some of the best diving in the world. I've never been there myself. I've seen it from a tour boat when I was in Panama. Looks forbidding. Which I guess is why they made the whole island a prison."

After thanking the professor again for going to so much trouble for her son, she escorted him to the back porch and waved him off down the street. Returning to the kitchen, she was surprised to see that neither of the men in her life had moved. Noting her son's crestfallen look, she suspected the professor's information was not what he wanted to hear.

"Okay, sweetie. You got your information. Was that the big surprise? You seem to be disappointed. Do you want to talk about it?"

Sorrowfully shaking his head, her son got up from the table and hugged her, saying, "No. It's okay, Mom. I just hoped it was a different island. I'm tired. I think I'll go to bed now. G'night, Uncle Matt."

Watching her son's bedroom light come on, Sunny turned to her still-silent brother. "That was weird. Sam never wants to go to bed. Something is bothering him about this—Hello? Earth to Matt! Come in, Matt!" she said, waving her hand in front of her brother's face.

"*Uh*, Sunny. I've got to get going." Seeing her surprised look, he continued, "I want to start putting out those feelers. I also want to get a copy of the detective's file on Jeremy's murder scene. I'll have to call in some favors for that one. I'll give you a ring tomorrow."

It was only after Matt's car was out of the driveway that Sunny remembered—her brother had recently investigated a story in Central America on an island off the coast of Panama.

CHAPTER 8

Sunny found Sam asleep in his bed at ten o'clock the following morning. It struck her as odd—he had been up at his usual 7 a.m. A morning nap was unusual for a boy his age, and seeing him there, his eyes closed, his breathing shallow, she felt a pang of concern. She sat on his bed and wrapped her arms around him, lying her head on his chest, murmuring reassurance that he was safe. After a few minutes, she felt his little hand glide softly over her hair.

"Mom? What's wrong?"

"Nothing, babe. I think you must have fallen asleep. Did you have a dream?" Sitting up, she peered closely at his face, looking for signs of fear or pain. If anything, he seemed extremely happy and relaxed.

"I guess I fell asleep after all. I wanted to see if I could talk to—uh. I mean, I was resting and—"

Once again, Sunny thought her son was not being entirely truthful. Her mother's intuition was never wrong.

"No problem, sweetie. Why don't you get up, and let's get you a snack? We haven't had a chance to catch up since I got home!"

Watching her son bound out of bed and drag her by the hand to the kitchen reassured her somewhat. It can't be too bad if he's still hungry.

After listening to her son's excited chatter about his trip to the lake, Sunny felt it was time to ask him about his animal drawings.

"Sam, I was wondering. Those were beautiful drawings you did of the parrot, monkey, and whatever that large rat-looking thing was so—"

"An agouti," came Sam's quick reply. That's the name of the large rat-looking things. It's kind of like a guinea pig but a lot bigger!"

"Oh, thanks, honey. I'll remember that. I could tell it was important for you to know where these animals lived and that you were disappointed when you found out it was Coiba Island. Why was that? Did you make a bet with G or one of your friends?" G and Sam were always trying to one-up each other. The victor always did a victory dance, singing, "I was right, and you were?" and the other had to shout, "Wrong." It was one of their favorite games.

"Uh, no. It was okay, Mom. I had—I just knew it would be— uh—another island."

Sunny felt a chill go through her as she saw her son's look of failure.

"Sam, look at me! In the eyes, mister. Something is going on here besides some animal drawings. Now I want to know the whole story, and I want to know it now."

"It's the boy," came the soft reply.

"The boy in your dreams?"

"Yes! I let down the boy. He needs me, and I let him down. I promised to find out where he was and that you would go get him. He could live with us, couldn't he, Mom?" Eyes pleading now, Sam continued, "G said she would like another grandson, especially if he looks and acts like me. The boy does look like me, Mom! But— but it doesn't matter now. It needs to be the right name!"

Seeing Sam's sad, almost desperate face, Sunny felt a pain in her heart. What had happened to her son? How could he believe the boy in his dream was real? Then she remembered that the therapist insisted he was dreaming about himself. She needed to listen. Taking a deep breath, Sunny pulled the drawings out of the folder and spread them out in front of her son.

"Sam, we'll find him. Tell me everything from start to finish." Reaching over to squeeze his little boy's arm, she continued, "I know you always said the boy in your dreams was not you but a boy who looked like you. In the last two weeks, I've learned that things are not always as they seem. I also know how wonderful it can be for someone to finally listen to you—no matter how weird your story is. So, I'm listening, son. I believe you. Let's help this boy."

"I always told you the boy looked like me but wasn't me. I can feel it when he is hurt or scared—just like it's happening to me. He was hurt and hungry a lot, Mom." Seeing her distress, he hurried on. "It's better now. A tall man with long silvery hair like a girl's took him! He's on an island now. That's where all the birds and animals are. He sent me pictures while I slept, and I drew them. There is a beautiful waterfall, and he gets to swim every day! It's better there, but he wants to live with us! The name of the island is Isla Seguro. He says that's Spanish for Safe Island.

After repeated reassurance that his mother would help, Sam happily grabbed his swimsuit and hurried down the street.

Unable to reach Matt, Sunny sat at the kitchen table. Lost in thought, she noticed her sister's blue vinyl album and flipped through the pictures while replaying her and Sam's conversation. Earlier, she spoke with Jackie, who offered to cover her shift for a couple of weeks. *Delaying her own vacation time for me. I am so lucky to have her in my life!*

"It's about time!" Sunny said aloud as she withdrew her vibrating cell phone from her pocket.

"Matt! I've called you thr—"

"Ms. Day. Agent Ables here. I'm sorry to have missed you. I have some additional information about Jeremy! The guy accused of murdering him—"

"Yes—yes," interrupted Sunny. "His father. What about him?"

"The DNA doesn't match. Proof he's not Jeremy's biological father," the agent replied grimly. If the kid is alive—maybe someday—that'll be a consolation to him. That is if we can find him."

"That tracks, Ken. In Raine's letter, she said she used her new lover's sperm; wait a minute! How did he become his guardian?"

So, how did this man get possession of the infant? Could he be her old lover? The one she was afraid of? She was so wrapped up in her thoughts that she almost missed the agent's reply.

"That's why I called, to tell you I am on my way to the Savannah County jail to talk with Ashton."

"I want to come too, Ken." Anticipating his rejection, she rushed on. "I need to—please. There might be some little clue he can give me that—."

"Sorry. No," came the flat reply. Knowing Sunny's stubbornness and determination by now, he said, "Look. I know it's not easy, and you're impatient—but you're just going to have to trust that I will ask the right questions."

So far, the FBI admits there are over a hundred children their task force can't locate, and I'm supposed to trust you?

Turning off the 5 o'clock news, Sunny put down the remote when the doorbell rang. On the porch stood her handsome, muscular, wavy-haired brother. The stubbled chin and red-rimmed eyes indicated little sleep.

"I've been trying to get in touch with you all day!

Hold on. Food first!" said Matt wearily, heading for the kitchen.

Sam burst through the kitchen door thirty minutes later to find his mother and uncle sitting at the table, his drawings scattered among empty plates and used silverware.

"Uncle Matt, you're here! Are you going to help us find him? He's going to come live with us! It'll be great—like having a brother and—"

"Whoa, fellow, simmer down there! Matt grabbed his nephew around the waist and drew him onto his knee.

Sunny watched as her brother gently questioned her son. He's in investigative reporter mode now, and it's working. Sam is cooperating and anxious to do anything to help them bring this boy here.

"Okay, Matt. If you're through grilling my son for a minute, I have some questions for you! Where did you rush off to last night after seeing Sam's pictures?" Seeing her brother's set features, she rushed on. "We're in this together, so spill it!"

Turning to look at his sister, Matt said,

"It's my island." Seeing Sunny's confusion, he explained, "The Panama assignment. The suspicious activities on a nearby island. It was Coiba."

"You mean, the same island Sam's animals come from?" she asked.

"Exactly. I was on the internet all night trying to find out more. Is it a coincidence that Sam suddenly draws pictures of animals that only live on this island?" he continued. Sunny looked at her son's disappointed face. He had hoped his hero, his uncle Matt, had found his island, Safe Island.

Sunny stood up quickly. She moved around the table until she stood behind her son's chair. She placed her hands on his shoulders and gently shook him.

"Sam. Please tell Uncle Matt what you told me last night. Remember? You told me the boy who looks like you but isn't you has a name." Feeling his little body go rigid, she quickly reassured him. "I know he told you not to tell anyone, honey. But how can we help him unless we know everything?"

"But Mom, he said we had to be careful! I had to promise!" said her son, obviously distressed at breaking confidence—a blood oath he called it.

Squatting down beside her son's chair, Sunny gently smoothed his dark, sweaty hair out of his eyes.

"Son, it's up to you. This is your secret, and you're going to have to decide. I just think it would—"

"It's Jeremy," came the quiet reply. "His name is Jeremy."

CHAPTER 9

Crank stepped inside the cool darkness of the building, scanning the interior for intruders. Assured that the electronically charged atmosphere held only expected staff, he felt his body relax. The large building on the compound's far side, far from the children's school and quarters, was called "The Eye" by island staff and comprised over 6,000 square feet divided into three rooms. Every wall was loaded floor to ceiling with computers, large plasma monitors, and all the accessory equipment needed to maintain security on the island. Kept private by a heavy soundproofed door, the large room at the back of the building was Crank's domain. The soundproofing was necessary; no one wanted to hear what happened in this room.

After punching in his security code, he swung open the door, surprised to see he wasn't alone. Monitor lights flickering off their faces made it easy to identify the room occupants. Hunched over the keyboard furiously striking the keys was a large, muscular black man named Leonard. His shiny bald head glistened with sweat even in the 68-degree room. Hovering over him was Rambo, Crank's best field operative.

"I know I told you guys to work on your project on your own time, but I didn't mean in the middle of the night."

Rambo whipped his head toward the figure leaning in the doorway.

"Boss! Shit! You almost gave me a heart attack!"

Crank's eyes fixed on the black man who had not even paused in his typing. He approached the two men, stopping when he reached Leonard's computer.

Looking up briefly before returning to work, Leonard said, "Hey, boss. Whazzup?"

"How's your secret project coming? And who wants to go first?" Pulling up a chair, Crank leaned back with his legs stretched out.

"C'mon, boss," said Rambo. "You said we could work on this in secret until we were ready to present it to you, and it's not quite..."

Watching Rambo flap his stick-like arms around—the guy couldn't talk without using his arms—it was hard for Crank to believe the skinny man with flamboyant gestures was their number one operative in the field. His size was an advantage. Hell, he could slip in through a doggy door. His small stature gave him an instant in with the kids, who followed him like the pied piper.

Giving up on the excitable Rambo, Crank focused on Leonard.

"Let's hear it. I don't want you guys wearing yourselves out unless this new program will help us. You are both too valuable to this organization, and we need you in top form every day, not exhausted by working half the night."

Slowly, the dark behemoth pushed back his chair and turned to face Crank. At over six feet four inches, he had to weigh at least 300 pounds, mostly muscle with little fat. No one ever saw him work out. As far as the staff knew, he spent all his time sitting in front of a computer. Slow to anger and devoted to the cause, he was a favorite of all the island's inhabitants, especially the kids.

Glancing at his co-conspirator, Leonard shifted forward in his chair. "Boss, the package we have now is like the one the FBI uses, and I'm not even going to ask again how we came to get it." When his deliberate pause did not bring any information from his steely-eyed boss, he continued. "Well, anyway. The major flaw in this package-at least for our purposes is that it treats all the victims the same. There is no 'timeline,' as it were."

"Yeah, boss!" said Rambo. "Their program can sort by age, height, and sex, but the most vital statistic is missing!"

Crank looked at both his employees. Rambo was almost dancing in his excitement, and Leonard was... well, it was hard to tell if Leonard was excited.

"Okay, I'll bite. What's the missing vital statistic?"

"Time!" crowed Rambo. "How much time they have left!"

Interested now, Crank sat up straighter and fixed his eyes on Leonard.

"How much time until what, Leonard?"

"Until they're dead, boss," came the soft reply.

Silence filled the room, the implication of this information hovering between them. Crank got up and paced around the room, almost afraid to ask for details. With that information, they could prioritize the snatches. They'd never be too late. No more busting their asses to get to the child only to find it was too late. He sat down and said, "Okay. I don't see how in the hell this would even be possible, but I trust you guys, so start talking. Rambo! Stop fidgeting and sit down! Leonard, tell me how it works. How would a computer figure this out?"

"Probability, sir," said Leonard. "The program takes all the data, weight, height, age, and body build of the abuser and the kid. Then, it looks at the type of abuse, the appearance of bruises or cuts, and the nutritional status of the child for their age. It also includes the physical strength of the abuser and any weapons used. Factor in millions of data from our database, including social security records, dental and physician documentation, and police reports. Everything available, and of course—"

"Yeah, and of course what?" came the impatient response.

"The video on the website," said Leonard. "It's incredible, boss. It searches for every little piece of audio and video information. It puts it all together, and whamo! We have a timeline." Finishing, he leaned back in his chair with a triumphant sigh.

Unable to keep quiet a second longer, Rambo burst into speech, "And the best thing of all is the program creates a death clock that keeps ticking and ticking. We'll know the status of each child continuously. The program will notify us if statistical information shows the abuse is accelerating."

"How close is it to being up and running so we can test it?"

"Already done!" both men said simultaneously before breaking into huge grins.

"You've been using this program without clearing with me first?" said Crank ominously.

"Boss. We had to see if it would work before we took it to you," said Leonard.

"We know how much this will mean to the kids. We had to be sure, " Rambo said.

"And are you? Sure, I mean?"

"For the last three months, we have been tracking the program's accuracy, " Leonard slowly replied.

"And?"

"Ninety-three percent!" yelled Rambo as he threw his arms up in the air, fists clenched. Plus, it's improving all the time!"

An hour later, the three men stood up to leave. They had answered all the questions satisfactorily—better than satisfactorily. With their limited staff and thousands of victims, this program would help the organization prioritize the snatches.

"Get to bed guys. You've earned yourselves some time off. If you want, give your report to the day shift and go to the mainland. I don't have to tell you what this will mean to those kids."

Both men solemnly nodded as they walked to the door, the idea of some R&R in Panama sounding pretty good. Their spirits were high as they walked toward the door.

"What about the judge's girl?"

The words said almost casually, halted them mid-step.

"The last snatch. Did I get to her in time? What did the clock say?"

Turning back to look at their boss, both men slowly shook their heads.

"Sorry, boss," Leonard said softly. "Her clock ran out of time the day you left her at the hospital."

"Jefe! Jefe! Wake up. It is time. There is news."

Crank cautiously opened his eyes. The morning sunlight cut through his head like a laser. His head and eyes ached, and he found himself lying on the lanai floor. Turning slowly toward his houseboy's voice, he squinted at a mass of brightly colored beads and feathers floating toward him. It must be a feast day for the Embera.

"Jefe! I came from my village. They told me news. Wake up! Wake up!"

Crank stood, swaying slightly over the little man, taking the tall chilled glass of pineapple juice with a trembling hand.

"I'm ready. Talk."

"There have been men around Panama. Mestizo. They come to my village and ask my people if they know anything about this island. Jefe. It was like last time that man who makes reports was in Panama. He stayed for a while and asked a lot of questions, and then he went. My Chief says he heard Mestizo say they have nothing to report this time and won't get any money from the man. I come back to tell Jefe." Relieved, Crank smiled.

"Thanks, Angel. I appreciate it, but it's nothing to worry about. They're working for that investigative reporter. He didn't find anything out the last time, and he won't now. He's one of many reporters worldwide trying to make a name for themselves, but our security is too tight. Now—I'm starving. Can you fix me something before—"

"It's not the same. Jefe. They asked about the saves and you, Jefe."

Thirty minutes later, Crank sat brooding in the calm silence of the administration building. This is a severe security breach. No one had ever connected the kids to the island. Occasionally, a reporter would land in Panama and start sniffing around. Still, Crank's business arrangement with the Panamanian government ensured they got minimal information. Usually, the mysterious happenings of the island were written off as military maneuvers.

The reporter would run out of expense money and leave.

"Greetings, Kamerade!"

Crank jerked his head towards the door, watching the tall, blond walk to the table.

"You are in a black mood today?"

I've had better days. We have a security breach." he replied irritably, watching as one silver-blond eyebrow arched, the only sign she was surprised by his surly response.

"There's a security problem?" came her quick response. All business now, she sat down at the table with a look that demanded information.

"Just hold on. The Chief's coming. I don't want to go over this twice. Once is bad enough."

Impatience in every movement, she got up and stalked to the room's refrigerator, pulling out her favorite German beer. Throwing back her head and taking a long swallow, she gave a long sigh of satisfaction before raising the bottle to Crank in invitation.

"Not one for me, thanks. I'm quitting—as of today."

Now seated across from each other, Gretchen leaned forward and said, "Does your sudden sobriety have something to do with this problem?"

"Yeah. But that's all I'm saying, so don't try your damn German interrogation techniques on me, Gretch. They won't—"

"Well, my two favorite people sharing a beer! And inviting their boss to join!"

They watched as their Chief closed the outer door and walked to the refrigerator, bending down to extract a cold longneck, saying, "Either of you ready for another?"

"Crank has given up drinking, Chief," said Gretchen.

Crank watched his Chief's involuntary start of surprise before standing up.

"Okay, let's hear it. I gather this isn't just a request for my company," said the Chief, all traces of good humor gone. "Crank, you called this meeting, so you start."

He told them about the death clock and promised to relay their congratulations to Leonard and Rambo.

"Now, the not-so-good news," Crank said at last. "I don't know how bad it is. It might be nothing, but I thought you both should know. Do you remember that last reporter? He was in Panama for several months asking questions about the island." Seeing both their nods, he continued, "He never found anything out and finally was called back home.

"Angel was at his village for a feast day, and he came back to tell me that some Mestizos were asking questions for someone. It may or may not be the same reporter. This time, he was asking different questions. At first, he wanted to know about specific animals on the island. Apparently, he isn't in Panama because later that day, he called and wanted the Mestizos to ask about any children seen at the docks or going to the island. The questions about the kid were very specific. "

"Kid? Or kids? Which is it?" asked Gretchen.

"Specifically, one kid. He wanted to know if a seven-year-old boy with dark hair had been seen in the company of a tall man with long silver hair."

Stunned, the three occupants sat busy with their thoughts, which, not surprisingly, were very similar.

"Damn Crank! That description matches you!" exclaimed the Chief. "How in the hell did this happen?"

"What about the boy?" said Gretchen, remaining calm while both men stalked around the room. "Do we know for sure which save he is looking for?"

"Yeah, I know," replied Crank quietly. "Due to the timeline and description, it's got to be the Tybee Island kid."

Sighing deeply, he sat back down at the table. "He wanted to know if anyone had seen a kid who looked like the description, and if so, was he called Jeremy?"

"Technically, a security breach would have occurred if someone remembered seeing the kid with Crank," said Gretchen. "Do we know for a fact that his questions went unanswered?"

"Angel couldn't tell me. He got the impression from the Mestizos that, so far, they hadn't got anything. Also, I always bring the kids on board in a sack or a box. They only get out when the boat is away from shore. The captain's people are highly paid to see nothing, but you never know."

"I don't like this, people," the Chief growled. "Even if they didn't get their answers this time, our security system has a definite flaw!"

"My security system is the best in the world!" exclaimed Gretchen, narrowing her eyes angrily at Crank. "The problem is in his section."

Never one to jump to his own defense, Crank smiled slightly and nodded for her to continue.

"When you were clearing him for the snatch, you overlooked something. One of the criteria is that the kid be a throwaway. No one wants him. Someone wants this kid back, and badly."

An hour later, Crank stomped down the path leading to the beach, too angry to notice the early afternoon sun filtering through the heavily scented jungle foliage and illuminating an already brilliant orange and red hibiscus blooms. Spotting the boat he was looking for moored to the landing, he quickened his steps.

"Captain Mike! How're you doing?" hailed Crank.

The bowl-legged Captain hopped off his boat and stalked toward Crank, chewing furiously on his unlit cigar. "How am I doing? I was on the other side of the bay, on a boat loaded with highfalutin tourists—paying customers, mind you—and I got this SOS call. You cost me a thousand bucks!"

"It's important. There's been some Mestizos asking about this island. They were working for that reporter here a few months ago. This time, he called asking about a kid. Can you ask any of your crew if they have been approached by—"

"No need to," came the gruff reply as the captain turned back to his boat.

"They already told you something?" Crank asked, following.

"No." The captain stopped so fast that Crank nearly ran over him. "My crew knows that if anyone ever questions them, they are to tell me immediately. They know where I am 24/7. I've been a captain for 25 years. I run a tight ship."

"I have a lot of respect for you as a captain, but you mean none of your crew would answer a question or two if the money was right?"

Settling stiffly on a nearby bench, the Captain squinted at the younger man. Settling his wet cigar to the other side of his mouth, he said.

"Sit down. I have a story to tell you. A seafaring story." He leaned closer to Crank, lowering his voice. "I sailed this sea for ten years before getting my boat. It would have been around 1965. As you know, there was a lot of smuggling. The Columbian drug trade was alive and well. There were some badass captains in those days; mine was the worst. Thaddeus Macrae, five-foot-tall, bald as a cue ball, and the coldest blue eyes I've ever seen."

Seeing he had Crank's full attention, he continued, "Yeah. I'm ashamed to admit it, but I was a drug runner. It's how I got this rig. It cost me my family in the long run. It was blood money, plain and simple. Anyway, back to my Captain, the old bastard, may he rot in hell. There were many odd things about him, but one of the oddest was that he never spoke above a whisper. Never. You know how noisy it gets on a boat. We always had to be on the alert for a command, and God forbid if you missed it."

"Captain," Crank interrupted. "It sounds like a great story, and I would like to hear it all, but—"

"Simmer down, pup. I'll get to the point. I learned how to ensure complete obedience from that odd, slightly insane man. We were deathly afraid of him, but we couldn't put our finger on why. But we noticed if a crew member screwed up or failed to follow a whispered order, he was gone the next day." "So, he fired him? That's it?" scoffed Crank.

"I didn't say he fired him. I said he was gone," the captain replied softly. "We were hundreds of miles from shore, and the crewman was just gone."

Crank blinked. "He threw them overboard? Is that what you're saying? So, if your crew screws up, you chunk the man over like a bucket of chum? So that's why your crew won't rat us out for money? Because they're afraid you'll kill them?" he said sarcastically.

Standing slowly, the captain chuckled as he began to walk to the boat. Crank followed.

"That works for most things but not when it comes to money. I just hadn't heard that story in a while and wanted to tell it. No,

I said I learned how to ensure complete crew obedience from him. His way works for most things, so I use it for every infraction except taking a bribe. Men will sell their souls to the devil or the briny sea for money. To keep them from taking money for information on this setup, I use the 25 percent system."

"What the hell is that?" asked Crank.

"I give them 25 percent more money not to give the information, no questions asked. It works every time. They get more money and don't have to swim with the fishes."

Back on board, the captain looked down at the confused younger man standing on the landing. Drawing a new cigar out of his pocket, he bit off the end with his tobacco-stained teeth. Shouting to be heard over the revving engines, he said, "Of course, I put it on the island's bill."

Later that evening, Crank walked through the jungle toward the waterfall. The full moon gave ample light as he walked the path. It was natural for him to move quietly after long years of military training. Anticipating the cooling relief from the tropical humidity, he suddenly realized someone was in the pool. He stopped. It had to be one of the staff. The children were in lockdown after dark unless there was a scheduled activity. He walked to the edge of the pool and looked down at the dark form frozen into stillness at his presence.

"Identify yourself!" he barked.

"It's me, Mister Crank. It's Jeremy."

"Jeremy! What the hell are you doing out here in the dark? There are poisonous snakes!"

"I know, sir. I couldn't sleep, so I slipped out," came the quiet reply.

"It's alright this time, but don't do it again. In a rainforest, there are very poisonous snakes. The Fer-de-Lance snake likes to stay around water, and its bite will likely kill you.

Crank dived effortlessly into the cool water. Emerging on the far side of the pool, he was not surprised to see Jeremy now sitting calmly on the other side. Flipping over on his back, he said, "Well, Jeremy, how goes it? Are you settling in?"

"Yes, sir. I like my room. I like school a lot."

"Yeah? I never liked school much. I've heard this one is good, and the teachers seem okay."

Swimming over to where the kid sat, Crank pulled himself out of the water.

"Jeremy, I was going to ask you this while we were traveling here but never got around to it. Did your father ever talk to you about any relatives you might have? An aunt or uncle, a grandparent?"

Watching the kid stiffen, Crank searched Jeremy's face.

"No, sir. He said no one even knew about me, and if they did, they wouldn't care anyway."

"Sorry, Jeremy. That must have been rough to hear. But you have people here who care about you. This whole island exists for kids just like you. Remember that you're a great kid with a lot going for you. Okay?"

Looking across the pool, the child smiled slightly, saying, "I know, sir. It's okay. I didn't believe him anyway because I knew I wasn't alone. Besides, he's not my father. He told me my father wouldn't want me either."

An hour later found Crank in the security building barking at his startled night staff.

"I need every bit of information you have on Jeremy's father. I want to search every database. I want DNA that proves he's the kid's father. And if he isn't, who the hell is? We always assumed he was the father because the police folder said he was. We thought it was verified. I also want everything available about this reporter, Matthew Day. His history, his family. The color of his favorite underwear. Everything! I think we've screwed up and screwed up badly. I better not be right. "

CHAPTER 10

"Sam. I'm here. I went swimming. I could feel you trying to reach me, but Mister Crank caught me, so I couldn't get away."

"Hi! Jeremy! It's okay. I went to bed earlier tonight. It took me a long time to fall asleep. I was so excited. Everyone knows, Jeremy!"

"What do you mean everyone knows about me? Did you tell your mother about me?"

"Yes! She's going to help! And Uncle Matt, too! They believe me. At least Mom does. Uh—I had to break my promise about your name. My mom needs it if she's going to help find you. I know it was like a blood oath, but..."

"That's okay, Sam. If it helps her."

"My mom needs to know where you are now. She gave me some questions to ask you. I hope I can remember them all. There were a lot. I wish I could be awake when I talk to you. It would help."

"What's the first one?"

"She wants to know if they are being nice to you. I told her they weren't hitting you because I could feel that, but she wants to be sure."

"No. No one gets hit here, even in school, if they mess up or act up. Some don't act nice in school, but they take them away, and when they come back, they're okay. I don't see any blue spots or blood."

"Okay. What about food? Mom's always worried about me not eating right."

"We eat what they call island food. There are a lot of fruits and stuff like carrots and lettuce. We eat chicken and a lot of fish. There are some things I don't recognize, but they taste good. There are short brown people here called natives. They paint themselves with this black paint. It's neat looking. Sometimes, they paint us. They fix the food for us."

"She asked me about something, but I'm not sure what she meant. Our teacher told us no one should touch us where we wear our underwear. She wants to know if anyone has touched you there."

"Once before I came to the island, but not anymore."

"Okay. I'll tell Mom. But if they try it again...run away or scream real loud. That's what my teacher and mom said to do. I think that's all the... wait! She said to watch for any signs on the island or mail lying around. I think she needs to know more to find where you are. You said Mister Crank caught you. Did you do something wrong?"

"I had slipped out to swim in the waterfall pool. I told you I do that at night. When I lived with that man, he would forget to lock me in, and I would swim at night in the ocean. I miss that

159

sometimes, but we're not supposed to be out at night here. It's dangerous. They say there are monsters out at night."

"Monsters! I've got to wake up now! I've got to tell Mom so she can come save you!"

"I'm just kidding! Some of the bigger kids told me that when I first came to the island. There's this guy here. He takes us into the jungle with nothing to eat. We have to find stuff out there. It's not easy. Nothing is cooked. We have to eat it raw. He says there are dangerous snakes out here. That's why we're locked up at night.

"It sounds like a bad place. My mom and Uncle Matt will get you out of there. I've got to sleep some now. G'night, Jeremy."

"G'night, Sam"

CHAPTER 11

Sunny glanced around the crowded restaurant. She hoped meeting Matt here would put him in a good mood—and maybe help temper his reaction to what she would say. The door opened, and she raised a hand to get his attention when he walked in. She patiently waited for her long-legged brother to fold himself into the booth.

"Sorry about the booth," she said.

"Okay, what's up?" His eyes held a distinctly suspicious look.

"Why does something have to be up? I just wanted to have a nice meal with my brother?"

"First of all, dear sister, you could care less if I don't like a booth. Your usual answer to my complaint about it is, 'Quit griping. If you hadn't hogged all the milk when we were growing up, you wouldn't be so tall now!

"You're right. I don't care if you don't like a booth, and the milk theory still holds up. Still, I needed to talk with you about a plan I—

"If this plan involves you going off to look for this Jeremy kid, then you can just forget it. Right now," said Matt.

"Sam talked to Jeremy again last night," she said. "They're touching him, Mattie. Where they're not supposed to, they also

161

lead him into the jungle and make him find food. Whatever he finds, he has to eat raw." Voice trembling now, she continued. "They lock him up at night so he can't escape." Seeing her brother's eyes darken, she added, "He says there're many children there. All ages."

"Sunny, you don't know what you're getting into. Coiba was a penal colony. Do you even know what that means?"

"Yes," said Sunny. "The island housed prisoners."

"Yes, but the prisoners weren't the ones who were locked up. The guard locked *themselves* indoors at night for their own protection. Supposedly, the government has relocated all of them. Still, they could never be sure with so much of the island's dense rainforest. Likely, some are still loose." Leaning forward, he added, "Sunny, these guys are murderers and rapists!"

"All the more reason we have to get those kids off that island," his sister said, undaunted. "Besides, you'll protect me and you know I can shoot a gun. Dad taught us all to shoot, and I'm the most accur—"

"There are snakes, too. Poisonous ones," said Matt.

Sunny turned pale.

"Very poisonous. The place is crawling with them, so I don't—"

"I like the idea of my nephew and the other children being in danger even less than snakes!"

"Sunny," Matt said, his eyes shut tight for a moment before looking at her again. "I know you're worried. I am, too. How about I go check it out first? I can be back in a week. I'll blend in much easier than you with your being female and that red hair."

"I'll dye it! I'm going, Mattie, with or without you. Mom will watch Sam." Sunny wiped the tears from her cheeks, straightened up, and said firmly, "There is only one way to find out for sure sure if Coiba island is where they took Jeremy. I couldn't live with myself if I sat here and did nothing."

❖

Ready for tomorrow's early flight and with her bag packed, Sunny sat at the table with Sam and her mother, playing Monopoly. Watching the evident love between the two made Sunny realize how grateful she was to her mother for being a "hands-on grandma."

Later, getting ready for bed, her cell beeped.

"Sunny? It's Ken Ables, FBI."

"Oh! Ken! I've been waiting to hear from you. Did you talk to that creep who kidnapped and abused Jeremy? Did they put him in one of those old run-down jails with rats or roaches?"

"Sorry, Sunny," Ken replied. "I wish I could tell you that he was in a damp, rat-infested dungeon and was being tortured daily, but the Chatham County jail is a fairly new facility."

"So what did you find out?"

"The news isn't good, even though it gives us more pieces of the puzzle.

This is going to be upsetting to you, but in a way, it might come as a relief and—"

"Please! Tell me! I'm stronger than I look," Sunny interrupted. "How could it be any worse than I have already lived through? The only thing I couldn't deal with was proof that Jeremy was dead. Oh! God! That is what you're calling to tell me? That monster did kill him after all!"

"No! Quit anticipating what I'm going to say and listen! Yesterday, I spent four hours grilling James Ashton. He's a mental mess. Broken. They've had psychiatrists in to evaluate him. It's not an act. I talked to the psychiatrists. They say he's grieving and full of guilt."

"For abusing Jeremy?" exclaimed Sunny. "Why shouldn't he be? Anyone who would take a helpless—"

"For killing your sister, Sunny."

Sunny abruptly sat down on the bed. She took the phone from her ear and stared for a long minute at the instrument, her mind unable to make sense of the new information.

"Sunny! Sunny! Are you there? Answer me, dammit!"

She lifted the phone to her ear. "I—I'm back." She took a breath. "Okay. The creep killed my sister, and now he has confessed to it. I will deal with that later, but what did he say about Jeremy? How did he even know about him? Tell me the rest.

Please, I'm ready."

"It's a classic case of an old boyfriend not wanting to let go. About a year before her death, they'd broken up. He had a violent temper, plus he was big into porn sites. She found cameras all over his place. He had filmed and posted their sexual activity. She told him to shove off. He became obsessed with her. He says he started following her. Says she took up with some new guy who left her when she was pregnant. Ashton watched as her pregnancy advanced, getting madder and madder. A few weeks after she gave birth to Jeremy, he followed her home from the babysitter one rainy night. Ashton says he just wanted to scare her by hitting the back of her car, but the roads were slick—her car skidded and went over the rail. When he climbed down the embankment, he found she was dead, but the baby was alive and unharmed. He got the baby out and took him before the police arrived."

"Why? Why didn't he leave the baby and call the police? They would've found Jeremy, and I would've been notified. All these years. He would've been loved, cared for, and safe." Sunny's voice was a whisper, tearful now as she imagined the fear and pain that filled the last minutes of her sister's life.

"I asked him that. He says he wanted to keep a part of Raine with him. So, he took Jeremy. He threatened her roommate if she ever told anyone about the baby. He hired an illegal immigrant to care for him until he got around five years old, and then she just came in during the day. She was the informant that told the

Tybee investigators about the abuse even though she will likely get deported. Most of the time, he just ignored the boy, but when he got to drinking—evidently, that was often—he would get angry again and take it out on Jeremy. He says the maid was responsible for relocating the boy downstairs to the shed. Probably to keep him out of Ashton's sight."

Ignoring the anger that surfaced at the last part of the agent's statement, she pressed on. "Did he ever know the other man's name, Jeremy's father?"

"Never got the name. Said the guy was a stranger in town. He'd show up, stay for a few days, and then disappear," said the agent.

Sunny remained silent, filled with disappointment at yet another dead end.

"Sunny, I know you want the guy's name," said the agent, "but Ashton did get some pictures we can run through the database."

"Pictures! When can I see them?"

"I don't have them with me. I haven't even seen them. The house's contents have all been cataloged and stored. Forensics is still going over everything. It will take me a while to get access, but I promise I will get them."

Smiling for the first time at the conviction she heard in the agent's voice, she said, "I know you will; and Ken?"

"Yes, Sunny."

"My family's so grateful for your help. Matt and I have a short getaway planned, and knowing you're on the case will help." Thinking of her "secret mission" and the possible outcomes, she continued

"And someday, maybe we can repay you with more information that will be helpful to your investigation."

"Thanks, Sunny. I'm on my way to the forensics lab. I'll contact you when I get the pictures. Hopefully, we can ID the father of Raine's children."

CHAPTER 12

Ken took the manila envelope from the clerk and walked towards the heavy glass doors, doing his best to look calm. Exiting the brick and glass structure of the Chatham County medical examiner's office, he felt the hot, humid Savannah air hit him in the face. Minutes later, he slid into the driver's side of his rented car and threw the manila envelope at his partner.

"Mission accomplished!" he said, reaching to turn the a/c knob to its highest setting.

"You got the pictures that bastard took of the mystery guy?" said Jax. "This is one for the books. They never release anything while the case is still being processed."

"It wasn't easy," he said, grinning. "Open the envelope. I can't wait to see the slimy face of a guy who would get a girl pregnant and then take off."

Undoing the fastener and lifting the flap, his partner said, "Remember, we don't know if the girl ever told him about the upcoming blessed event. I was thinking while you were misrepresenting the hell out of our jurisdiction to the M.E. that our old friend Ashton could have killed him, too."

Backing out of the parking space, Ken thought about his partner's remarks. He was right. That crazy son of a bitch could have done both of them, but it just didn't feel right. Why would he have held back on one murder when he had just confessed to murdering the girl? What would he have to gain? Plus, he was so nuts he probably would have confessed to President Kennedy's murder with a bit of persuasion.

"Son of a bitch!" exclaimed Jax

Glancing at his partner, he pulled over to the shoulder and threw the shift into park. Picking up the first eight-by-ten graciously enlarged by the friendly M.E.'s office, he was suddenly face to face with someone he had never thought to see again. The picture was of a man in his middle thirties with short hair and the high cheekbones indicating Native American ancestry. Electric blue eyes flashed out of his face, turned bronze by the sun. He laughed at the camera, pale hair glinting almost silver in the sun. Stunned, Ken hurriedly looked through the other pictures.

"It's him," said Jax. "It's Rand. These pictures would have been taken about six or seven years ago before he went off the grid. He was still an active operative then. He must have visited Atlanta on his time off."

"We're going to have to report this to the bureau," said Ken. Looking at his now silent partner, he continued. "Just not yet. Rand was a friend as well as a partner. There was no one I'd rather have on my team. He had my back more times than I can count. And yours, too."

"Yeah—yeah. You're right," Jax said. "You remember when we were in Columbia undercover, which was going fine until someone recognized you? Then all hell broke loose. They scattered like a bunch of roaches when you turn on the light. Damn, it was dark in that jungle. We couldn't have seen anything if it wasn't for our NODs! Suddenly Rand comes riding up on a damn horse. Old nag with a swayback. He's galloping through the brush, whooping and yelling—picking off that scum one at a time and hitting them in the leg so they couldn't run. Got at least half of them. Meanwhile, we're standing there with our mouths open, and he suddenly turns the nag and rides slowly back to where we're standing. He gets off as calmly as you please and says, 'Fellows. I want you to meet Petunia.' Never did find out where he got that damn horse."

Smiling, both men sat for a moment, lost in other memories of good times and some not-so-good.

"What's our next step?" asked Jax. "We know that Lewis is more than likely the father of Ms. Day's kids. We don't know if he ever found out the girl stole his sperm. We also don't know if he's alive or not. If he showed up later after Thailand, Ashton could have killed him, or he could have been killed later in some covert mission. So, my friend, what will you tell the Day family? I can imagine their reaction when you tell them the man that impregnated their dead family member was FBI, and we don't know where he is or if he's even alive.

In the following silence, Jax stared out the car window, a grim look on his face. He knew what had happened to Rand. He was dead. When Jax reported that Rand was at the egg farm in Thailand, she ordered the hit. It was easy to gather some of her guys from the village to "dispose" of Rand immediately. By the time they finished, he was miles away following up a fake lead.

"You still got that friend in personnel?" Ken said abruptly.

"You mean Sheila?" his partner said, grinning wolfishly. We get together now and then. I think she has been moved to Internal Affairs. You want me to pump the lovely Sheila for information on Rand's last known whereabouts?" Sighing heavily, Jax continued, "Alright. If you think I must, then I must. The things I do for this job."

"Yeah, yeah," Ken replied sarcastically. I appreciate you taking one for the team. We need to know what I.A. knows. Once we're up to speed, we can start our quiet investigation."

"While I'm busy sacrificing myself, where will you be? Talking to the Day family?"

"I want to get a warrant for surveillance at the Day house. I can get the judge to issue it since they are part of an ongoing investigation, and now, with the connection to Rand, there'll be no problem. Sunny mentioned taking a short vacation. I think with her brother. The grandmother and boy are home. They are fixing to have major trouble with their cable."

"I'll let you know if I get anything more from Sheila. I doubt it, though you had me dog I.A. for months after Lewis disappeared, and I got nothing."

Jax put the passenger seat back, put on his sunglasses, and closed his eyes. They had gotten nothing, of course, because he had made sure of it. He wasn't worried about this new stuff or the Day family. All this was before Rand "disappeared," so Bolo's trafficking organization was safe. He'd yet to meet the leader, man or woman, but he'd heard enough things to know he never wanted to.

The persistent redhead discussed in Texas would have been pleased to know the FBI agents had fallen for her vacation decoy. She was in a tropical paradise but not to catch some sun— she intended to catch a kidnapper.

Sunny stretched luxuriously in her narrow bunk bed. Bright tropical sunlight poured through her shuttered window into the tiny room, magnifying the simple, clean lines. Concrete floors— wood accents and starched white sheets spread over twin bunk beds—had looked heavenly to her when they had finally arrived in Santa Catalina late last evening. The plane trip to Panama City had been a piece of cake compared to the six-hour drive to this place by the ocean, where they would hire a boat to get them to Coiba.

She had to hand it to her brother. He could speak Spanish like a native and had no trouble hiring the jeep and navigating the way. Of course, his insistence they pretend to be young newlyweds interested in surfing and canoodling was icky. She could see his point, however. The need to blend in was paramount since they intended to avoid getting official permission to visit Coiba Island. Allowing one more stretch, she swung her legs over the side of the bunk and absentmindedly scratched a bug bite.

"Quit scratching. You'll get them infected, and that's all we need."

Startled, she turned her head in time to see her brother swing through the door. Clad in an old T-shirt with fading letters that spelled "Catch the wave!" and long khaki shorts, he looked carefree and years younger.

"I wasn't scratching!" she hastily lied. "Besides, I am a nurse, so if anyone knows how to prevent infection, it's me! After all, who was the one who forgot to bring bug spray in the first place?"

"Me." he said good-naturedly. "But bugs don't bite me. I don't know why. I've been in some of the worst bug-infested jungles in the world. Not one bite."

"I'm happy for you. Does your uncanny luck extend to getting some food? I'm starving! It's about 10 o'clock, so we missed breakfast."

"Not to worry. The lovely Italian lady that runs the place said she would save something for us since we got in so late and—"

That was all Sunny needed to hear. Jumping off the bed, she rushed into the small bathroom to put on her shorts and her equally disreputable T-shirt, which said, "Surfers do it better!" "I would've loved some input on selecting our outfits, brother dear."

"Sorry, sis. There wasn't enough time for fashion consulting. I bought them from that guy at the airport. He gave me the name of a contact here who should get us to Coiba in the middle of the night without asking any questions. "

"Why can't we go to Coiba like normal tourists, check it out first, and then go in at night?"

"A waste of time", said her brother. "Remember? I've already been on the island. The Panamanian government has an ANAM station there. They restrict you to small parts of the island. Coiba is a big island. It's about 10 miles wide and 30 miles long."

Snatching the room keys off the table, he ushered Sunny outside into the brilliant sunlight. Holding hands like the newlyweds they were supposed to be, he stopped so suddenly that Sunny's arm popped back.

"What're you trying to do? Dislocate your bride's arm?"

"I just thought of something." Dropping his sister's hand and pacing the narrow path head down, frowning, he continued. "I don't know why this thought just popped into my head, but there was something strange about that ANAM police station."

"Strange? Like what?"

Sitting on a bench, he tipped his head back and closed his eyes tightly. Speaking slowly, he recounted the first meeting.

"We came in that afternoon. It was a chartered boat. The captain was a crusty old sob, bowlegged as hell. His name was Captain Mike." Sitting forward, he said, "The ANAM guys were there before we even got off the boat. They checked our papers."

"Well, what looked or felt wrong? "

"They had the right color and uniform style. Also, the logo on their sleeves looked official. It was the men. They were all very muscular. They looked more like bouncers at a local bar. They were also taller than your average Panamanian. Their haircuts were military-style. When we went into their quarters to finish the I.D. check. Everything looked top dollar. The equipment. The furnishings. Yet the outside of the building needed paint and a new roof."-

Frustrated now and trying to understand where her brother was headed, Sunny plopped down on the bench beside him.

"I don't get it. The guys looked in shape and had good equipment. Is that all you have? "

When Matt did not answer, she continued.

"Maybe they work out. Like, what else is there to do on a deserted island?"

Turning to look at her, Matt said slowly, clearly thinking aloud, "I don't think they were Panamanian at all. They were some ex-military group. There were three there that day. They all spoke fluent Spanish, but—that's it. There was no trace of an accent when they spoke to me in English. Different from a person where Spanish is their first language and they've learned to speak English. They spoke like English-speaking people who have learned to speak Spanish."

Still confused about the significance, she quietly waited for him to continue.

"Why didn't that hit me sooner? It could have made all the difference for my investigation when I was there the first time."

"I don't get why this is important in finding Jeremy. An exmilitary group? Why would they be interested in kidnapping or harming children? Can you—"

"I don't know how it relates to Jeremy, at least not now. But it relates to the mysterious building materials being shipped to the island—metal buildings and supplies like the military would need."

"You think some government is kidnaping the children?" asked Sunny.

Standing up abruptly, Matt said, "I don't know what to think. I don't have enough information yet. Let's get something to eat. I always think better on a full stomach!"

Hauling Sunny up from the bench, he marched her down the path to the little thatched-roof restaurant.

"I tell you, the son of a bitch is alive!" Jax hissed as he strode toward the baggage claim area at the Austin airport. Several travelers glanced at him as they passed.

"You are wrong," came the oily voice snaking its way into his earbuds. "I know he is dead. I took care of him myself."

"Look, you asshole! I just got some new intelligence from I.A.! They say he survived the beating! He's not with the FBI anymore. He has gone underground, and they've lost touch. I want the money back!

"No refunds, cabron! He was one tricky bastard to kill, but it was done, I assure you. Do not call me again unless you have an order." The line went dead.

Watching the unclaimed baggage slowly make the circle, cold sweat dripped down his chest. Rand's alive? At least he was three years ago before they lost him. Did Rand go back to Raine? Did he know he had a son? Maybe that crazy bastard, Ashton, offed him later. Wouldn't that be ironic? One of the best undercover FBI operatives was killed by a crazy alcoholic when a skilled assassin couldn't get the job done. Bolo's not going to like this.

Jax took a breath, his mind shuffling through the possibilities. He hadn't been seen or heard from in over three or four years! He could not have been undercover that long without the FBI knowing. He must be dead. Maybe Bolo didn't need to know after all.

Smiling grimly, he grabbed his battered black case from the revolving silver tray of offerings. Rushing from the terminal into the late-night Austin heat, his thoughts churned. It was going to be a long night.

❖

"C'mon Sunny! The boats here!" whispered Matt, sticking his head in their room.

Dressed in black pants and a turtleneck, with her hair under a black knit cap, he was surprised to see his sister's small, dark form sitting motionlessly on the bed. "What's wrong? Sunny? We got to go. Now!"

"I—I just can't go, Matt."

Closing the door, Matt sat down next to his sister.

"Are you scared? Is that it? It's okay. You can stay—"

"What if he's dead?" she whispered. "Or we have the wrong location and come up empty-handed?" She looked up at her brother. "I'm not scared of the island. I'm scared of what we'll find out about Jeremy. I— I don't think I can take knowing for sure."

"C'mon. Where's all that fighting spirit? We've come this far. Besides. What if we can help some other child? Even if it's too late for Jeremy?" Surprised at the lack of response from his normally firecracker sister, he played his ace card. "Tell you what. Why don't you stay here and relax? I'll slip over to the island. Have a look around and be back in a few hours. I figured this adventure might be a little too—"

"Might be a little too much for me? Was that what you were going to say? I'm not some fragile, helpless little thing. I've taken martial arts, and I can bench press my weight! You know I'm not about to let you go there by yourself. You might need me!"

Snatching her black bag from the bed, she hurried through the door, tossing one last order to her now smiling companion. "I know what you just did, smart ass!"

An hour later, Matt turned to smile at his sister, barely visible in the darkness. Black grease smeared heavily on her face.

"Did you get a look at the captain?" she asked.

"No, Matt answered. "What he's doing could get his license taken away. He'll probably stay out of sight any—"

"It's the same one!" Sunny whispered urgently in his ear.

"Same what?" Standing in the bow of the fishing vessel, Matt continued to peer into the inky darkness.

"I heard one of the hands call him Captain Mike. Isn't that the same captain that took you to Coiba the first time?"

"Well, I'll be damned. Nice little sideline he's got going," laughed Matt. "I told you he was a crusty old bastard."

Soon, the dark shape of the island came into view. They were silently escorted over the side into a small dark dinghy accompanied by two crew members. Idling engines and the gentle slap of waves against the boat's sides were the only sounds. Matt had told her they would land closer to the island's north tip, away from the ANAM station. Using the hotel's Wi-Fi, she learned that ANAM stands for Autoridad Nacional del Ambiente, the National Environmental Authority. Due to its largely unexplored ecosystem, environmentalists worldwide have been on the Panamanian government to protect the area from exploitation. Visitors were strictly supervised, making it difficult to visit any island areas other than the ranger station and a few miles of coastal beaches.

Sunny and Matt watched the dinghy slowly disappear from view before trudging inland, leaving the long strip of beach behind. Looking at the dark interior, Sunny could not believe there were any inhabitants.

Following Matt closely as he silently threaded through the dense vegetation, she was impressed that her brother could see where he was going. After what seemed like hours, he finally stopped by a large tree. Glad to see his breathing was slightly labored too, Sunny dropped her backpack and sat down with her back against the tree. So relieved to finally rest, she didn't even care that the spongy ground was soaking wet.

"You stay here. I'm going to look around," said Matt, looking down at his sister resting against the tree. Sensing that reinforcement of his instructions might be needed, he squatted down and looked her in the eye. "And I mean it. Stay here! It may take a while. You have supplies, so get something to eat while you wait. You can contact me, but only if it's an emergency. I have it set on vibrate, so text me."

"Are you quite through?" asked his sister in a frosty tone. "Because if you are through, then I can tell you there is no way in hell that I'm going to sit here while you go off into God knows where without me. What if you step on a snake? " Matt stood up abruptly.

"I'm not going to step on a snake. You're just throwing that in because you think I'm scared of them like you are! Besides, the boots we're wearing are snake-proof anyway, so you might as well—"

Standing nose to chest with her brother, Sunny hissed loudly, "Matt, it's not going to work. I'm going!" "C'mon, Matt. Let her come. In fact, I insist." Startled, they froze.

The voice had come out of the darkness, low and amused.

A gun appeared in Matt's hand and then disappeared just as quickly in a blur of movement. Big shadows surrounded them on all sides, and bits of light glinted off guns and helmets. Sunny watched as her brother's arms were grabbed and jerked behind him.

Lunging forward, she yelled, "Let him go! Don't hurt him, you bastards! We're United States Citi—. Oomph!"

Suddenly, Sunny was surrounded by male hardness, top to bottom and side to side. Looking way up at a strange alien-looking head, she realized that all the muscle now holding her in place was only one man.

"Let go of me, you big jerk! How dare you manhandle me this way! After all, I'm a —"

"I know. I know. You're a United States citizen," came the terse reply. "Take them to the lock-up. We'll interrogate them later."

He shoved Sunny away from him into the arms of a much smaller man. He silently disappeared into the darkness, giving one last command that made Sunny's blood turn to ice.

"Rambo. Keep the men off of her. This one's mine."

Sunny was exhausted. It was rough going through the dense vegetation, and the mushy floor was slippery. She and Matt fell several times, only to be hauled roughly to their feet. Not one word was said by her captors, but Sunny felt obligated to give full rein to her red-headed temper and filled the air with her threats. Finally, she got tired of talking to herself and put all her energy into taking one more step.

Who were these people? Matt had said there was military here at one time. He thought the ANAM guys at the ranger station might be military. Whose military? Their leader didn't have any Spanish accent. What could all of this have to do with Jeremy's kidnapping? Were they on the wrong track? Would she ever see her son again?

Finally, the silent party came into a clearing. They halted so quickly that Matt and Sunny bumped into each other and fell onto the water-soaked ground.

After being roughly hauled to their feet, she looked around at an empty clearing.

"Why are we stopping?" she asked the nearest soldier. He was the slightly smaller man the leader had commanded to put them in "lock up." Suddenly remembering he had been called Rambo, she addressed him by name. She had read a book once that advocated creating a relationship with your kidnapper.

"Uh. Rambo, is it?" Getting no response, she continued, "Rambo! There is nothing here. Are we going to sleep outside? Isn't there somewhere inside we can go? I'm tired and wet."

While Sunny was trying to appeal to Rambo's better nature, one of the other men walked away from the group and reached out his arm. Pulling it back toward him in one swift movement, suddenly, there was a large rectangle of light in the darkness. As Sunny and Matt glanced at each other, they were roughly shoved toward the lit area. Several men entered the first after walking up what looked like stairs. At least it looked like stairs were under their feet, but they weren't visible. Matt leaned toward her and whispered,

"Son of a bitch. It's invisible paint! I heard the military had the technology. The buildings and the stairs are coated with it. That's why I couldn't see anything from the helicopter during my first visit! "

The guards discouraged more communication by roughly shoving their captives through the light. Given no opportunity to look around while their eyes adjusted, the brother and sister were hurried along a corridor and into another room. Without saying a word, the team filed out of the room, banging the door shut behind them. The room was large and had bunk beds along one side. There was another door that opened into a bathroom. Sunny headed for it while Matt prowled around the room.

After quickly washing up, Sunny stood at the bathroom door, watching her brother move furniture.

"Matt? Wha—?" she began. Stopping when her brother frowned at her to be quiet. She knew that frown, having been on the receiving end of it since childhood. He pulled a small metal cylinder from the cuff of his sleeve.

After holding it up and sweeping the room, he smiled and said, "I was checking for electronics."

Sitting in one of the room's two chairs, he looked around and frowned.

"Nothing. Which is strange. They would want to watch ushear us if this is an interrogation room."

"Who are these people? Are they military? Are they ANAM? Drug smugglers?" Sunny asked, her voice rising as her imagination blossomed. Sunny sat on the nearest twin bed and thought about how tired and she was and how she would love some food, a hot shower, and some sleep.

The next instant, the door flew open, and a big, black, baldheaded giant stood in the door, carrying a tray piled high with steaming plates of food and a package under his arm. Convinced she was hallucinating, Sunny continued to gaze at the apparition. He was splendid. He was dressed in white clothing, which stood out in stark contrast to his ebony skin. His bald head glistened in the artificial light.

"Dammit, Leonard, get out of the doorway! There's no way anyone can get around you!"

Since Matt was standing between Sunny and the giant, she leaned to one side in time to notice the strangest sight. Behind the giant were two skinny arms with flapping hands, trying to push into the room. Moving slowly, the behemoth named Leonard walked to the table to set the food tray down, allowing the occupants of the room a chance to see the owner of the skinny arms. At first glance, looking at his small, wiry frame and delicate childlike features, it would appear a thirteen-year-old boy was ordering this giant man about. However, the knotty muscles, goatee, and dark, intense eyes indicated a much older man. She realized he was Rambo, one of her captors.

Having finally gained access to the room, he walked quickly up to them.

"Let me introduce myself. I am Rambo." He paused, looking expectantly at the stunned brother and sister, waiting for the usual smirks this unlikely name always brought. By this time, his audience was so confused that he could have said he was the Easter Bunny without getting a reaction.

Undaunted, he continued.

"Yes, well. I am Rambo, and this is Leonard. I'm sure you have many questions, but unfortunately, I cannot tell you more than that now." Holding his hands to ward off all their questions, he said, "I know it's confusing. I want to assure you that you are safe at the moment. The boss will see you in the morning, and after you answer his questions, he may answer some of yours." Indicating the table with a sweep of his hand, he went on. "This package includes some clean clothes and bath soap. Feel free to use the bathroom facilities. The door isn't locked, but it is guarded."

"Wait a minute," Matt said. "I demand to know by whose authority we are being detained. Are you the Panamanian police?"

Glad to see her brother finally snapped back to the present, Sunny stood beside him to lend support.

Smiling graciously, Rambo responded, "Tonight is not the time. Eat! Rest! Tomorrow, the boss will talk with you." Rambo stopped. Frowning, his gaze on Sunny he continued, "Just a bit of advice before we go. The boss is not a patient man, especially in the morning. I would answer his questions thoroughly and not give him any problems."

Watching Leonard solemnly nod in agreement over this advice, Sunny felt a chill of apprehension up her spine. Remembering their leader's parting shot that she was to be kept for his use only did nothing to reassure her.

Jerked back to the present by the door shutting as the men departed, Sunny hurriedly walked over to the table and began to fill her plate with food. Who knew fear could make you so hungry?

"We got to be careful what we tell these guys," said Matthew, joining his sister at the table. "We need to know who they are. What government do they represent? I got a good look at their equipment on the way here. I've learned a lot about military-issued equipment during my career. Their rifles and the thermal night scopes they're using are top of the line. I think we can rule out some guerilla faction."

Seated across from her brother, Sunny watched as he fell on his food, mainly using his hands. Wrapping a giant tortilla around the meat mixture, Matt took a huge bite chewing silently with a blissful look on his face.

"C'mon, Matt!" Sunny burst out. "They have got good equipment! They aren't guerilla forces, so who the heck are they? Why did they take Jeremy? What would soldiers need with abandoned abused children?"

Sunny's interest in food had disappeared, so she shoved her plate back and got up from the table, pacing furiously.

"Mattie, I'm scared. This is so sinister. There's a lot of money being spent on this island. That invisible paint stuff. All those supplies shipped here! Their military equipment! Is the Panamanian government involved in human trafficking? I saw a special about it. There are people that sell women and children to use them as sex workers!"

"Sit down and quit wringing your hands," Matt commanded, bringing his sister back to the chair and gently pushing her down. "You're taking very little information and creating this whole scenario. We don't know if they even have Jeremy. The only thing I know for sure is that these people are not Panamanian. I should've figured it out my first time on this island."

"If they're not Panamanians, who are they?" Sunny asked, sensing the confusion in his voice.

"They're American, sis," Matt replied slowly. "Their equipment is standard issue for the United States Special Forces."

CHAPTER 13

Jax sat in the dim room, listening to the task force leader's voice. It was another mandatory meeting about human trafficking—as if he needed a briefing. He wished he'd never gotten involved with Bolo's organization. Glancing quickly around the darkened room at the twelve other agents, he slid down comfortably in his chair and closed his eyes to the flashing gruesome images displayed on the white screen, letting his mind return to the meeting yesterday in New York.

He had arrived at the fourteenth-floor lobby promptly at 11. The receptionist directed him to a chair and disappeared behind the polished metal doors. He still felt the contained panic as the minutes ticked slowly by. The refrigerated air turned to icy clamminess when mixed with the sweat forming under his hand-tailored dress shirt.

"Sir? She will see you now."

Seconds later, he stood in awe of the panoramic view from the seamless glass expanse. Walking toward a massive expanse of metal that made the word "desk" laughable, he made out a small, still form. Petite with long, blue-black hair, it was plain to see that Bolo was an Asian woman.

"How good it is to see you in person, at last. We have never directly spoken, and that is the way I prefer it. However, sadly, there seems to be some problem now making this necessary. Please, sit down."

Jax watched in fascination as one tiny feminine hand with three-inch scarlet nails waved him to a chair. The lack of emotion on her face and the almost metallic cadence in her voice made the woman seem unreal and menacing. More cold sweat formed in his armpits, and he was suddenly aware of how dry his mouth was.

Grateful for the chair's solid feel, Jax leaned forward and said, "Uh, I'm glad to meet you, Ms. Bolo."

"It is just Bolo. Please continue. It was mentioned there was some problem with a contract regarding your friend. Please refer to him as your friend. No names, please."

"Oh, sure. I mean—that would be fine." Speaking carefully, Jax continued. "It appears that a contract between you and I was not concluded as I had thought. There was a mistake made." Unnerved by the lack of reaction, he continued, "I mean. I thought it had been concluded, but the person delivering it—screwed up."

"You were paid, yes?"

"Yes! And I intend to complete the contract myself.

You have two weeks; I need proof that the contract was completed. I am sure you understand that failure is not an option. You may go." Jax watched as her tiny hand buzzed for her receptionist.

Seconds later, he was in the elevator, descending to the lobby. He had never been closer to death. He thought it had been completed when Rand never resurfaced. Maybe he should have asked for proof. With the deadline in mind, he texted an immediate request for leave. Maybe that jealous son of a bitch Ashton offed him after all, and he could have a nice vacation. Whistling cheerfully, he headed for the door to hail a taxi.

Crank looked down into the petite redhead's light blue eyes as she lay in his arms. It was a beautiful spring day, and they had found a private spot by the lake.

Moving out of his arms, she pulled her shirt over her head and raced towards the water, laughing and peeking over her shoulder. He felt a strange unease as she swam further, her head and flashing arms now barely visible. The setting sun made silhouettes, but no female form was visible in the water. Heart racing, he started running toward the water. He could feel the adrenalin filling his limbs as it had so many times before when sensing danger. He opened his mouth to scream her name, but—

Crank sat up in bed, choking and gagging, wrenched from his nightmare, with a lump in his throat, making it hard to breathe. Leaning over between his shaking legs, he coughed hard and spit something on the floor. Still groggy, he tried to focus on the slimy pale pink mess on the floor. Slowly, recognition set in.

Bubblegum?

"Good morning, Jefe." Said his smiling native houseboy. You were lying on your back, making noise. I thought you were missing the beer again. I gave you bubbly gum instead, like you said." Hastily slammed doors followed the roar from the bedroom.

Angel's family knew the Jefe was not happy.

"Damn, Angel," bit out Crank as he stalked to the bathroom. "What were you trying to do? Choke me to death in my sleep...of all the stupid things to do to a person."

Flushing the toilet and washing his hands, Crank continued his tirade, not worried he could be heard all over the compound. Not expecting any answers from his houseboy, who knew when to shut up, he walked back into the room.

"Yeah, I *do* chew a lot of bubble gum. It helps me not miss drinking. I figured it worked when I quit smoking, so why not? But I like to chew it when I'm awake," he continued as he stopped in front of the small still form. "The operative word here is *awake!*"

Crank watched the small Embero native digest this new information. His Jefe's anger did not shake his composure, and he seemed in no hurry to process the matter.

Giving up, Crank pulled on his khaki shorts and a black Tshirt. He slipped his feet into his sandals and said grumpily, "If you're through trying to kill me, how about some breakfast... I've got a lot to do today."

He walked out on the lanai and sat down, pleased to see his chilled glass of fresh papaya juice waiting. Settling into the chair, he leaned his head back, staring at the thatched ceiling, shafts of sunlight winking at him as he moved his head.

The approach of his still-silent servant made him feel guilty for his anger.

"Uh. Angel. Look, I'm sorry I yelled, but man, you need to understand, " Crank said somewhat desperately. "You don't *ever* put something in the mouth of a person sleeping—or unconscious, for that matter. They can choke to death."

Watching Angel quietly and efficiently arrange breakfast on the table reassured Crank that he had gotten through to the little native. *No argument? Great! Cause he can argue the hell out of you if he doesn't understand something—*

"Thank you, Jefe, for your reasoning. I will need to ask the spirits about this. Then we can discuss it together." *Aww. Crap!*

Not wanting to be late, Crank strode up the path to headquarters, still bothered by last night's dream. Since coming to the island, Crank had been haunted by recurring dreams, which made no sense to him but were occurring more frequently.

In one, he is entering a small village—the sound of a woman coming from one of the smaller huts. At least the sound seems human, but just barely. Several dark shapes run to the hut and enter the only door—the interior lights up with a flickering yellow light. He ran to the glassless window and looked in— filled with dread only to abruptly wake sick to his stomach. These damn dreams are why he started drinking.

Approaching the invisible administration building, he remembered his disbelief when told about the "invisible paint" that, thanks to nanotechnology, directed a person's vision around and over the object, rendering it invisible to the eye. It was one of their most significant security features, eliminating any discovery from the air. Surprised to see his boss pacing back and forth on the gravel path, he quickened his step.

"Morning, chief! What's up?" said Crank as he approached the silent form.

"What's up? Is that your question today, Crank? What's up!" came the response.

Crank could feel the other man's tension and anger coming in waves. Approaching cautiously, he said, "Uh, well. I probably have some other questions. Like, what are you so pissed about so early? It's only 1100 hours. The day's young."

"I don't need you to be a smart ass right now! How come I wasn't notified when you decided to capture two of the island's visitors?" The Chief's voice rose slightly in volume.

"Then keep them in isolation and, in general, terrorize United States citizens!"

"Oh, you've met the female. She is awfully proud of that. She kept throwing it in my face last evening. Like she was the only U.S.

citizen in the area. Who the hell does she think we are? Iranians?"

"Since your terrorist team was in full garb, how the hell would she know who you are? Did you by any chance identify yourself, or was your departing remark to keep her for yourself meant to reassure her?"

Crank winced when he heard the last question. He took a few seconds to answer, still confused about why that remark had slipped out. Watching the veins bulging in his Chief's forehead, he decided he better try to calm him down before he had a stroke.

"Calm down, Chief. I was coming to brief you. They were secure, so I didn't need to wake you from your beauty sleep. It could wait. Let's go inside so I can tell you all about it," said Crank, walking toward the building until his Chief's next words stopped him cold.

"I wouldn't go in there if I were you. You think I'm pissed? Gretchen is inside, and don't try your sense of humor on her because, as you know, she doesn't have one. You better brief me now."

Quickly putting more distance between himself and the building, Crank walked back toward his boss.

"Last night's surveillance picked up a dinghy coming ashore. It was that old scoundrel, Captain Mike. He took their money for the trip and then notified me. We were waiting for them. We took them back to my building for the night. I didn't interrogate them. Rambo and Leonard fed and treated them like guests. Rambo tried to get their identity from them, but they didn't have any documents. So, we had to get some DNA samples. That could have gone better from Rambo's account. But we should know their identity soon. I think I know who the guy is. I hope I'm wrong."

"Well, don't keep me in suspense." drawled the Chief.

"I think he's the reporter who was asking questions about Jeremy. I need to find out who the girl is. Maybe his assistant?"

Getting no response from the Chief, he turned back toward the building.

"Might as well get it over with. The longer you make Gretchen wait, the madder she gets."

Swinging through the door, Crank was surprised to see several more people in the conference area than expected. The blinds were drawn against the morning sunlight, making it difficult to distinguish the occupants. The two standing against the wall were easier to recognize. Leonard and Rambo.

Crank turned and looked down into the most beautiful, baby-blue eyes he had ever seen. Topped by shoulder-length red-gold hair, the toned, petite form stood so close to him that he would have touched her body if he had taken a deep breath. To be more exact, his chest would have touched her nose since she was at least a foot shorter. About 100-110 pounds of redheaded fury—just what he needed today.

"I demand to know the answers to some questions! How dare you people hold us captives!"

"Sit down, Red! I'll be asking the questions for now." Signaling to his men to escort her back to her chair, he understood when they hesitated for a second.

Looking at the other captive, he saw the man quietly studying *him.*

"Don't *you* have any questions to demand answers to?" Crank asked dryly.

"Yes, I do. But I figured that Chief Plankton and you will answer them when he returns."

Seeing his Chief enter the room and walk to the head of the table, Crank heaved a sigh of relief. The older man was experienced at interrogation and negotiation and had the patience that Crank lacked.

Plankton cleared his throat, drawing all eyes to him.

"First, let me apologize to you and your companion for the treatment you have received at the hands of my staff," he said, addressing Matt. His eyes shifted noticeably, making it easy for all occupants to tell who he held accountable.

Crank frowned and shifted restlessly in his chair.

"And," continued the Chief, "I know you have many questions. Unfortunately, for security reasons, we must know who you are and what your purpose is here. Why *are* you both coming to the island in the middle of the night dressed for reconnaissance?"

"*Unfortunately,*" echoed Matt, "we will need some answers first. You are not Panamanians. That much is clear. Your equipment and buildings are military issues, the most recent and technologically advanced military equipment available. Your accents are American, even when you speak Spanish." He stopped and smiled calmly at the Chief before continuing. "You're flying under the radar for some reason. A reason we may not even need to know at this point." Seeing the frown on Crank's face and the complete lack of expression on the Chief's had him reassured that he was right. "So, Chief Plankton? How am I doing so far?"

Everyone in the room watched as a blonde woman with platinum blonde hair came to stand by the Chief. Her tall frame stood stiffly and silently as if to let her Chief know she was there to assist if needed. Her eyes touched briefly on Matt before cutting to Sunny, lingering there with a thin smile, the only expression on her face.

Smiling to acknowledge the support, the Chief introduced his Security Head.

"This is our Chief of Security. You may call her Gretchen. Understandably, she is concerned about any information being given that could make our operation vulnerable. However, since you have already noticed these things, it won't hurt to validate your impressions. Before we continue, though, I would also like to introduce someone you have met previously and not under the best circumstances." Gesturing to the still-silent Crank, he continued. "This is Crank. He oversees operations, and I'm sorry, but that is all I can tell you now. Let me reassure you that his handling of your visit—" Stopping, he fixed his eyes on Crank. "—mostly was according to policy on dealing with intruders. "

Sunny watched as Gretchen walked over to the chair beside Crank. Exchanging looks told her that Gretchen had a bone to pick, and Crank could care less. When Gretchen had seated herself, the Chief continued.

"It's your turn. What are your names, and why are you here?"

"We need some assurance that we will be allowed to leave this island unharmed," Matt said. "If we can have your word, as a military official. I will accept it."

Sunny and Crank erupted out of their chairs at precisely the same time and with identical expressions.

"Matt, you can't tell them anything yet! We need—"

"You're not getting any damn insurance policy!" growled Crank. We want to know why you're here and fast. If you think last night was rough—" Crank's threat was interrupted by the feel of a small hand pushing into his side. Surprised again at how fast the tiny, enraged woman could move, he looked down into her furious face as recognition settled over him.

"How dare you threaten my brother! He could take you apart in two seconds. He knows self-defense moves that—"

"Lady! Quit pushing me! Go sit down! Now!"

Sunny looked up into Crank's icy cold face and felt the bite of his fingers on both arms. With a swift, practiced motion, she shifted her weight, twisting her hips to the side. The sudden movement caught Crank off guard, and his grip loosened just enough for her to break free. Matt was on his feet and coming around the table behind Crank. After that, everything was a blur. Fascinated, she watched as two physically matched men squared off.

"Crank! Matt!" shouted the Chief. "Return to your seats. There will be no fighting here. This is a negotiation, dammit!" Sunny glanced at the Chief of Security across the table as the two men stiffly sat down.

"Chief Plankton, could I speak with my, uh, companion in private for a minute?" said Matt, not waiting for permission before he hauled Sunny up and marched her into the darkest corner of the room.

"Will you quit antagonizing him?" her brother hissed. I'm trying to get some information before I decide what to tell them!"

"You decide? You mean 'we' decide, don't you?" said Sunny.

"*We* decide. Now listen! I don't know what they're really up to, and I don't know if there is any connection between them and Jeremy's kidnapping. I think we can trust them not to be involved in something that would be a danger to kids. Sunny, we tell them our story and see if they know anything." Feeling her jerk of protest, he continued. "Listen, sis. We're fairly sure this is the island Jeremy is transmitting from, for want of a better word. This is a big island. They could help us find him!"

Sunny found her head nodding to agree to something every fiber of her being resisted. But she held her tongue and returned to the table with her brother. After seating Sunny, Matt turned to the Chief.

"Sir, we have decided to tell you why we're on the island. We're looking for someone and need your help. This island is big, and the vegetation is almost impenetrable. We would never be able to do it on our own. However, there is just one stipulation." Matt paused, giving Crank a cold smile. An unspoken challenge flashed between the two men. "We talk only to the Chief."

Sunny winced at the curse that exploded in the room.

CHAPTER 14

Sunny lay in the dark, listening to Matt's quiet breathing, thinking back to her earlier call to Sam.

"Sam, it's mom. Please listen! I only have a minute."

"Mom! G! It's mom calling! Mom, did you find him? Why are you whispering? Did you find Jeremy?"

"Not yet, son! Please do something, and it's very important! When you go to sleep, ask Jeremy if there's a waterfall surrounded by big orange and yellow flowers on his island. I need to know!"

"I already know that, mom. There is! He's told me about it lots of times. He goes swimming there, especially at night when all the other kids are asleep. It's his favorite place, but why are—"

"Okay, that's great! Tell him to meet me there tonight after everyone is asleep. Tell him to be sure no one sees him. He's to hide until he hears me calling his name. Hurry, repeat it back to me! I don't have much time!"

"He's—he's to go to the waterfall tonight—when everyone is sleeping. He has to be quiet and hide until he hears your voice.

Is that right, mom? Do you think you're on Jeremy's island? Does he know you there cuz—"

"Sam, I know it's hard for you to do all this waiting. It will be over soon. Uh. I have—have to go, sweetie. I love you. Tell G, Uncle Matt, and I will be home soon."

Feeling homesickness wash over her again as she remembered the sound of her son's voice, she quietly turned on her side and pulled the almost dead cell phone out of her bra. No one had bothered to look there.

That afternoon, as they were escorted back to their building, Sunny noticed a definite difference in her captors. Rambo was downright chatty, and Leonard, though silent, would give her a gentle pat occasionally. They apologized profusely for having to blindfold her and Matt and explained over and over that they were under orders. She winced when Rambo tied the cloth around her head, which immediately had him apologizing and retying it so loosely that she had to wrinkle her nose to keep it in place. Walking along the narrow path, she could hear birds singing and feel the stinging slap of branches hitting her body. It was the same gravel-type path but a different route. She was sure of it. Somehow, she could tell by the sounds. Suddenly, she could hear the roar of thousands of gallons of water hitting rocks—a waterfall. It had to be.

Seconds later, she bumped into Matt and pretended to stumble. Since their wrists were unbound, she could easily land on both knees and fall forward, bracing with her hands. As the guards scrambled to help her, there was plenty of time to look over the top of her blindfold. She was right. There was a beautiful grotto surrounded by orange and yellow hibiscus with giant heads. Sparkling water tumbled into the pool. It wasn't until later that she formed her plan to call Sam.

For now, she needed to find a way out of this room. She looked over at her brother, his chest rising and falling gently. She wished she could wake him, but he'd only try to stop her. She had to see if Jeremy was here and would allow no one to stand in her way.

She slipped silently from her cot and walked softly to the bathroom, easing the door shut. The window over the sink was high, but she had to try it. Bracing one hand on the wall, she reached for the towel rack beneath the window and climbed up on the sink, praying it would hold. It's a good thing she was a light weight.

Moments later, Sunny winced as her feet hit the leaf-covered ground outside the bathroom window—a sound so alien in the stillness of the night that she froze in a half crouch, waiting for some hard hands to drag her back inside. She thanked the full moon for its brightness and walked to the front of the building. Standing still, she concentrated on hearing the faint sounds of rushing water and then moved in that direction.

Minutes later, Sunny stood silently at the pool's edge, peering anxiously into the many shades of darkness. It was as if the moon was purposely lighting the pool, making the mist from the waterfall glisten and dance.

"Jeremy?" she whispered. "Jeremy. It's Aunt Sunny. It's alright. Come on out."

Creeping closer to the water's edge, she stared into the trees, her body tense, listening for any little movement.

"Aunt Sunny?" said a soft voice directly behind her. Whirling around, heart racing, she came face to face with her nephew.

Immobilized, she stared at the boy, her mind unable to comprehend what she saw. The boy held his ground and let her come to him. A face identical to her son's—almost. It was an older boy's face, more angular than Sam's, but almost certainly what he'd look like in a year or so.

Unnerved by his calmness, she tentatively touched Jeremy's face.

"It is you," she said, almost in a whisper. "You look exactly like your brother Sam."

Unable to stand it another second, Sunny enfolded him in her arms, bending down to kiss the top of his head, tears streaming down her face. After a few seconds, she felt his thin, stiff body relax, and his arms went around her waist. They stood that way for several minutes, with Sunny crying and Jeremy holding tightly.

Finally, she reluctantly let him go, suddenly aware they were standing in a moonlit spotlight. She pulled Jeremy back into the shadows.

"We only have a few minutes. Are they treating you well here? How far away are they keeping you? Do you get enough to eat?" Seeing his slow smile at the last question, she stopped.

"Sam said you always worried about him eating okay. He says that's what mothers do. What was my mother's name? Did she love me? What happened to her? Will you take me home with you so I can be with Sam? I am his older brother...he'll need me."

Smiling at the idea that this child, who had never had any support or nurturing, would be worried about Sam.

"Oh, Jeremy, your mother's name was Raine. She was my sister, and she loved you very much! Your mom died in a car accident when you were just an infant. I have a photo album at home with pictures of you and her. And absolutely, you're coming home with me!" Sensing urgency, she sat down on a smooth rock, pulling Jeremy beside her. "The problem is, Jeremy, I'm still unsure what is happening with this place. I know you were brought here away from that abusing bas— um—man. But I still don't know why. I can tell you one thing... when we get away from here, the authorities are g—"

"Well, well, well. It's my little nocturnal redhead out for an evening stroll with one of the kids who has been repeatedly ordered to stay in at night."

Instantly recognizing the voice, Sunny jumped up from the rock, thrusting Jeremy behind her, trying to locate the danger.

"I found him! I found Jeremy! I knew you bastards were lying!" she hissed quietly, not wanting to alert the whole island. She struggled to keep Jeremy behind her, who, for some reason, was trying his best to get in front of her.

"It's okay! It's only Mr. Crank," said Jeremy as he finally pushed in front of her. "He's the one that saved me! He won't hurt you. He often sounds angry, but that's just his way."

Losing her grip on the wiggling child, Sunny stood helplessly by as her nephew quickly darted to the side of the pool, where she could make out a dark form. Words tumbling over each other, Jeremy talked excitedly to the now silent giant. Fear galvanized her into action, and she ran to them.

"Jeremy, come here! Now!" she said firmly in what Sam called her "mom" voice. For some reason it didn't work on Jeremy. However, he did turn to meet her as she ran up.

As the clouds moved across the moon, the entire area was illuminated. Sunny was stunned as she looked from the grown man to the boy. Even in the moonlight shading of their faces, it was clear how much they resembled one another. They looked like father and son. That was impossible, but here they were, before her eyes—

She crumpled silently to the ground.

"Help her!" Jeremy yelled as he ran toward his aunt's still form.

"Simmer down, kid!" growled Crank, confused about what was happening. Bending down, he gently scooped her into his arms, barking over his shoulder at Jeremy. "Let's go. Stay right with me, and don't, I repeat, don't get off the path!" He glared down at Jeremy, who was anxiously running alongside him, keeping one hand on his aunt.

"Mr. Crank. Is she going to be all right? She's going to take me home to my brother, Sam. I have to get home to him. He might need me. He doesn't have any brothers. At least not the ones that are alive yet; I'll have a real home. She's my mother's sister!" He finished almost out of breath from Crank's long-legged stride. After a quick gulp of air, he continued. "I just found out my mother's name! I never knew it. That man said I didn't need to know it because she didn't want me anyway. But she did! He lied!"

Arriving at his headquarters, they both quickly walked up the ramp, Jeremy running ahead to hold open the door for Crank. Still talking, he demanded, "Don't you want to know her name, Mr. Crank? You said I didn't have anyone, but now I do, and I know my mother's name. Don't you—"

"Okay, kid. Tell me her name, for Christ's sake!" he growled since it appeared to be the only way he would get through the door.

"It was Raine!" the child cried the name breathlessly. "Like a rainy day! She was Aunt Sunny's sister! Isn't that a beautiful name, Mr. Crank? Mr. Crank?"

Crank stopped, images flashing through his mind. Nightmares finally coming to life. For a moment, he felt like he might fall to his knees. Leaning against the entrance door, still holding the limp form, thousands of lost images bombarded his consciousness.

"Sir! What happened? Are you alright?"

Crank realized he was still standing at the door holding the unconscious woman. Looking at her pale face, he finally realized why she seemed so familiar.

A few hours later, Crank stared at the silver strands of moonlight darting across the waves. Still shaken by the flood of memories, he leaned forward and massaged his aching temples. It was no wonder Sunny had looked so familiar. She and Raine looked enough alike to be twins.

After handing Sunny over to an agitated Rambo, he departed for his favorite spot on the beach, needing time alone to process the thoughts swirling in his head. Jeremy had said his mother had died in a car accident. He cursed himself for not being there, for disappearing and never returning, and for his memories staying hidden so long. Raine had been so sweet and caring, different from her spitfire, man-eating sister. Maybe if he had been there, she wouldn't have picked an abusive loser to father her child.

His headache intensified as more thoughts wracked his brain, bringing him to his feet. Nightmarish images he usually saw while sleeping. Each picture stood out like a scene from a movie, answering long-asked questions before flashing to the next one. Like his life as an FBI agent when he'd met Raine. The attack and why he had no memory before waking up in the hospital. The Chief had told him he'd been in a coma after a nearfatal car crash which he now knew was bullshit.

Lost in thought, Crank suddenly felt the hairs come to attention on the back of his neck. Muscles tightened, fists clenched, and he whirled around. He saw a brief movement at the tree line. Not knowing who to trust anymore, he watched the area for a few minutes before focusing on the silent form studying him from the darkness.

"Well, Chief. Just the man I wanted to see," said Crank snarled.

"You okay, son?" asked the older man quietly.

"I'm going to say this one time and one time only. You have lied to me. I don't know why, and it doesn't matter. But from this point on, I want the truth."

In the last hour, the roles had changed between the two men. At one time, the younger man had looked up to his superior as a man of truth, commitment, and honor. Knowing there had been a conspiracy to keep him in the dark about the true reason for his memory loss changed his perception of everyone—especially his Chief. In under an hour, he regained years of lost memory and experience. The new knowledge aged him and gave him a new maturity and authority that was absent before. The older man could see it in his voice and stance. Crank wanted answers, and he wanted them now.

Noting the silent nod from his Chief, he started pacing up and down the sand, head down, almost as if he was talking to himself, only needing the other man for validation in case his faulty memories were wrong.

"My real name is Randall Lewis. I've worked as an FBI operative since leaving the Army Rangers. I'm in the Special Forces unit for Crimes Against Children and was working on a case when I met Raine Day in Savannah. I never told her my real name or what I did for a living. The last time I saw her would have been almost eight years ago now, and—"

"Randall," interrupted the Chief. "We didn't know anything about Raine. You didn't come onto our radar until later, or we..." Abruptly stopping, Crank turned to face the Chief.

"I'm getting to your part in all this. We had a team of agents investigating reports that in areas of the world where you wouldn't expect to see them, a lot of Caucasian children were turning up on our human trafficking reports."

Resuming his pacing, Crank continued, his speech halting at times as long-dead memories were pulled to the surface.

"I took off on my own and was asking questions in Bangkok. After a few days of getting nowhere, I got a tip from a native saying that there was something I should see. He was just a scrawny, dirty street kid. He didn't want any money, which I thought was strange because he was starving. He said I had to go alone. I knew it might be a setup, but he was so anxious I agreed to follow him."

Crank sank on a still-warm rock, watching the waves creep toward him, only to scurry back to deeper water. Sweat formed on his forehead as he struggled to get through this recall of events.

"It was a three-mile walk through some of the densest jungle I had ever had to hack through. By the time we got there, it was almost dusk. About ten small round thatched huts and several long rectangular metal buildings surrounded a clearing. I could see several natives going in and out of the huts. The huts were lit only by their campfires. I could hear the hum of a generator supplying the light for the long buildings. "

Feeling slightly sick, Crank took a deep, slow breath before continuing. "Moans were coming from one of the huts, and the noise soon turned to harsh screams. It sounded like a woman. It sounded like she was being tortured, and I took off running to the hut while my guide hung onto my shirt, trying to drag me back! I finally got to the hut and looked into the hut's only window. A native woman was struggling to give birth. Sweat was running down her body as she pushed the baby from between her legs. Three other women were helping her. All of them were pregnant. I thought it must be a native custom that only pregnant women could attend a birthing. I didn't give it too much thought at the time. I was just grateful they weren't killing someone in that hut. The kid kept pulling me toward one of the barracks. They were well-lit from the inside, and there wasn't anyone guarding them. Just to be sure, we kept to the outside of the circle and looked in a back win—"

Crank abruptly stopped his pacing. "Of course! I remember now! I knew there was something strange about that building. I didn't think about it at the time. It had glass windows—good quality ones. The whole building was of good quality. There was a compressor unit on the back wall. The damn place was air-conditioned! That explains all those generators and—"

"Damn, man! I don't care about the building. What was in it?"

Jerked out of his reverie by the voice behind him, Crank stood up to face the Chief.

"Don't you know?" he said, his voice dripping with sarcasm. "You seem to know damn little for someone who went to all this trouble to keep me from going further with the investigation. Exactly, what's in this for you? Why didn't you just let me die, then no one would have found out?"

Frustrated, the Chief clenched his fists.

"Listen here, you son of a bitch! This organization had nothing to do with whatever was happening at that village or your investigation! We can go into that later. Just tell me what the hell you found that was so important. Someone almost beat you to death to keep it a secret!"

Crank walked to the surf's edge and stood for several minutes staring at the waves before returning to the Chief.

"I guess I can go ahead and tell you because, more than likely, I will end up killing you anyway. It was kids, all ages, from infants to three or four years old." Seeing the older man's body jerk in surprise, he continued. "White kids... with blonde or red hair. Boys and girls. The ones who were awake had blue eyes. Not sure about the rest. "

"What the hell? How is that possible?" sputtered the Chief. "Where in God's name could they get all those kids with those same characteristics?"

Sitting down on the rock, Crank leaned back and said with a slow drawl, "The guys who captured me told me all about it. They didn't think they had anything to lose. After all, they planned on killing me. They dragged me into another building. There were three or four of them. Big bastards. Not natives. I think they were Mexicans. They would work me over for a while, and then when they got tired, they would fill me in. You see, in the States, there are millions of little unborn fertilized embryos sitting in commercial banks waiting for mommy or daddy to remember they're there. Sometimes, they don't get implanted for whatever reason. The bank will destroy the embryos after a certain time or at the client's request."

Coming to sit beside Crank, the Chief said quietly, "Go on."

"You see, Chief, that's why we were seeing all these white kids show up in the sex trade. In China. Indonesia. Africa. Blond or red-haired white kids with blue eyes are highly sought after. So, the banks cull out the embryos with those characteristics and sell them to human traffickers. Very lucrative business." He sneered. "Of course, other color combinations are valued also. They're probably being created in similar setups."

"But that doesn't make sense. I'm missing something here. What good is a bunch of frozen embryos?"

Looking at a wave lapping at his boot, Crank drawled, "That part's easy. All those native girls. The pregnant ones. They were the surrogate mothers for the embryos. They have the kids. Take good care of them. Then, when they're about four to five years old, they are sold as sex slaves. "

Standing up, he looked down at the man still sitting.

"So, the two and three-year-old kids by now are seven or eight and have been living in hell because someone stopped me from getting those bastards. That is, if they're still alive. Make no mistake. If I find out you had anything to do with that, I *will* kill you. I want to know who created this organization. I want you to take me to him."

"That was always the plan, Randall," said Chief quietly. "We were just waiting for you to get your memory back. If you didn't, then things could continue. He created the organization for you."

"He? He who? Why for me? Dammit, I want some answers!"

"You'll have them. The head guy can be in Panama tomorrow. That's all I can tell you."

"This is to stay between us: and one other thing, Chief. Randall Lewis is dead. My name is Crank."

From a thicket of brush about twenty yards from where the two men spoke, Gretchen shifted restlessly, listening to the tense exchange. She stepped further back into the shadows. Walking swiftly back to the compound, she slid her cell phone from the pocket of her black vest. "Crank's real name is Randall Lewis, that FBI agent who was attacked and lost his memory. I thought you might want to know. His memory has returned." "There will be an agent named Jax coming to the island. Do nothing until I contact you."

Gazing for a long minute at the view of Manhattan from her penthouse window, Bolo touched the pad on her intercom with her long scarlet nails.

A loud, frustrated scream jerked Matt from a deep, dreamless sleep. Groggy and slightly disoriented, he realized it was his sister. The next second, he stood at the bolted door, banging hard and yelling.

With both hands on the doorknob, he twisted the handle furiously only to find it turned easily. He charged into the now silent room, fearing the worst, only to see his sister sitting calmly in a chair flanked by Rambo and Leonard. Rambo's hair was sticking out in all directions. A white T-shirt hiked up on one side like he hadn't had time to finish putting it on. Glancing from Rambo's dazed expression to Leonard's calm one, he stalked over to his sister, who had still not even acknowledged he was in the room. She stared straight ahead with no expression on her typically very expressive face. It was the silence that was so eerie. His sister was never quiet.

The group looked like they were frozen in time. No one moved a muscle or made a sound. Silently, Matt edged around Leonard's colossal body and took his sister's hand. He gently guided her to their room and quietly closed their door.

He watched as his sister drifted aimlessly around the room. It was fascinating to see. His usually extroverted, animated sister had gone to another place. She often accused him of going somewhere deep inside his head, where he blocked out everything and everybody. It must be genetic.

Sunny saw her brother standing before her, clapping his hands and telling her to return to earth. She blinked and looked at him for the first time.

Matt released a relieved breath.

"Sit down in this chair before you fall or something. You're white as a sheet. You scared the hell out of me, screaming like a banshee one second, and then nothing. How did you get outside our room?"

He leaned forward to grasp her arms. "Wait a minute. Did those creeps come and get you out of the room while I was sleeping? Did they do any—"?

"No!" said Sunny. "I crawled out the window. I screamed because when I came to, they startled me."

Seeing the thunderclouds begin to gather in her brother's eyes, she exclaimed.

"I found him, Matt. I found Jeremy. He's alive."

Matt glanced at his sister to see if there were any obvious signs of trauma.

"You found Jeremy?" he sputtered, still unsure what had happened while he slept.

"Yes!" said his sister ecstatically. "He's perfect! He looks like an older Sam. His face is more angular, and he's slightly taller, but he is beautiful! Just like our Sam."

Seeing the tears in his sister's eyes, he jumped in to distract her. "Okay, you found Jeremy. Tell me every detail and include everything. How did you find him?"

Fifteen minutes later, all details were revealed, and Sunny grilled relentlessly. At least, that was how she felt. She did not tell him the real reason she fainted. It could have been a trick of the light, making Crank and Jeremy look so much alike. She attributed it to nerves. They sat side by side on the bed, both lost in their thoughts. Matt was reviewing all they knew and thinking about how they would get the kid out when there was a loud knock, and the door swung open, revealing a changed Crank.

Gone was the smartass, top-gun attitude they had witnessed on other occasions. This man looked formidable and remote. His silver-blue eyes glinted with a cold light. Sunny had a feeling the smartass part was still in there somewhere.

"The first thing I need to say is there have been a lot of new developments. I can't tell you everything at this time, unfortunately. It is unlikely I can ever completely fill you in."

As Sunny jumped up from the bed, Crank raised a hand to ward off any questions.

"I know you have questions, but first, let me tell you what I can relay. You have found Jeremy on your own," he continued, looking pointedly at Sunny. "You may not believe me, but I am glad he has people who care about him. But since this has been such a significant security breach for the island, I plan to propose that I would—"

"Yes," interrupted Sunny. "I'm sure you do have a plan. Well, I have one, too. I plan to take Jeremy off this island and bring him home and then let the FBI know what is going on here at the first opportunity. I know from Jeremy that there are other kids here. God knows what is going on, but I'm sure..."

Hearing a groan from Matt, she paused to look down at him. He ran his hands through his hair and slowly stood up.

"Excuse my sister," he said wryly. "She has not learned the fine art of hostage negotiation." Turning to his sister, he continued, "Sunny, usually when you want someone to release you, it's not a good idea to tell them you are going to turn them in once they let you go."

Sunny looked furiously at both men. "Matt," she said, trying to keep her tone even. "I want to learn everything about the kids on this island and how they are treated. I'm prepared to keep an open mind, but I need to know more."

Turning to Crank, she continued. "Crank, let me learn about your system here. That way, I could spend time with Jeremy, too, getting to know him better."

Unmoved by her plea, Crank continued as if she hadn't spoken.

"As I said, I have a plan to propose. You are both welcome to explore the system we have here. I will instruct everyone to cooperate with you. You will have free access to everything but the command center. I am in Panama most of the day tomorrow. Still, at 0800, Ruth and Sophia Green, two department heads on the island, will come to get you and start your orientation."

Sunny eyes widened. "Thanks so much, Crank! You'll never know how much this means to my family! I never imagined you would be open to this, knowing once we get off the island..."

Crank was already swiftly walking to the door. Sunny's blood froze at his last words before closing the door.

"But Sunny," he drawled. "I never said you would get off the island."

CHAPTER 15

Feeling the morning sunshine gently warm her shoulders, Sunny stretched and shifted her position on one of the large smooth rocks edging the lagoon. Dangling her feet in the crystalclear water, she inhaled the heady aroma of tropical flowers. Nearby, next to the pool, Matt quietly talked to his nephew. The boy had been waiting when they had arrived here this morning. She had watched as, with a massive grin, he flung himself at Matt. While the two hugged, she gave them privacy by walking around the waterfall. After all the abuse Jeremy received from a man, she was relieved to see no hesitance from Jeremy towards her brother.

Sunny swished her foot in the cool water, her thoughts returning to Crank's impassive face and his last words. The moment shocked her into silence. But now she knew that Matt must leave since she had decided to stay. Someone had to take care of their mother and Sam. Someone had to alert the FBI about what was happening here now that her cell phone was dead. Either way, she refused to leave Jeremy behind.

Sonny's reverie was interrupted by sounds coming from the direction of the path.

"Sophie, dear! Can't you hurry?"

"I'm coming, Ruth! I'm right behind you. Goodness, you're in a hurry today!"

Two short, plump older women, obviously identical twins, were hurtling toward them. Dressed in khaki with short, curly grayish-brown hair, they skidded to a stop as Jeremy ran to them, leaving Matt and Sunny to follow.

"Oh! Dear! I am so sorry! I almost ran right over you!" said Ruth with a beaming smile at Jeremy. We were supposed to meet you at 0800 sharp, but Sophie was late as usual. She couldn't find her glasses, which she doesn't need. I don't, and since we're identical twins, she doesn't either...but..."

"Forgive her, please!" came a softer voice behind Ruth. "She thinks she knows more than me because she was born a few minutes earlier. I do need bifocals, and..." She hesitated, glancing at her sister. "So does she. She won't admit it."

Finally, silent, two pairs of twinkling eyes focused on Sunny and Matt, who had yet to make a sound. Jeremy, however, had no such problem.

"Hi! Ms. Ruth, Ms. Sophie! This is my aunt and uncle. I told you I wasn't alone! They found me, and now they will take me home with them. I have a younger brother, Sam, and..."

Looking down at the boy, Sophie smiled gently, saying, "Jeremy, I know you did, and here they are! How exciting for you! It's a miracle, that's for sure!"

Looking rather sternly at her sister, Ruth interrupted. "Jeremy. It's good to see you so happy this morning, but we've been asked to take your aunt and uncle around the complex to show them where you live and go to school. We are a little late already." Seeing Jeremy's mouth open with an apparent request, she patted him gently on the head. "And no...you may not go with us," she said firmly. "We passed Ms. Samantha on the path. She said you have a math test today, but we will release you early to spend time with your new relatives."

Watching her nephew run down the path, Sunny smiled and turned to the pair, saying, "You probably already know our names, but please call us Sunny and Matt. We're so grateful for this opportunity to learn about Jeremy's environment." Matt extended his hand. "I'm glad to meet you. Could we start with you telling us who you are and your role on the island?"

"I am Ruth Green, the island's psychiatrist." Gesturing toward her shyly smiling sister, she continued. "This is my sister, Sophie Green, director of medicine for the island. As you can imagine, the children have tremendous mental and physical hurdles to—"

"Yes, they do, poor dears," interrupted Sophie. "But they are so precious, and most adjust wonderfully."

As the group slowly walked along the path into the island's interior, the sisters gave background information regarding the mission and the formation of Safe Island. Ruth was the narrator, even though Sophie tended to finish her sentences.

"The planning for the island began over three years ago, and we know little about that. It seems an anonymous benefactor decided that the system in place to deal with children who have had severe abuse wasn't efficient or comprehensive. The states didn't have the money and professional intervention needed for these poor children. So, he decided to create another option—a safe place in a controlled environment that would nurture, heal, and educate them. Prepare them to function in the real world. They approached me about heading up the psychiatric department about two and a half years ago. I then enlisted Sophie to—"

"You see," interrupted Sophie, "both our husbands had passed away. Our parents were dead, and we had no children. We were heavily involved in the states' administrative side of the child welfare system. We were disillusioned at the inability of that system to address the complicated cases of children with severe abuse issues. The foster system, though it tries, is just not set up to handle these kids. We watched as they went through the system and eventually committed violent crimes or committed suicide. They were just too damaged, and their pain was too great. I guess...we were just burned out and ready for anyone to show us a different option."

"You have to know," burst out Sunny, "that what you do is illegal. Kidnapping is a federal crime no matter what the justification!"

"Oh, yes," said Sophie, bobbing her head vigorously. "This was explained to us in great detail."

Matt smiled encouragingly at the ladies and said, "So you never knew who was behind this setup. How do you get your paychecks? Do you leave the island to visit relatives or take a vacation?"

"We can leave the island if we want, of course. We're not prisoners," replied Ruth. "Our money is electronically deposited. They trust us to know that a security leak would compromise our children, and we would never do that!"

Several minutes later, they arrived at a beautifully landscaped area with gravel paths leading to nowhere.

"This is where all the children live," said Ruth, making a sweeping gesture with her arms that included all the paths. "Of course, they're in school now. You've already been introduced to our invisible structures. It took forever for us to get used to them. Sophie kept running into them. We're always building new ones as more children come. There's also a new playground. It is visible but in a heavily forested area for safety reasons."

"Sister!" said Sophie. "Let's take them inside the quarters! They are lovely! Just lovely. Each one holds ten children. There is a live-in married couple who assists in forming a family environment. They are trained sexual abuse counselors. There are also native staff who cook and clean during the day. Wait until you meet the Embera natives. They are so good with the children."

Matt and Sunny watched as Ruth marched confidently up the ramp, put out her hand, made a fist, and pulled sharply. A door-sized picture appeared, and she walked through it. Still fascinated every time they witnessed the effectiveness of the nanoparticle paint in completely obscuring a structure, Sunny and Matt followed the sisters inside.

The interior of the building was built using a wagon wheel design. A vast common area in the middle included the kitchen and great room. The modern kitchen was spotlessly clean, and after inspecting the cabinets and refrigerator, Sunny could tell the children were well-fed with healthy foods. She also noted the large chart on the wall that indicated the assigned daily tasks like setting the table or sweeping the floor. Tears filled her eyes when she noticed Jeremy's name in several spaces.

Next to the kitchen was a long dining table made of dark native wood that Sunny didn't recognize. Twelve matching chairs surrounded it. The den area was filled with bookshelves and comfy couches. There was also a substantial flat-screen TV hung on the wall. After scanning the contents of the bookshelves, she was pleased with the well-rounded selection of nonviolent books and DVDs. Eleven bedrooms came off the common area. The cheerfully colored rooms were comfortably furnished. It was clear from the different toys and sports equipment that individual tastes were considered.

There were two small Embera women busily cleaning. They greeted the visitors with huge smiles before quickly returning to their tasks. Sunny had learned some things about their tribe while on the island. The little women had long black hair and brown skin marked with black ink designs. Their brightly colored beaded clothing mimicked the beautiful birds indigenous to the rainforest. The house couple was picking up supplies in Panama. Making a mental note to meet them later, Sunny followed Matt and the sisters into the bright sunshine. Ruth continued the tour as they walked along the path to the school.

"The structures were designed so there was no 'better' bedroom. We want them to focus their emotional energy on learning to live in a community. However, their room is entirely their own space. All children are taught to request permission before entering someone else's area. Also, each room has an adjoining bathroom. After what these children have been through, they need to have privacy. Every room has an intercom switched on at night in case someone has a nightmare."

Sophie, who had been uncharacteristically silent, chimed in.

"As you can imagine, dearies, there are many nightmares at first. We wanted the counselors to be able to hear them so they could be with the child. They also tape the nightmare and turn it in to Ruth for their sessions. Some of it is very hard to hear. Poor Ruth." Shaking her head, Sophie caught up to her sister, and linking arms, they continued up the path in silence.

Matt and Sunny glanced silently at each other as the party approached another clearing with gravel walkways. Since early childhood, they could look at each other and know what the other was thinking. Right now, they were thinking the same thing. The ideals that resulted in this detailed setup with emphasis on the needs of abused children had come from personal experience.

An hour later, they sat on the smooth rocks by the waterfall, dangling their feet in the cool water and watching the curious, brightly colored fish swim around them.

"This is the most fantastic setup for kids I have ever seen," Matt said. Every possible detail has been addressed. Down to the type of clothing the kids wear. No buttons or zippers that would require assistance, so their sensitive areas are never touched by anyone but them unless necessary." Turning to his sister, he continued. "Did you get a look at the classrooms? Big open windows with birds sitting on the windowsill! The curriculum is so well-rounded. These kids will be able to get into any university in the world. All the languages taught! The character classes! Do they have those in the US? Teaching kids what it is like to be a community member but encouraging individual achievements. Did you see Jeremy's face when the teacher called on him? He was confident and assured. You could tell he felt valued and respected there. I wish I could've gone to a school like..."

He noticed the distracted frown Sunny had on her face. "Don't tell me you weren't impressed. I saw your face during the tour. Something else is bugging you, so spit it out!"

Shifting to face her brother, Sunny took her feet out of the water and placed them on the sun-warmed rock. "Something is bothering me, but it's just a feeling. I can't pin it down—not with the setup! That was amazing. I can't tell you how glad I am that Jeremy has had the opportunity to attend a school like that. Heck! I wish Sam could go to a school like that!"

Matt stood up and stretched, giving Sunny a hand. With a huge yawn, he said, "Aw, come on, Red. Women always have to worry about something! That school was perfect! You saw it with your own eyes."

"That's it!" she shouted, grabbing her brother's arms, her eyes suddenly wide.

"What, for God's sake?"

"Didn't you notice? Their eyes! Almost all the kids except Jeremy and a couple of others... Think of all the children in the classrooms we saw today... Didn't you notice anything strange?"

Her stared at her, his expression growing restless. "No, I didn't notice. What about their eyes?"

"Not just their eyes, it's their hair too. Didn't you notice anything strange?"

Seeing her exasperated brother throw up his hands and walk towards the path, she continued hurriedly.

"Except for Jeremy and maybe one or two others, they all have blue eyes and blonde or red hair. We saw almost 150 kids today. Statistically, that has got to be impossible!"

Before Matt could answer, she felt a cold chill going down her spine. The tiny hairs at the back of her head began to prickle.

"Very astute of you, Ms. Day," came the cold female voice, which could only belong to Gretchen.

Whirling around to face the six-foot-tall woman, Sunny automatically stepped back a foot. The unfriendly blue eyes continued to look down at her even as Matt came to stand beside his sister.

"Now that she mentions it, Gretch," said Matt. "It does seem a little odd to me, too. Do you have any information about something that seems to be a huge coincidence?"

Narrowing her eyes at his shortening of her name, she responded curtly.

"You will need to ask Crank. He can tell you if he chooses. I will tell you nothing. You are interlopers on this island and will not likely be allowed to leave. I will not waste my time."

Turning abruptly on her heel, she rapidly walked away.

"I wouldn't believe anything she said anyway!" fumed Sunny. "But I am going to find out from someone."

"I agree," Matt reassured her hastily. We will find out, but I am due in the command center right now. Crank has arranged for Leonard and Rambo to give me a tour even though he initially said no way." Seeing her start to follow, he put up his hand. "Not you, Sunny. He doesn't feel it's the place for a woman." Seeing the frown on his sister's face, he continued.

"It's not a sexist thing. Okay? He feels it would be too distressing to see some of the things they monitor because of what Jeremy has gone through. Also, in my job in war-ravaged areas, I have seen a lot of things that still give me nightmares. Seriously, in this case, he is trying to be considerate."

"I doubt that!" said his sister frostily. "However, it doesn't matter right now. I'm going to Crank's house. The sisters let it slip that he was on a mission last night so that he would still be asleep. There are a couple of questions that I need answered."

"You're going to wake up a man who was out all night saving a child in danger to ask him a couple of questions?" he said incredulously.

"I know it's not the nicest thing I've ever done," she replied defensively. "But I need Crank at a disadvantage. Maybe he will be too sleepy to lie." She smiled and walked down the path away from her brother.

"What answers are so damn important that it can't wait?" shouted her brother.

Sunny ignored Matt and continued walking. After asking for directions from several native women, she walked up the gravel path to a thatched-roof bungalow. Looking up into tall, slender trees covered with lacey-looking leaves interspersed with thick ropes of vines, she felt the triple canopy of the rainforest standing guard over the villa. Breezes made a gentle motion in the tallest trees. Stepping into the covered verandah that ran the whole house width, Sunny noticed the gentle puffs of dust accompanying each movement of the Embera man's broom.

"Hello!" said Sunny.

At her greeting, he stopped what he was doing.

"I'm Sunny! I just wanted to see Crank. He's expecting me," she said in a friendly but firm voice.

"My jefe is sleeping," he said softly and resumed sweeping.

"Uh…I know! He said to wake him up when I arrived," she said, forcing a wide and hopefully innocent smile.

By this time, she was standing right in front of him. The small cocoa-colored man was dressed in the usual native dress. A bright red loin cloth hung from his waist and ended at the top of his thighs. All visible parts of his body were covered in intricate black markings. Long dark hair was held with an intricately beaded tie. As he calmly continued his sweeping, it was clear she had been dismissed.

"Now, look here," she said, growing impatient. "Crank expects me; he will be very upset with you if you don't wake him up. Don't you know who I am? I am an important visitor to your island and Crank said I was to be given every cooperation. Take me to your master now, please!"

The native laid his broom against a chair and looked up the short distance into Sunny's face. His dark eyes looked deeply into hers for at least a minute. He appeared to be considering something. Finally, he gently took her hand and guided her into the dwelling. Pulling her through a large room that served as a kitchen and living room, he stopped in front of a closed door. Dropping her hand, he turned to face her.

"My name is Angel. I know who you are. You are the woman who arrived with her brother to find the child. I know Jeremy. He is smart and wise for his age. I teach him all about the forest. How to protect it. How to survive in it. He learns quickly. Mr. Crank is not my master. He is my Jefe or 'chief' in your language. I owe him my life."

Sunny blushed, embarrassed she had tried to steamroll him into doing what she wanted.

"We never wake up, Jefe. He does not like this. He will yell. Very loud. Scaring the birds from the trees. Even if he has a nightmare, we do not wake him up. He is a good jefe and will answer all Angel's questions but does not wake up happy. You have fire hair, and that means you have courage. If you want to wake up Jefe, stay by the door and call his name. Do not touch him."

Thoroughly exasperated by now, Sunny said, "I have a brother who is the same way. A real grump in the morning, but I know how to do it, so thank you for the warning, but I will be fine."

In silence, Angel walked away, leaving Sunny facing a closed door. Suddenly, she heard another door slam shut from the other side of the house and saw two native women hurrying down the path, chattering in their language.

Crank sighed and turned over, hugging his pillow. He kept waiting for sleep, but his mind had other ideas. His trip to Panama that morning kept replaying in detail. Chief and he had arrived at a modern high-rise downtown at 0700. The plush interior and wall-to-wall glass verified the big money this organization had. The Chief had been oddly quiet, though he didn't seem upset or nervous.

"Will you gentlemen follow me?" asked the sleek, professionally dressed Panamanian receptionist, escorting them into the office suite.

Staying with this organization might be best, thought Crank. FBI doesn't pay much.

"I won't be coming in, Crank. This is your show now. Good luck!" smiled the Chief as he closed the door behind him.

"Randall. It's been a long time."

"It took a minute to notice the man seated behind the massive desk. Recognition took even longer. No more the tall, robust, and frightening authority figure of his youth, his father, Jackson Lewis, was a small, shriveled shell, with silver hair and wrinkles, nervously tapping his pen on the desk.

"Not long enough, dear old Dad. I thought you were dead by now. Figured you would drink yourself to death. You're not looking too good."

"Sit down, please. You're right. I don't look good, and I don't have long either. I have been hanging on, hoping your memory would return so you could take over." Smiling weakly, he continued. "I know I was a crappy father. Maybe it was genetic, but my father made me look like a saint. I was determined to be a different father, but the alcohol brought out all the rage. I quit drinking 12 years ago. I know saying I'm sorry is not enough after what I put you and your mother through, but that's why I created this organization to correct many wrongs. Even though the organization is vast and international, I have always been in control." Seeing his son's sneer, he stopped talking.

"What does that have to do with me? Why pull me into it? I want no part of you trying to save your soul," said Crank

"I didn't plan to, but when I found out I was dying and you had lost your memory, I thought maybe we could come to an arrangement if it returned. If it didn't, the organization could continue with another leader, but you would always have a job." He sighed weakly. "There are always struggles for control in an organization, but you are my heir. I want you to take over for me and expand the organization."

Silence reigned as father and son looked at each other. Exasperated, Crank got up.

"You know I would rather die than take anything from you, so you dangle this big carrot in front of me. Here's the deal. No negotiations. I will assume responsibility for this organization's work. I will put people in place to run it and step in when necessary, but my life is on Safe Island, not in an office. Get your lawyers to write the paperwork, and I will sign it to be effective when you can't work anymore."

At the door, Crank turned back to his father, "And by the way, you're right. Saying you're sorry is not enough."

Sunny gently turned the doorknob and entered the darkened room. Slivers of afternoon light pierced the now-sleeping man. A ceiling fan gently stirred the edges of the white sheet that almost covered him. Quietly, she walked to the side of the bed and gazed at the long length of the hard-muscled male tangled up in bright white sheets. He was naked under the sheet, she could tell and seemed younger and less threatening somehow. She thought he looked even more like Jeremy and Sam with his long eyelashes. She moved closer.

"Well," drawled a husky voice. "Like what you see, doll?"

In the time it took her brain to register she was moving, Sunny lay spread out on the bed, pinned down by a—and now she knew for sure—naked man.

"What do you think you're doing!" she gasped as she struggled to dislodge the solid mass that completely covered her.

"Nothing yet...at least until I get a better look at what is under those clothes. Before I do, care to tell me what the hell you're doing in my room?"

She looked into his eyes and the sensuality and danger she saw there made her mouth go dry.

"I... I wanted to... ask you some questions," she finished lamely. Fighting her body's desire to melt into his. "You said... you said you were available for questions!" she snapped. Her face flushed; she was beginning to get angry at being manhandled in this way. "So, get off me, you big oaf! I can't breathe! Wait until Matt hears about this! He is going to kick your ass from one end of this island to the other, and then you'll be sorry!"

Crank suddenly rolled off her and stood up. She lay unmoving, warily watching this perfectly proportioned man walk to the bathroom.

"You getting out of that bed, or do you want to wait for me?" Sunny jumped up and hastily rearranged her clothes. Running her hand quickly over her hair as she attempted to regain control of this situation.

"If you've had your fun for the day tormenting a helpless female, I'll meet you out on the verandah when you are properly dressed!" she said haughtily, stalking from the room.

Fifteen minutes later, a freshly showered Crank exited the house onto the verandah. Barefooted and wearing only loose white cotton pants, he looked around for Angel. He knew he had been there because two tall glasses of icy fruit juice sat on the table. Sunny sat at the table, drawing circles in the wet glass top. The filtered sunlight dancing off her red hair turned it to liquid flames.

"Angel!" yelled Crank, startling Sunny out of her reverie. "Where the hell are you?"

Within seconds, Sunny watched in amazement as the small native appeared before Crank. His smooth brown face showed absolutely no sign of fear or worry. She noticed he stood almost toe to toe with Crank, making it necessary for him to bend his head back to see his Jefe's face.

"What in the hell were you thinking, man?" said Crank harshly. "You know better than to let anyone enter my room when I sleep! What if she had startled me and got hurt? If you're not trying to kill me with that damn bubble gum... you're letting strange women into my room!"

Jumping up from the table, she ran over to Crank, putting her hand on his arm.

"Please! It was all my fault! He had nothing to do with it. I sneaked past him and went to your room!" she lied hastily.

"Jefe," said Angel calmly. "She, with the fire hair, has great courage. You should choose her as your woman. She will warm your bed and give you many fire-hired babies. It is meant to be. That is why I let her in."

For once, neither Crank nor Sunny had anything to say. No one moved or spoke for several minutes.

First to find her voice, Sunny sputtered.

"Well! I never! Angel. The women in my country have more to do with their lives than sit at home, cook, clean, and make...make ba...anyway. That is the most ridiculous thing I have ever..."

Crank continued to glare down at the little native. As Sunny's speech sputtered to a stop, he spoke.

"Go get us some food for Christ's sake!" he barked and stalked to the table. He took a long drink of the chilled juice.

Angel walked into the house, shutting the door. Relieved that it seemed the native was to be spared to live another day, she just stood there, still, confused as to how things could have gotten so off track when all she wanted to do was ask some damn questions.

"Are you going to stand there all day? Sit down and have a drink. Angel will bring us something to eat in a minute. The native women are fantastic cooks," said her suddenly amiable host. Cautiously, she approached the table and sat down opposite Crank. Shaking off the last few minutes, she carefully arranged her face into a polite smile.

"Does that usually work for you?" came the amused drawl from the other side of the table.

"Uh...does what usually work for me?" she replied, entirely off-balanced by this infuriating man.

"That fake cooperative smile you put on when you are about to try to manipulate a man into giving you what you want."

Feeling a flush beginning to creep up her face, she narrowed her eyes and said frostily, "I don't know what you're talking about."

Chuckling, Crank reached out a long, tanned arm to grab his glass. Draining the contents with one long pull, he put the glass down and called loudly for his servant. Within seconds, two fresh glasses of iced fruit juice appeared, and Angel silently reentered the house. Cranks' next words were so unexpected that Sunny jumped.

"You look so much like her but are worlds apart in personalities. She was sweet, spontaneous, generous, and a free spirit. The world was a better place for her being in it, " he said softly.

Sunny felt tears form in her eyes as she looked at the last person, she knew to see her sister alive—the man her sister had loved and wanted babies with.

Seeing the tears, Crank leaned forward and took Sunny's hand.

"After a bad injury, I had amnesia for years. When I saw you, it started coming back to me. I was in the FBI, so I couldn't tell Raine where or what I was. The times we got together were filled with fun and laughter. I would be gone for weeks on a mission. My last mission was when I got injured and lost my memory." Looking deeply into Sunny's eyes, he continued. "I didn't remember she existed, so I never went back. Knowing that

Jeremy is Raine's son makes sense. He is a great kid. I wished his father hadn't been such a bastard."

Sighing deeply, he let go of Sunny's hand and stood up. Continuing almost as if speaking to himself, he muttered, "I just wish I could have been there when the accident happened. Maybe I could've saved your sister."

Sunny wiped her wet face with shaking hands and stood up. Walking around to stand in front of Crank, she said hesitantly.

"I...I guess it is time to clear up...several of your misconceptions."

Seeing his silvery eyes sharply focused on her, she took a deep breath and continued. Convinced he did not know that Jeremy was his son made this conversation harder.

"First, it wasn't an accident. It was murder. An old boyfriend ran her off the road. She was dead at the scene, and he kidnapped Jeremy.

Sunny watched, fascinated, as Crank's face started changing. The angles sharpened, and eyes narrowed to slits. Feeling a chill, she continued.

"Secondly, Raine did not fall in love with anyone after you left. She...uh...saved...some of your sperm from the last time you were together."

Ignoring the sounds of disbelief and anger, she continued rapidly.

"She had her eggs fertilized with your sperm and froze them. She willed most of them to me."

She stepped back as cold waves of anger reached her.

"What's the third thing?" he said tightly.

"Uh...what?" she said.

"You said 'several things.' That usually means three. So what is the third 'misconception.'" Gone was the gentle, consoling man that appeared earlier.

"Now...I know this will come as a shock..." she started.

"As opposed to the first two things?"

"I know you're furious at my sister. I was shocked, to put it honestly. But as you said, she was a free spirit. But she loved you. She wanted something to remember you in case you didn't return."

He paced restlessly around the verandah, she waited quietly, watching for some clue that he was ready to hear more.

"I left a watch there if she wanted a damn keepsake," he said dryly.

He was standing on the other side of the verandah, the shadows highlighting the sharp planes of his face.

"The third thing. What was it?"

"Crank," she said softly. "You could probably figure this out on your own given time...and...if you think you've had enough today, we can discuss this later...after all. I have thrown a lot at you...OUCH!"

She looked down at two hands gripping her arms.

Shaking her slightly, he said, "Tell me, dammit!"

"Raine used one of the embryos!" she cried. "After she died, I used another one! Raine's Jeremy and my Sam are your sons! Identical twins from the same egg! There are six more embryos still in the bank!"

❖

The quiet on the verandah was deafening, and Sunny winced, regretting her bluntness. If she thought he had looked cold and hard before, it was nothing compared to the frozen mask of shock she now witnessed.

"I'm sorry, Crank," she said. "I didn't mean to blurt that out. I mean... I know how I would feel if I found out I had two children on this earth for six or seven years and didn't even know it. Plus six frozen embryos but that's..."

"Just stop talking," came the hissed request. He looked down at his hands, gripping her arms, and slowly let them drop to his side. He turned and stepped away.

Rubbing the red marks on her arms, she had to strain to hear his soft words even though she felt it was an intrusion into some private moment.

"Son of a bitch! That's why I felt different about Jeremy than the others. He's my kid. Of course! He's mine. How could I have not seen it? Same features and coloring. Same resilience and watchfulness, but why the hell wouldn't he be watchful? After what he had been put through. God, I wasn't there for him or his mother. And I have another son I haven't even met!"

He walked to their table and sat down, running shaky fingers through his hair.

Seeing his hurt confusion destroyed any hard feelings. Sunny put her hand on his arm, feeling his muscles quivering. There was nothing helpful she could say. Because of her sister's actions, they were family now, making everything different.

"How do you know any of this for sure?" came the quiet question.

She took a deep breath and began to explain the story of the Savannah fertility clinic, the embryos, her use of one of them to have Sam, and her discovery that Raine had used one, as well. "I just didn't know where her baby was or if he was still alive... until I found Jeremy," she said.

As shadows lengthened on the verandah, Sunny explained the events surrounding her sister's murder and the path that had led her and Matt to him. She told Crank about the trip to Savannah, the FBI agents, and finding Raine's picture album, which proved Jeremy's existence.

Dredging up all this saddened her and brought home once again the reality that she had lost her little sister. Head down and taking deep breaths, tears slid silently down her face. Gentle arms pulled her close. His warm body radiated strength, protection, and safety.

"I know how hard this is, but I must know every detail," he said.

Drawing a steadying breath, she smiled bravely and nodded.

Reaching for the still-icy fruit drink, she took a long, satisfying swallow. Sighing deeply, she continued.

"We knew at one time she had a live birth, but we didn't know for sure that Jeremy was her son despite the likeness. I needed more to be sure. So, Ken Ables ran a DNA match for Sam and Jeremy. They were a match. That was a bad day for us because, at the time, we still thought Jeremy had been murdered." "Ken Ables?" he said softly.

"The FBI man I told you about. He has been helping us. Well, I mean, at first, he thought I was nuts, I'm sure, but—"

"How much does he know about this island? Does he know you and Matt are on this island?" he asked sternly. "Was there an agent named Jaxson Creed with him?

"Are you kidding?" Sunny asked incredulously. "No way. He would have found some way to stop me. I will fill him in when we return home, and there was never any other agent with him. The only reason he was helping is that there is some similarity between Jeremy's case and a bunch of others they have been investigating. Abused kids assumed murdered. Lots of DNA without bodies. All evidence points to the abuser. DNA mysteriously appears in databases, though there is no record of these poor children receiving medical care or...." Suddenly, a light went off in her brain, and everything became clear. Her startled gaze flew to Crank, who was smiling grimly at her.

"Oh my God! It's you! Your organization! That's what you do! Take them away to safety and get the abuser convicted. How could I have been so stupid...!"

He leaned down gently to take hold of her chin and tipped her face up.

"Sunny. This is about my sons. I need to know everything. We will come back to the other things later. So, what else does the FBI need to learn? How did you make the connection that Jeremy had been kidnapped and taken to this island? Sunny freed her chin and quickly got up from the table, putting some distance between them. Sometimes, she found it hard to think when she was close to him.

"I know this is going to sound bizarre. And yes, I can tell from the smirk on your face that this whole thing has been bizarre, but hold onto that thought, and maybe this won't seem so unbelievable."

Seeing his nod, Sunny tells him about Sam's nightmares, the animal drawings, and the twin telepathy between the boys, which leads her and Matt to connect Jeremy to Safe Island.

Finally finished, Sunny sat back and listened to the music of the tropical birds filling the air, giving the man sitting across from her time to digest everything.

After a long silence, she said, "I know this is a giant leap for you to take... to even think about... believing this story. But there are well-documented cases regarding telepathy between identical twins if that helps. How else would Matt and I have been able to make this connection, which happened to be correct? Jeremy is alive. Jeremy is on this island. I have found him. He is your son."

CHAPTER 16

Sunny needed to work out some stress and entered the spacious but silent gym. Hoping for a partner match, she started her stretch routine, relieved to hear the soft swish of the automatic doors.

"Shall we start? I was surprised to see you scheduled." Gretchen smiled. Hard muscles rippling in her sleek black catsuit she padded barefoot to Sunny. "I will go easy on you since most of my training is military."

Already feeling disadvantaged and threatened, Sunny replied cautiously, "I've trained for years, and Matt has also worked with me, but it's just a friendly match anyway, right?"

"I rarely do anything just for fun, Sunny. Plus, I don't like you. You and your brother put the island at risk and question my security measures. You cause trouble for my lover with your lies about the fake sons. He does not believe you either. He is just playing you along." Gretchen suddenly struck Sunny square in the chest, knocking her backward. She hit the ground hard, the impact driving the air from her lungs.

Gretchen loomed over her, lips curled into a victorious sneer. "You're outmatched, Sunny," she said, her voice a low growl.

Sunny's vision blurred for a moment, but she forced herself to focus. With a burst of adrenaline, she rolled to the side just as Gretchen's foot came crashing down where her head had been. Using the momentum, Sunny pushed off the ground and sprang to her feet, her breathing heavy but controlled.

Gretchen came at her again, but this time, Sunny was ready. She parried a punch with her forearm, then sidestepped a kick with a quick shuffle. In a fluid motion, Sunny closed the distance and delivered a sharp elbow strike to Gretchen's side, followed by a spinning heel kick that connected with Gretchen's jaw. The impact sent Gretchen stumbling back, but she didn't go down.

Instead, Gretchen wiped the blood from the corner of her mouth and smiled, a dangerous glint in her eyes. "Not bad," she admitted, her voice tinged with grudging respect. "But it's not enough."

With a roar, Gretchen launched herself at Sunny, using her superior strength to drive Sunny back. They exchanged a flurry of blows, each move faster than the last. Gretchen's attacks were relentless, her strikes heavy and punishing, but Sunny danced around them, using her agility to stay one step ahead.

Just as Gretchen seemed to gain the upper hand, pinning Sunny against the wall, Sunny twisted her body at a sharp angle, slipping out of the trap. She delivered a quick jab to Gretchen's throat, followed by a knee to the stomach. Gretchen doubled over, gasping for air.

Gretchen wiped the sweat from her brow, her chest heaving. "This isn't over," she spat, her voice full of venom.

Sunny nodded, wiping a trickle of blood from her lip. "It is for me," she replied, walking off the floor.

CHAPTER 17

After a long hot shower, she headed to meet Matt, still thinking about Gretchen. She had been in tough matches before, but this felt personal. The woman was dangerous, and she hated Sunny. Her pride had suffered, so there was no telling what she could do. But her reactions were extreme. If she and Crank were lovers, could it be jealousy?

Putting thoughts of Gretchen away for now, she focused on what Crank had told her. The organization, though illegal, was performing an essential mission to protect exploited children. Exposing what was happening here would ultimately put countless lives at risk and endanger innumerable children for many years to come. How could she ever let the FBI know about Safe Island? She couldn't. At the same time, why would the people here ever trust her not to reveal their secret, especially after all she had said? She knew she had to convince Matt to bring her mother and son here to live, at least for a while. *I need more time here and miss them terribly.*

She found her brother sitting on a smooth rock, edging the waterfall pool, dipping his hand in the cold water and splashing his face, his expression somber.

"I don't know how they do it day after day," he gasped, seeing her approach.

"Do what?"

Taking a deep breath, he straightened with tears glistening in his eyes.

"Watch the things done to those kids. I know why they do it. It's the only way to catch those bastards, but God, what it must do to their souls to know some of them will already be dead by the time they rescue them."

Sitting down, Sunny put her arms around her brother and gently hugged him. "We're not telling the FBI about this place," she said quietly. "Not ever."

During lunch, she told him about the visit with Crank, all she had confessed to him, and all he had told her. To her surprise, Matt agreed with her decision to bring G and Sam to the island. He would journey home, avoid the FBI, and, with luck, they would never know he was even in town. The hitch was that neither could devise a good way to get Crank and Chief to allow Matt to leave.

"I can't just sneak away," said Matt. "That damn captain is on their payroll. We can't trust him. Even if I could stowaway, he docks so sporadically it could be a month or longer."

"I thought of that," replied his sister. "Maybe if we tell them we agree, support their operation, and promise not to tell the FBI. "

"After telling them ever since our capture that you're going to turn them in?" Matt asked. "Do you think they will buy that? Crank is ex-FBI. They use paranoia as a way to stay alive. He'll never fall for it."

Two hours later, they entered the invisible building to meet with what appeared to be the whole administrative staff of the island, all seated around the long, gleaming metal table. Crank leaned against the wall behind Sunny.

"Nice to see all of you today," Chief said, seated next to Gretchen, who glared as they sat down.

Before he could begin, Matt stood up to address the Chief.

"Chief? I want to speak. I'll be as brief as possible."

Seeing the Chief's nod, Matt continued addressing the group.

"Today, Sunny and I were treated to a tour of your wonderful facility and school. To say we were impressed is putting it mildly. It seems as if every mental and physical need has been evaluated and addressed for these kids. I've been to Crank's area and observed what his staff is exposed to daily."

Matt fell silent, observing the glances of sympathy sent Crank's way.

"Suffice it to say you have our admiration and respect for what you accomplish here. We also realize that you function outside the scope of and without the permission of international law."

Sunny glanced around the table. They sat tensely, waiting for Matt to continue. Chief stood up slowly and looked Matt in the eye.

"We're aware of our vulnerability, Matt, so we keep our operation secret. We also know it's a relatively small operation and are busily creating similar setups on deserted islands worldwide. *If* we are left undisturbed, we will one day be able to rescue these kids earlier and reduce deaths significantly.

"We agree, Chief," said Matt, looking at Sunny, who nodded. "We agree with your mission and will do everything possible to support it. We have decided not to tell the FBI, Interpol, or anyone about your mission. You have our word."

Sunny could feel the release of the tension that had permeated the room. Gretchen was seemingly unaffected by this meeting, and the security chief's small, cold smile hadn't changed.

"Mr. Day, that's good news to hear," said Chief. "Of course, you understand that, in this instance, your word may not carry the day. Especially since your sister has been very vocal about her intent from the start."

Sunny felt the heat rising in her face when all eyes turned to her. "Uh...yes...You're right, Chief," she said. "Initially, I was very skeptical about your intentions, but can you really blame me?" She glanced quickly at Crank, who was staring into space, then slowly stood, taking a quick drink to wet her lips. "As Matt said, we have had unlimited access to your organization. We admire all your staff. The kids I saw today were healthy and happy, though I am sure they still have a lot of residual issues. They love all the staff. You saved my sister's son, Jeremy. If Crank had not rescued him, he'd likely be dead by now. How can I be anything but supportive of an organization that had done all this for him and other children?"

She looked each member in the eye, "I swear I would lay down my life to protect this island and its children. I...I have not yet figured out how to assist your mission, but know I would never divulge anything about this island."

"I second everything my sister said. I hope you will be willing to trust our vows of silence because we have a favor to ask." Waiting for the whispering to subside, he continued.

"Sunny understandably misses her son Sam, Jeremy's identical twin. She wants to stay here to continue to learn about your mission and to see Jeremy. I want to go home and put my mother and nephew on a plane back to the island. I need to go back and report to my boss. I can only stay here for a while since it would raise questions. I want to visit intermittently. Sunny can request an extended leave of absence due to family issues without anyone getting interested. This will be an excellent place for the boys to get acquainted and be in what we feel is the most beautiful environment in the world. I assure you I will not contact the FBI in any way while I am there. We know by now that your group votes on most things and will wait outside for your decision, which I hope will be favorable. We are respectable, trustworthy people. I have worked with the FBI before and protected a lot of information. You can trust me."

Minutes later, sister and brother sat on a bench awaiting the verdict.

"Something troubling you, sis? That frown is going to leave lines, and you know…"

"What is up with Crank and Gretchen? They might have been on the moon for all their attention to the meeting. I understand about Crank. He's still probably shell-shocked from learning he's a father of 2 living boys. Touching her still tender lip, she continued. "I had a match with Gretchen today, and I think if she could have, I would be dead now. She never liked me, but something has made it a lot worse." Agitated, she stood up and paced.

Matt quickly stepped in front of her, bringing her pacing and muttering to a stop.

"I noticed your lip, but I figured someone snuck a move past you during your workout. At your level, the matches get intense. You're saying this felt personal?"

"Very, but we can talk about that later. Didn't you find it odd that the two people in that room who are paranoid and object to everything we want to do didn't respond?"

"You're right," he said. "Gretchen and Crank! They didn't say a damn thing the whole meeting. I say I'm leaving, and still nothing. Gretchen acted like this was her last meeting before retirement!"

"Exactly!" said his sister. Maybe she's already figured she's going to kill us anyway?"

The sister and brother stopped pacing and turned to each other. Seeing his sister's distress, Matt put his arms around her. "It's going to be okay. We're just guessing. We don't know anything for sure. Let's wait for the vote, and then we can go from there. "

They stepped back as the door opened, and out filed most of the committee members, smiling gently and patting their arms as they walked by. As Gretchen stalked past them, Sunny was pleased to notice the stiff gait and bruises on her face. She could hear loud voices coming from the conference room.

Matt led her back into the room. The Chief was sitting at the table; his face turned ruddy from some strenuous reactions to something Crank said. Crank was sitting on the edge of the conference table, idly swinging one leg and leaning toward the Chief to speak quietly. Crank noticed them and got to his feet, smiling.

"Come on in and sit down. We just about have this all worked out. Right?"

The Chief's grew redder, but he nodded curtly in reply.

Sunny sat down, already forming her arguments against Crank's obvious objections.

"I don't know what Crank is saying, Chief, but surely the majority rules in this organization, so if he's..."

Seeing the look on the Chief's face made her stop in midsentence. The way Crank had sat on the table, speaking quietly to the Chief, how the older man had yet to say a word since they re-entered, how even now he avoided looking her in the eye— the balance of power had shifted. Crank somehow had become the one in charge. Sunny looked over at her brother. She could tell that he picked up on it, too.

Matt was used to this. He had done investigative reporting involving many military coups, during which power seesawed within minutes. "Crank, I gather you are in charge now, so I will address our request to you," he said quietly, smiling. Does the majority still rule, or has this become a dictatorship?"

"Not a dictatorship," Crank responded. "I assume Sunny has filled you in, so you know I'm a former FBI special agent?" At Matt's nod, he continued. "Also, you know I am the father of Raine's children? You are aware of the need to keep that information under wrap. Again, he noted Matt's nod. "I have a lot at stake in this decision and..."

Sunny stood and moved toward him hands clenched.

"I knew it! I knew somehow you wouldn't go along with it!" Tears in her eyes, she continued. "I miss my son! I am not leaving without Jeremy! I want to know more about the island, and whether you believe it or not, I think what your group is doing is amazing! But since you're so para..."

"Red! Sit down and listen for a change!" came the barked command, causing her to flop back in her chair, head down with tears sliding down her face.

Crank walked over to her side of the table. Leaning down, he gently lifted her chin. Fingers brushed lightly over her cut lip.

She had no choice but to look him in the eyes.

"Who did this?" he said, frowning, gently touching her lip.

"Gretchen and I worked out in the gym. The match was supposed to be practice, but it got personal. I'm ok. Tell me your decision, please."

"Matt can bring Sam and your mother to the island—to us. He is my son, too. She is both kids' grandmother. I want to meet them both."

As her eyes cleared and shone with relief, he gently let go of her chin and straightened up, addressing Matt, who was smiling.

"You can bring your mother and Sam back to the island. But make no mistake. If you alert the FBI, I will kill my son's only uncle to save these kids. Which would be a shame since I like and admire you," he said grimly, leaving everyone in the room assured he meant precisely what he said.

Matt smiled coldly, stood up, and shook the other man's hand, saying, "That might not be as easy as you think, but you have nothing to worry about. I would never compromise the safety of my sister and my nephew. And I like and admire you. It will make for good family relations at Thanksgiving. Right?" Crank's reply was stalled by the Chief standing up.

"Okay. Let's get all the cards on the table. Everyone but Gretchen voted for your request. As you've noted, there has also been a change in leadership. But for now, we would like to keep that a secret. Later on, we will make the rest of the island privy to everything. I was only put in charge until Crank regained his memory. The benefactor of this island organization always hoped his memory would return. Now, I will be second in command if I desire, though I am considering retiring here and doing a lot of fishing. "

Crank looked at Matt. "When did you want to leave the island? We need to set you and Sunny up with secure cell phones so you can communicate without worrying about the transmission being hacked. We will give your family false identities while you travel so the FBI will not be alerted. That will take us a few days."

"That's true," replied Matt. "I did take some precautions. We traveled under fake names, and our cells were secure. Hopefully, that was enough."

"That's good to know," Crank said with a smile. Turning to Sunny, he continued. "I will spend some time with Jeremy tomorrow morning exploring the island. Would you like to go along? Matt will be busy being briefed on his trip by Rambo and Leonard."

Nodding her head enthusiastically, she said," That would be great! I have wanted to see more of the island, and any time I can spend with Jeremy is valued. What time should I be ready?"

Minutes later, all details relayed, both men wished them goodbye.

❖

After a long, hot day of exploring the island, they finally arrived at a secluded stretch of beach, the golden sand glowing under the late afternoon sun. The ocean breeze caressed their skin, carrying the scent of salt and tropical flowers.

As the others headed into the ocean to snorkel, Sunny spread out her beach towel and let herself sink into the sun's warm embrace. The rhythmic sounds of the waves lulled her into a peaceful slumber, where the line between dreams and reality began to blur.

In her dream, Crank's muscular form moved with sinuous grace, his every step a tantalizing promise. This was no longer just the heroic figure of her dreams; something more was happening. The sight of him sent a thrill through her—a sensation that started as a flutter in her chest and spread downward, igniting a quivering excitement in the pit of her stomach—the excitement left her breathless, her mouth dry with anticipation. She awoke to the sensation of warmth on her skin, and when she opened her eyes, Crank's shadow loomed over her, his broad frame blotting out the sun. His hand was extended towards her, fingers slightly curled in invitation. Without a word, she took it, feeling the roughness of his palm against her own. The simple touch jolts her as if their connection was electric. They began to stroll along the shoreline, still holding hands as if it were the most natural thing in the world. The air between them was charged, each step bringing them closer physically and emotionally. He asked her about Sam, her mother, and where she had grown up. As she spoke, she opened up to him in ways she hadn't expected. His presence was reassuring, and she could feel the walls she had built around her heart begin to crumble. In turn, he shared stories of his own— his sister and brother, who lived in Seattle, who believed him dead. The sadness in his voice when speaking of them touched something deep inside her.

Their conversation turned lighter as they laughed about Raine's quirks, and Sunny couldn't help but notice how Crank's eyes softened when he talked about her. But then, he admitted something that made Sunny's heart skip a beat—even though he liked and respected Raine it had not turned into love. The revelation left Sunny feeling a strange mix of relief and hope. As they continued their walk, she drew closer to him, their shoulders brushing, sending shivers down her spine. There was an intensity in how he looked at her, something unspoken but deeply felt. She realized that their connection was more than friendship; it had been simmering beneath the surface, waiting for the right moment to bloom.

When they finally turned back, the sky was painted in hues of pink and orange, the sun dipping low on the horizon. As they walked, Sunny asked about his parents, sensing that there was more to his story. Crank's expression darkened slightly as he mentioned his mother's death and refused to speak about his father, only muttering that he was a "useless son of a bitch." His pain was palpable, and Sunny squeezed his hand without thinking, offering silent comfort, happy that now with his memory returned he could reconnect with the rest of his family.

Crank paused as they reached the camp's edge, turning to face her. His eyes locked onto hers, and for a moment, the world around them seemed to fade away. Without a word, he leaned in, his lips brushing softly against hers in a kiss that was both tender and full of passion. When they finally pulled apart, Sunny felt she had awakened to a new reality where Crank was no longer just a hero but something much more.

CHAPTER 18

Sunny waved at her brother standing on the deck of Captain Mike's boat. Watching the native crew hopping over deck ropes and pulling up the anchor, she smiled, waving again at her departing brother. With a spring to her step, she walked down the beach, waving at the ANAM guys who were doing their duties at the station. It was a gorgeous day. Not a rain cloud was in sight, even though the wind had picked up. With Matt gone, she would have the opportunity to spend time with Crank unchaperoned. Mattie had been checking out her potential boyfriends since she was a teenager, and he watched Crank closely. Spirits buoyed at the idea of freedom; she eagerly approached her new villa.

The moonlight barely penetrated the dense canopy of the jungle surrounding Playa Hermosa, casting eerie shadows over the deserted beach. The gentle lap of waves against the shore was the only sound as a small dinghy approached the shore. A figure emerged from the darkness. Dressed all in black, Gretchen scanned the area with a practiced eye.

The dinghy's engine shut off, and Jax stepped onto the beach, his expression hidden behind a dark visor. He carried a duffel bag slung over his shoulder. The two met at the edge of the water.

"I see you've managed to get here without attracting attention."

Still silent, Jax shined a light on her face.

"Turn that light out, dummkopf!" said Gretchen angrily, turning away and stomping through the foliage. "Let's get to your camp, and we can talk."

Satisfied he had identified his contact, he turned off the light and followed.

Traveling miles inland through an almost impenetrable jungle, Jax was sweaty when they arrived at a cave entrance hidden by foliage. Entering the cave, he was relieved it was cool, dry, and loaded with provisions. He had stayed in worse places. Dropping his bag, he sat on a rock, took a big swig from his canteen, and looked up at Gretchen. Even in the dim light provided by a lantern, he could see her impatience.

Gretchen studied the man reclining before her. His tight black clothing displayed his powerful body. His strength and FBI training were essential for this operation.

"Sit down. Looking up at you is giving me a neckache!" said Jax.

Stalking away like an angry cat, Jax couldn't help but appreciate her retreating form. The way she moved, all coiled tension, made him smirk. She settled on a rock a few feet away, her eyes narrowing into slits as she leaned forward, voice sharp as a blade.

"We need a plan. What does Bolo want?"

Jax's smile faded. "She wants us to eliminate any threat to her organization. Originally, I only needed to take out your Chief of operations. It turns out he's an undercover FBI agent on the CAC task force who witnessed Bolo's operation in Thailand. His real name is Randall Lewis. But now that his memory's back, we have no idea who he's told."

Gretchen's eyes flashed. "So far, the Chief also knows about the 'embryo farm,' but Matt and Sunny will find out soon."

"That makes four. Crank won't be easy, but I'll handle him," Jax said, his tone cold and final.

"If you had handled it right the first time, we wouldn't be in this mess," Gretchen shot back, her voice dripping with disdain. "In my country, such incompetence would never be tolerated." She raised a hand to cut off his protest, her eyes hardening. "Bolo told me she wants the kids off the island. She's got plans for them. A boat will be waiting offshore. When the time comes, her people will extract them."

Jax's temper flared at her words, his voice a low, dangerous growl. "I didn't know she wanted the kids! I planned to get him alone, get the job done, and get off the island. Now, there are three other people to remove. This is turning into a real shit show! How did you let it get this bad?"

The air between them crackled with tension as they rose to their feet, mere inches apart, muscles coiled, hands clenched, each daring the other to make the first move.

"Security was contained until the person you didn't eliminate regained his memory! They were a small organization Bolo just wanted me to monitor," said Gretchen, exasperated. "Anyway, we are wasting time! We need to separate our marks. Did you bring the supplies I ordered?"

Pulling open the duffel bag, Jax removed some items. Peering closely in the dimness, Gretchen said, "Yes, C-4 and detonators. We will use this for our diversions. We will plant devices on the ANAM building and on the East side of the island to detonate simultaneously, away from the beach and away from the kid's school. Their emergency plan is to lock kids in the school building if there is danger. The Mestizos can pick off the rest of the staff when they move the kids. If we do this at night, the blast will kill the sleeping ANAM park rangers. Crank's group will have to separate into pairs to investigate the separate explosions.

"We will do this tomorrow night at midnight. You take the ANAM station. I will work on the Southwest end of the island. I'll need daylight to set charges. No one will think anything if they see me there. You can stay hidden until dark. It won't take long to do one building." Snarled Gretchen. "You can handle that, my soldat?"

Jax dropped the duffel bag and smiled lazily at Gretchen. "I get Crank. Bolo wants proof he is dead, and I'm taking no chances this time."

They moved with practiced efficiency, each handling their tasks with precision. Gretchen began preparing the C4 while Jaxson organized the detonators. The atmosphere was tense but focused, the weight of their mission pressing down on them.

❖

Two days later, Ken sat in the breakroom, sipping his morning coffee and enjoying the peace and quiet. The noisy entrance of a long-time surveillance specialist, whom Ken had known for years, disrupted his thoughts.

"Hey Ken!" said Ralph as he shook Ken's hand.

"Hi Ralph, how's it going?" said Ken, pointing to the freshly made coffee. "Sit down. The coffee's fresh."

"Like to...can't right now. Did Jax contact you last night?"

Ken shook his head, saying, "Jax? No. I haven't seen him in a few days. He had some personal business to attend to. Why?

"He came by yesterday morning. He wanted to review some of the Day house surveillance in the last week and seemed surprised that Matthew Day was back." He said, shaking his head. "Day must have some intelligence training. When he got home, the talk was general initially, and then he took the older lady and the kid outside to his car, which we had also bugged.

Shrugging his shoulders, he continued. " Jax reviewed the transmissions.

Something must've been significant, because he took off quickly, saying he had to report to you."

Feeling uneasy, Ken abruptly stood up and reached for his phone. Running his fingers through his short hair, he barked orders into the phone.

"Get someone over to Jax's. Find him and have him report as soon as possible! If you can't find him there, locate him electronically. I want to know where he is!" he demanded, Sliding the cell back into his pocket.

"Ralph. I need you to e-mail all the information you gave Jax last night."

Cell in hand and tapping the screen, Ralph said. "You should be able to download and print what you need now. Anything else?"

Smiling slightly, Ken shook his head.

"That's all for right now. Thanks, Ralph." He said over his shoulder as he headed to his office to read the files.

An hour later, Ken slowly swiveled his chair away from the glowing computer screen, his gaze shifting to the office window. Leaning back, he laced his hands behind his head, the weight of his thoughts pulling his brows together. He couldn't shake the disbelief gnawing at him—Rand was alive and living in Coiba under an assumed name, according to what Matt told his mother. It seemed impossible. Sure, the man had always been a wild card with a penchant for risk and a mind that questioned everything, but his loyalty to the FBI was ironclad. Rand could recite the manual by heart, rules and all.

Ken shook his head, still trying to piece it together. *What could have pushed Rand to vanish like this, to tie himself to such a dubious operation?* Matt and Sunny might be convinced they're on the right side, but Ken knew better. Where money flowed freely, corruption was never far behind, and the law... well, the law had no place in whatever mess Rand had stepped into.

A wry smile tugged at Ken's lips as he imagined Rand's reaction to the news—two sons and six unhatched embryos. In the old days, that revelation would have sparked endless ribbing from the guys, and Rand would have taken it all in stride, grinning as he dished it back just as hard.

But those days were gone. Ken's smile faded as he stared out the window, the burden of his duty settling heavy on his shoulders. Rand had to be brought in, no matter how much it twisted Ken's gut to do it.

Jerked out of his reverie by the ringtone on his cell, he touched his cell's speaker key.

"Did you find him?" he asked. "Everything's gone? He's at the airport? No! Don't detain him. Just put a tail on him. Tell them to report straight to me. No one else and no written reports until I give the word."

After listening for a few more minutes, he terminated the call. Jax's apartment was abandoned. His checking account and credit cards were closed. The car was left at the apartment, and he'd bought a ticket to Panama leaving in an hour. Ken had always wondered where Jax had been when Rand was nearly killed. As his partner, Jax should have been with him. Was Rand set up? Also, around that time, Jax supposedly inherited money from a relative to explain his new car and apartment. It seemed suspect to him, but IA had cleared him. Had they been wrong?

Standing up, he snatched his keys, left the office, and headed to the airport.

Matthew woke up lying crossways in his sister's bed. It was late last night when he got in; it was Sam's bedtime, so Matt briefly answered some of his questions. After they were alone, he was able to at least tell his mother about Crank, Sam, and Jeremy's connection but little else. On the plane, he had decided to come clean with his mother and, to some extent, with Sam. If they went to the island, the knowledge they didn't have could be dangerous.

An hour later, they were sitting around the dining room table, finishing off what Matt liked to call one of Mom's waistline increasing breakfasts.

"I need to share more information with you both. As you already know, we found Jeremy. He's happy and getting healthier every day!"

271

Matt paused while Sam jumped up and down, pumping his fist.

"I knew that first! We dream talk every night! I have a brother! I have an older brother!" Stopping to take a breath, he asked. "Uncle Matt? We're going to see him? On the island? And mom, too? I'm going to go swimming and meet all the other kids there! He says there is one kid there that can touch his chin with his tongue! Do you know how hard that is to do? I've tried over and over. Jeremy too... Neither one of..."

The doorbell ringing brought his questions to a halt.

"Hmmm. I wonder who that is," said G. "We're not expecting anyone. Sam, could you answer the door? Please remember to ask who it is first."

From the dining room, everyone could hear Sam ask the caller's identity. With lightning speed, Sam jerked open the door and told someone he had an older brother who would come live with him.

"Hi, folks!" said Ken Ables, smiling, entering the kitchen. "Sorry to interrupt you so early, but we heard Matt was back from vacation, and I have some things we need to discuss."

"You heard I was back, Ken?" Matt asked. "Now I wonder how you would have that information so quickly. You don't by any chance have this house under surveillance?"

Smile gone, Ables replied, "Yes. Could we go outside and speak in private?

"No, we're through with secrets around here." Smiling at Sam, he said, "Sam, can you go play next door for about an hour, bud? You know Jeremy is okay, and that is the most important thing. The rest is grown-up stuff."

Sam glanced at his grandmother to see if she was okay with him leaving. He smiled when she nodded her head. Matt continued when the door slammed shut and the agent was seated with a cup of coffee and two giant fluffy biscuits in front of him. Remembering his promise to keep the island organization a secret, he let the agent lead the way, thankful he had put off telling the whole story to his mom and Sam.

"Ken, what can I do for you?" said Matt

"Matt, you might as well save whatever story you plan on telling me. I already know a lot, but perhaps you could fill in some blanks." When Matt nodded, he continued. "We've been monitoring your home and cell lines. Any transmissions that have occurred in and around your house since you left. We had a warrant, as your family was considered part of an ongoing investigation."

Addressing Matt only now, he said, "I know you are here to bring your family back to the island. From Sunny's calls, I know that she is there learning about this organization that abducts abused children and raises them on the island. "I also know you are convinced this organization is on the up and up, but so many questions haven't been answered. Who are the people who make up the organization? Where does this unlimited money come from? They are breaking international laws right and left. You can't be comfortable with that."

G stood up and smiled. "I am going to leave you boys to discuss things. The important thing for me is that my entire family is alive and well at the moment. "

Waiting till his mother was safely out of the room, Matt replied. "I understand that your view as an FBI agent will hardly be unbiased. However, there are many ethical issues to consider. Is it okay to break laws that are not serving a certain population? Maybe. In this case, the world has let down children who, through no fault of their own, are subjected to repeated physical torture and sexual exploitation, which eventually kills them or leaves them unable to function in our world. Sex trafficking is a billion-dollar industry that is flourishing, and no one is doing anything to control it effectively. This is a relatively small operation when you consider the number of kids they can get to, but every child counts."

Matt stood up and tiredly brushed his fingers through his hair. Looking out the window, he said, "I was there! I see the children when they come there...so bruised...so fragile...so scared. I see how they blossom, grow physically and emotionally, and are prepared to live productive lives. If they hadn't snatched Jeremy, he would likely be dead. So in answer to your question about where the money comes from..."

He turned slowly to look the agent in the eye. "Frankly, Ken. I don't give a damn."

An hour later, they all sat on the porch drinking iced lemonade. G and Matt sat together on the swing. Ken sat on the first step, drinking from his icy cold glass. The only concession that Matt had been able to get from the agent was that he would reserve judgment and proceed under the radar until he was sure. "There's something else we need to talk about," Ken said. "It's the real reason I came over here today. On her last call Sunny told Mrs. Day that the person they called Crank was really an ex-FBI agent that had lost his memory after being beaten almost to death in Thailand. He was my partner and friend, Randall Lewis. We were told he died. Then he resurfaces in this organization. His partner in Thailand was Jaxson Creed. I had suspicions about his part in Rand's death but could never prove anything. Two years ago, he was assigned to my task force. He's disappeared. Intel tells us he is now on his way to Coiba Island."

Matt jumped up from the swing to stand, glaring over the seated agent.

"What the hell, Ken! What are his orders?" he barked.

"He's gone rogue! I just found out he cleaned out his accounts and his apartment." Standing up to face Matt, he continued, "This problem is bigger than Safe Island. Rand and Jax were investigating some intel we had received. Our information indicated that unscrupulous commercial embryo banks were selling the embryos on the black market. Impregnated native women gave birth and took care of the kids until around the age of three or four. At that point, they were sold into the sexual slavery markets. We don't know what Rand found, and Jax denied any findings. Said it was a 'wild goose chase.' According to Jax, he lost touch with Rand in Thailand and couldn't locate him. This was about seven years ago. Jax was there when we got Raine's accident investigation folder. Ashton had been stalking Raine while she and Rand were together. Later we got the DNA match on the twins that proved he was their biological father. That was before he went missing in Thailand. We got the intel of his being alive and on Coiba during Sunny's calls."

Taking a minute to take a deep breath, Ken was not surprised to see the white face of Mrs. Day.

"Mrs. Day," he said gently. "You don't really need to be here for this. It is pretty bad stuff and I..."

"I can take it, Mr. Ables," she said somberly. "Please continue. I can break apart later."

He watched Matt searching his mother's face. Matt nodded for Ken to continue.

"Jax is on his way to Coiba. Did he sabotage the mission and sell Crank out? Is he going back to finish the job? Are they in it together? Even though I can't explain how Crank got involved in Safe Island I can't accept that he would go so far down the rabbit hole as to be involved in black market baby production. If he is on the up and up, then he as well as everyone else on that island are in danger because Jax won't leave any witnesses this time."

Mrs. Day stood up, calmly folding the shawl she had been using. "Sam and I will be ready to leave in an hour," she said, and walked into the house. She tossed the next statement over her shoulder as she shut the screen door. "We are family and we stick together. If my daughter and grandson are in danger, I will be close. You can leave Sam and me in Panama."

Matt stared at the shut door, knowing it would be pointless to argue with Eugenia Day about her family.

"Well, that's that. I guess we're all going to Panama." Looking at the still-silent agent seated on the porch steps, he continued. "What's your plan?"

Getting slowly to his feet, the agent took a deep breath and said, "I am due a lot of vacation time. I wanted to take some of that time before retirement, and a week or two of island living sounds just about right."

When he saw Matt's grin, he hastily said, "Don't get any ideas, Day. I am always an FBI agent, twenty-four-seven. If Rand is dirty, I'll bring him in; make no mistake about that. Can all of you be ready by late this evening? It will be better to do all this at night. I'm going to assume, knowing Rand, you already have false identities for your family. When you get there, stay put until I contact you in Santa Catalina."

A few minutes later, walking down the steps with Matt, he asked, "Have you got any hardware, and is it registered under your name?"

"Yes and no," said Matt. "Not traceable."

"Sure, you don't want to rethink bringing everyone to this party? It could get bad really quick. If Jax is as deep in as I think, he'll be desperate. Jax and Rand are lethal; who knows how many others are on the payroll. We could be walking into a nest of snakes."

"Don't worry; my mom is easier to manage than my sister. She and Sam will be safe at the hotel."

Near two thousand miles away, Sunny was lying on the chaise on her verandah, sipping an icy glass of papaya juice. Feeling the breeze gently ruffle her hair and brush across her bare legs and knowing her family would be arriving soon had this displaced Texan pretty happy. Remembering the fun she had last night on this same verandah when many island staff had converged to socialize. The impromptu guest list included all the committee members except Gretchen. Sunny was at a loss to explain how the food and guests all arrived at her place. She liked to think it was because they were beginning to accept her into their community. It was interesting to see them outside their workplaces or the boardroom. Everyone was talking and laughing. The tables had huge platters of steaming seafood and local fruits and vegetables. She got to catch up with Leonard and Rambo. She had become close to the pair during her "captivity." The big, silent, smiling giant and his smaller, wiry friend were adored by all the kids. In the waterfall pool, they would ride on Leonard's shoulders. He would dive under the water with the squealing, laughing kids. The fact that they would let a man get that close to them indicates their feeling of safety. She also got to know Bubba better. He had such an open, honest face that you get the feeling he has never met a stranger. He and Nelson appeared to be close friends of Crank. The native women silently went from table to table, replenishing food and drink for everyone. All the staff treated them with courtesy and respect.

Sunny opened her eyes to find Crank standing over her, smiling. Her first instinct was to jump up and put her arms around his neck, but remembering what Gretchen told her she resisted the impulse.

"Hi," he said, his voice low and husky.

"When did you get back?" she asked casually, standing up and walking to the counter to pour him a glass of juice, avoiding his eyes. "Uh...sorry for the mess. We had a little party last night, and it ran late, so I asked the helpers to clean up later today so they could rest."

Taking a deep breath, she smiled and handed him the chilled glass. He was frowning.

"What's up?" he asked, and before she could answer, he continued, "Don't bother lying because it won't work with that expressive face of yours. So give. Did anything happen while I was gone?" Sitting on the porch swing, he patted the cushion beside him.

His tone disarmed her, and she decided to ignore Gretchen's tales for now and sat beside him on the swing, turning slightly to face him, her hand on his knee. "I didn't mean to be distant. I just have something on my mind. I just wanted to be sure that with everything going on, I didn't leave out any information you would need to be sure Raine's children are yours, so..." She stopped when she saw his frown of concentration turn into a smile.

"Well, babe. DNA doesn't lie."

Deciding to let the first part of that comment pass unchallenged, she jumped up from the swing in amazement at her stupidity. She had told him about the FBI matching the donor sperm to the kids, but that didn't prove it was his sperm. Raine could have changed her mind, or there could have been a mix-up. Before she could even address it, he stood up and took her hands.

"I had my DNA matched with Jeremy's, Sunny. There is a 96% chance he is my son. One day, when you see pictures of me about his age, you'll see why there was little doubt anyway. Is that all that was bothering you?"

It was then she knew Gretchen had lied. She had been right not to trust the woman.

He slowly pulled her into his arms. Up against his body, he used his strength to press her even closer, resting his chin on the top of her head and gently kneading her muscles along her back and buttocks. She moaned softly.

"God, I missed this even though I never had it. Sounds weird, doesn't it?" he chuckled softly.

She was drowning in sensations. Every time he pressed her impossibly closer to his hard body, she felt a delicious pull starting in her belly button and spreading all the way to her thighs. Her nipples tightened so hard they were painful. Face flaming, she braced her hands on his chest and pushed. They looked into each other's eyes, messages flashing soundlessly between them until he sighed and put her gently away from him. They stood apart, breathing unevenly, eyes locked. Crank jerked his eyes from hers and walked to the verandah's edge, where rain was now dripping silently off the roof. Several minutes passed, and Sunny felt her body relaxed, exposed and vulnerable, as if she had lost something she needed very badly. So she did what she always did when the tension was high. She babbled.

"I...I think I need to go in. It will be time for school to be out soon. Uh...Jeremy usually comes by, and we do his homework. But...of course...If you want to see him, you must stay. He is your son, so you certainly have a ..."

Without turning around, Crank said, "Tell him I will see him later today. I really think I should leave now."

He walked off the verandah and into the rain without so much as a glance back to Sunny.

In silence, Sunny walked into the house more confused than ever.

Shaking rain from his hair, Crank walked into Headquarters. Leonard, as usual, was at his computer, Rambo fidgeting around him, talking.

"Anything happen while I was gone? Any wild partying?" Laughing at the guilty expressions on their faces, he said, "Relax. I know everyone had an island party at Sunny's last night. Just because I'm gone doesn't mean I'm out of the loop. Any intel from the other operatives in the field?"

"All have reported in, and there were two successful saves. They're on their way here now," said Rambo.

"And Matthew Day? Did he get his family on the plane?"

"Yes, sir. Mr. Day put his mother and Sam on the plane for Panama an hour ago as planned. There's something else, though, sir. We think there was a glitch in the security system late last night. The alarms went off on the south end by Playa Hermosa, but we couldn't see anything on the cameras. We got the dogs out, but they couldn't find anything either. Course that side of the island is not as well visualized by the satellite."

"What did Gretch say about it?" asked Crank

"She's the one that said it was a glitch and that there had been no breach. So we called everything off," said Leonard. "We wanted to look a little closer, but she is Chief of Security, so..."

"I'll talk to her. It probably was a glitch. They do happen in the best of systems, but just to be sure, send more patrols in that area with the dogs for a few days."

Angel was sitting on the floor at the verandah's edge, waiting for Crank.

"The cold one, jefe," standing up, Angel began, using the name the island natives gave Gretchen. "You asked us to follow her. We did."

Crank let out a breath. Gretchen's odd behavior had prompted Crank to have his native intelligence squad keep an eye on her. She needed to make better security decisions. They all had recently issued high-tech secure cell phones. Crank had noticed Matt and Sunny were carrying the old-style black ones. It was a big slip for someone of her standards, which set off warning bells in his head. There were also long, unexplained absences. So far, the only intel he had was that she was often roaming the island's perimeter and talking on her cell.

"Let's hear it," Crank said.

"The cold one is still going around the island, but today she stops often and sticks bubbly gum between rocks and in dead trees."

"Bubbly gum?" said Crank, wrinkling his forehead in thought. "Angel, this is important. I need to know the size, shape, and color of what you found between the rocks."

The native turned around and went silently into the house. Restlessly drumming his fingers on the tabletop, Crank prayed for patience. A few minutes later, he watched in fascination as his helper returned with three items: a piece of sandwich bread, a sock, and a small black CD player remote. Angel carefully placed the three items on the table in front of him. Crank sighed and said, "Size?" Angel pointed the bread.

"Shape?"

Angel again pointed to the bread.

"Color?"

Angel pointed to the bright orange sock. Crank felt sweat break out on his forehead and a tightness in his chest. Carefully, he picked up the small remote, dreading the answer he said.

"And this?"

Angel silently took it from Crank's hand and placed it in the middle of the bread.

Crank jumped up and started pacing the floor.

"Jefe? We can bring you some from the rocks so you can see..."

"Hell no! Don't touch it! What you saw is used as an explosive. To blow things up! How close to the compound is she?"

Two hours later, after trekking to the island's southwest end through nearly impenetrable jungle the three men stood looking down at a square piece of orange playdough with a black blasting cap in the center.

"Shit!" said Bubba. "That's Semtek alright. No doubt about it. What is that crazy bitch up to?"

"Semtek?" said Nelson, bending close and peering through his glasses curiously.

Scanning the perimeter, Crank said, "It's the best damn explosive created so far. A Czech man was the genius behind this. It's odorless, very stable, and the rain won't affect it. Terrorists love it and have smuggled large amounts despite the Czech government's efforts to stop the flow."

Turning to smile grimly at Nelson, he said, "You're in the presence of the best demolition expert in the military."

An unsmiling Bubba took a bow when Crank pointed a finger at him.

"Thanks, but that was a while ago." He bent down and pulled the material from between the rock. "Not big enough to do much damage. She's setting up many fairly small charges in the most remote part of the island. So far, there is nothing in the compound that the guys have been able to find. A diversion?"

"She's in Panama getting supplies until tomorrow. We need to keep this just between us and the chief. We don't know if she's acting alone. Just wish I could figure out who she's working for," said Crank as the men returned to the compound.

"How are we going to play this?" asked Bubba. "Do we stop her at the boat dock when she returns, or are we going to Panama to find her? I don't like letting her back on the island, but we need to interrogate her."

"We'll be meeting this afternoon with Chief and come up with a plan," said Crank. "If we don't find out who she works for and we take her out, they'll just send in someone else."

Each lost in his thoughts, the men continued silently down the path.

Watching the three men walk away, Jax extricated his long form from the hollowed-out tree. Stretching, he felt his tight muscles relax in the humid air.

He was surprised to see with his own eyes that Rand was alive. He had no idea how the agent had survived but did not intend to let that last for long. He smiled as he walked to his camp to get some sleep before it got dark. In a few hours, it would all be over. He could disappear with his offshore money. It would last a long time in some third-world country.

CHAPTER 19

Sunny and Crank stood on the pier watching as Captain Mike's boat tried to approach in choppy water. Sunny's hair was rain drenched, strands whipping across her face. The rain slicker and hood she wore did little to keep her dry. Gazing at the darkening skies and frantic waves, she turned anxiously to Crank.

"How bad is this storm going to be?"

She watched as he tore his gaze from the struggling boat to her hand on his arm, reminding her she was trying to keep her distance. Dropping her hand, she looked up to see him smiling. Droplets of water spiked the long lashes surrounding his silver eyes. Rain fell from his hood to stream down his face.

"Luckily, it is unusual for this area to have severe storms. There may be some high winds and rain, but we're prepared. The structures are built to withstand high winds." He nodded toward the now-docked boat and said, "Old Captain Mike is probably cussing a blue streak. But it will affect him more than us. The wind comes up, and his profits go down. He doesn't like that."

Minutes later, they were surprised to see only Matt and Gretchen get off the boat.

Sunny was disappointed. She rushed to hug Matt, bursting with questions. She ignored Gretchen.

"What happened? You were supposed to stay and send Mom and Sam."

Embracing her, he said, "Calm down. Everyone is okay." Then he whispered in her ear, the wind making it difficult for her to get everything he said. She understood that she should play along and not ask any more questions. She thought he told her mother and son were in Santa Catalina but could not be sure.

They started walking down the pier. Captain Mike, Gretchen, and Crank were in a huddle by the boat. The portly, bow-legged Captain was chewing furiously on a soggy cigar. Whatever he was saying to Crank was not being received well. Sunny knew the signs. Narrowed eyes said Crank was not happy. Gretchen seemed her usual cold, aloof self.

"Keep walking," Matt said. "I need to take you somewhere private for a few minutes to catch up. "

Minutes later, they shed their rain gear on the verandah table. Wiping his face on the towel provided by their native helper, Matt waited until she went into the house to speak.

"I have to make this fast. I don't know how long we have before Crank shows up. You know he's going to have questions."

"What happened, Mattie? You did say Mom and Sam were in Santa Catalina?"

On the lookout for Crank, he sat at the table with his sister.

"Yes. Keep your voice down. These natives hear everything. I

THE CHILD SHE LEFT BEHIND

was getting ready to tell Mom and Sam everything when Ken Ables showed up. The FBI are on to us, Sunny." Seeing the alarm on her face, he continued. "It's not as bad as it sounds. Ken has agreed to take some vacation…"

"He's coming here?" she exclaimed. "You know we promised—"

"Are you going to let me talk?"

Seeing his sister's set jaw and fiery eyes told Matt she would cooperate, but she was unhappy. During the next few minutes, he hurriedly brought his sister to speed on all events.

Then, his sister spoke calmly.

"So, just to be sure I have this right, only Ken and this agent, Jax from the FBI, know about the island. Jax may be either in collusion with Crank or out to kill him. Jax is probably already on the island. Ken is probably somewhere on the island, or will be soon, and neither knows the other is there. Mom, Jackie, and Sam are in Santa Catalina, and I can't get to them because of the storm. Good job, bro," she finished dryly.

"Yeah. Good job, Matt."

Sunny didn't have to turn her head to know who was there.

Standing to face the man in the doorway, Matt said, "Knew you would turn up eventually. As you have heard, the trip didn't turn out as expected."

With panther-like grace, Crank moved to the table, sitting down and leaning back with long legs extended. "I noticed that when you got off the boat. You said Ken and Jax are likely on this island now. As far as you know, Jax is prepared to kill me. Since I regained my memory, I've wondered where the hell Jax was that night. He said he was right behind me when I sent him my location. I was set up."

Walking to the door, Crank said, "I hope you're right to trust Ken and bring him to this island, Day, but you better hope none of these children are harmed in any way by your actions, or I will kill you."

"None of this was his fault!" Sunny shouted, jumping to her feet. "The cell phones were not secure! Why don't you kill your security chief!"

Crank mumbled and walked out into the rain. She jerked around to her brother.

"What did he say? I couldn't hear it!"

Eyes narrowed as he gazed at Crank's departing form; Matt tossed a raincoat to her.

"I think he said, 'Already on the list, Red.'"

The rising wind made it difficult for them to reach headquarters and nearly impossible to open the door. Finally, inside, they shrugged off their rainwear and were handed a towel by Chief.

Looking around the room, Sunny gasped at the condition of Ken's face. His right eye was purple and swollen, with a small cut on his cheekbone.

"My God, Ken!" exclaimed Sunny, looking accusingly at Crank. "What happened?"

"Ken decided to resist my men when they discovered him on the island. He's lucky he doesn't look worse."

The agent shrugged and asked, "What do ya'll feed those noneck bastards, anyway?"

"Not much to do on the island but work out and eat," came Crank's laconic reply.

Walking around to the head of the table, he surveyed the four seated occupants. "I wanted to keep the number of this little gettogether small for now. Ken? You want to say something?"

Ken leaned forward and folded his hands together, addressing Sunny and Matt. "Jax is after Rand because of the mission I sent them on. I realize now that Jax is corrupt and probably has been on the black-market payroll for a long time. He probably contracted the hit on Rand, which failed. This has all been verified through my sources in the States." Looking around the room at the silent group, he continued. "While in that jungle, Rand stumbled onto an 'embryo farm.'" Seeing the questioning glances, he raised his hand.

"Let me finish, and I will answer questions afterward. The sex trafficking trade can get more money for Caucasian or lightskinned kids with blond or red hair and blue eyes. The traffickers, always looking for a way to maximize profits, figured out a way to produce a steady stream of kids with the most desirable traits. Bogus labs and adoption centers contacted commercial storage banks and made proposals to the owners. Of course, most refused because the organizations seemed sketchy. They never reported any of this to the FBI. A few centers jumped at the chance; that was all the traffickers needed to get started."

Crank stood up and began pacing the room as Ken continued, "The deal included the sale of unwanted embryos that matched the current most desired traits created through some genetic rewiring. Once the genetically modified embryos were obtained, they were flown to Thailand, where they were implanted in native women in remote areas." Ignoring the sounds of outrage, he continued. "Crank was led to one of the egg farms by a native kid paid to take him there. It was a trap, arranged by Jax.

"Jax never showed," said Crank. "It was several South American dudes. I remember thinking that was strange. What the hell were they doing in Thailand? After a few minutes of their tender care, I no longer gave a damn where they came from. I woke up in a hospital and didn't remember anything: my name, my job, nothing. After I healed, the organization approached me about Safe Island. My dear old dad, the bastard, had been following my career. More about him later, but he knew the true goal of our mission and had me followed. They found me in a ditch by the village and brought me to a hospital." Shaking his head, he looked at Ken. "He must have a hell of an investigation team. Better than the FBI, apparently."

Ken interrupted. "Hell, man. We would have found you if Jax hadn't been sabotaging every effort. The Mestizos told him you were dead when they threw you in the ditch. He found out when I did that you made it. He has come to finish the job."

Crank stood up and faced Ken with a grin. "I haven't had a chance to say how good it is to see you. You were always a great partner and well-respected in our group. It's good to have you on this operation. I realize you are operating outside the FBI, and I want you to know I appreciate it, But one thing I need to clarify. Randall Lewis, an FBI agent, no longer exists. You could say I've gone rogue. My name is Crank now; just Crank." Seeing Ken's nod, he addressed the others. "As for Jax, we have several guys on him now. If he tries to move this way, they will get him. Until then, they have only been instructed to observe. We want to see if he has a contact on the island. So far, no one has approached him. The more significant threat is Gretchen, our security chief. She was on your boat. Matt, you and Ken didn't see her because you were below deck the whole time. Our native staff had reported she was wandering around the island's south end planting explosives yesterday."

Sunny jumped up, her protective instincts full-blown. "We have to get the kids off this island! I'm going to see Jeremy—"

"Everyone relax!" Crank barked, gesturing for everyone to sit. "It's under control. All the explosives had been replaced with fake ones, and Gretchen was followed everywhere she went. There is no immediate danger."

"What about the kids? They are everywhere on this island during the day and in different lodges at night," Sunny rose, pacing furiously, her voice shaky with fear. The chief came forward and gently led her to the table.

Sunny dropped and covered her face with her trembling hands, taking big gulps of air.

Crank went to her side, gathering her in his arms, murmuring things no one else could hear. Visibly calmer, she shook her head in answer to his unheard question.

"Until this ends, the kids and all staff are confined to the school. All doors and windows are automatically locked as part of the security system," announced Crank.

Minutes later, everyone was seated, and icy fruit drinks were placed on the table. Matt had never seen his sister look so shaken. She was such a spitfire that he sometimes forgot everyone had a breaking point. Seeing her leaning on Crank with such complete acceptance and trust was surprising.

"We think the explosives were set up as a diversion," said Chief. "Why, we don't know. We intend to allow her 24 hours to show her hand. If not, she will be brought in and interrogated. We haven't caught her and Jax together yet, but obviously, they are communicating. Ken? I believe you had something to say?"

"We feel that Gretchen is connected with the sex trade organization. It's possible they placed her here to monitor this setup in the first place. We have verified that both Jax and Gretchen are connected to Bolo. Now they know Crank is alive and has intact memory. He is a threat, along with anyone he has told. First, I imagine they would want the kids. They are valuable commodities. The diversion at the island's south end would draw us away and leave the kids with less protection."

"What did they gain by letting you operate for several years? Why not shut you down before now?" asked Matt

"We are making expansion plans, Matt," said Crank. "I can only tell you the expansion will be huge. Also, we would be focusing more on early detection of abused children and finding out how these children came to be in the abuser's care. Which, of course, will eventually lead back to the embryo centers and Bolo. They got wind of this through Gretchen, and after Crank regained his memory, they decided it was time to move. They want information on the money and power that supports us. As we discussed, my father is the head of the organization, but he won't share his contributor's name. He did say there were world leaders involved. Bolo wouldn't like that at all."

Crank continued. "I know this is not going to be a popular decision, but I want you all off the island until it is safe."

Feeling Sunny's body tense up, he gathered her more tightly against him.

"We can take you all to Santa Catalina," Crank said, "where Sam and your mom are. We need to leave in two hours before the storm gets any worse. I will come to your villa at 1100."

Standing up, Crank walked them to the door and watched as they silently trooped down the path. Turning back to the other men, he smiled, shrugging his shoulders. "I expected more of a fight out of Red. Glad to see she has learned to follow orders."

Two hours later, the small troop led by Crank fought the rising wind and torrential rain to the dock. Captain Mike was pacing up and down with a sodden cigar clamped tightly between his teeth. He walked up to Crank, shouting, "Whose hair-brained idea was it to make passage in this weather? I bet it was yours. If the money weren't so good, I would tell you to stick the idea up your—"

"Enough," said Crank. "They have to get off this island. If your damn boat sinks, I'll buy you another one." "You sure as hell will!" he spat out.

Turning away from the still-fuming Captain, Crank took Sunny's arm and led her away from the group.

"I got something to tell you, and you won't like it," he said.

"What is it?" Sunny asked. "I don't know if I can take any more."

Gently grabbing her arms, he brought her up close to him. "You can trust me. I will do anything within my power to protect the boys. I thought you were beginning to accept that."

Sighing deeply, Sunny raised her eyes to his. She held so tightly against him that she could hear the rumble of the words before she understood what he was saying.

"I just found out Jeremy isn't at the school with the other kids. I talked to him earlier and told him about the threat and that I was his father and would keep him safe. He argued about leaving me, but I thought we had it settled."

At first, it was as if he was holding a piece of wood. Every muscle in her body tensed. She lifted her head from his chest and looked into his eyes. Gone was the hard-won trust and faith.

"Wha...what did you say? Jeremy is lost somewhere on this damn island with killers and explosives. Do you seriously think I'm going to leave him? You must be delusional!" she screamed, turning to run off the dock.

Grabbing her coat, he whipped her around to face him. His hand's steel bands around her arm, he glared at her. "I told you I just found out. I am going to find my son! You will have to trust me, damn you!"

Suddenly crushed against his chest, hard lips met hers, then softened as the kiss deepened. Suddenly, he groaned and pushed her away.

Dreamily, Sunny smiled briefly and then snapped to attention. "Don't think you'll talk or kiss me out of this! I'm not going..."

"Sis?" Mattie suddenly stood at her side, grabbing her arm. "You have to get on the boat. I overheard Crank, and I'm staying."

Shivering in her too-large rain slicker, Sunny watched the two most important men in her life walk down the dock inland.

Thirty minutes later, Sunny waved goodbye to Captain Mike, who agreed to leave her a little down the coastline. Focused on getting to Jeremy, she started inland. Every step was a struggle against the slick, treacherous ground beneath her feet. Wind howling and rain lashing, she blindly stumbled into a cave and was immediately engulfed by pitch blackness. The howling of the wind was muffled now, replaced by the distant drip of water echoing within the cave. Relieved to be out of the storm, she waited for her eyes to adjust.

Spotting a sleeping bag and scattered provisions, she took a few cautious steps forward, her heart pounding in her chest and every nerve tingling with the awareness that she was not alone.

Hearing a faint shuffle of feet behind her, Sunny started to turn, her instincts sharp, but it was too late. Within seconds she was locked in a brutal choke hold. She struggled, but her attacker was tall, strong, and moved with the precision of someone who had done this a hundred times before.

"You should have stayed away, little girl," a cold voice hissed in her ear, the words laced with a thick German accent.

Recognizing her attacker, Sunny bucked against the grip, twisting her body to gain leverage. But Gretchen was taller, her slim, muscled form radiating lethal efficiency. Sunny's vision began to blur as the chokehold tightened, cutting off her air. She had seconds, maybe less.

Her survival instincts and training took over as Sunny suddenly shifted her weight, dropping to one knee. The unexpected move threw Gretchen off balance, loosening her grip just enough. Sunny slammed an elbow into Gretchen's ribs, eliciting a sharp gasp of pain. She followed with a spinning kick aimed at Gretchen's knee, which was blocked with fluid and practiced moves.

The two women faced off, the flicker of distant lightning casting eerie shadows across the cave walls. Gretchen's cold blue eyes gleamed with malice, her lips curling into a mocking smile.

"It's over for you, my friend," hissed Gretchen. "You know too much. It is out of my control now. It was never personal. I tried to get you to leave. I knew you would be trouble, and I was right."

Gretchen suddenly lunged, her fists flying with deadly accuracy. Sunny parried the blows as best she could, but Gretchen's strength was overwhelming. A punch to the gut sent Sunny reeling backward, gasping for breath. Before she could recover, Gretchen was on her again, a flurry of kicks and punches driving Sunny deeper into the cave. Sunny's back hit the cold stone wall with a sickening thud. She barely had time to register the pain before Gretchen's fist connected with her jaw, snapping her head to the side. Tasting blood, Sunny slid slowly to the cave floor. The world spun, her vision narrowing to a tunnel of darkness.

Gretchen stood over her, breathing heavily. "You should have left when you had the chance," she repeated, her voice icy with finality.

Gretchen knelt, smiling, her face inches from Sunny's. "Head wounds really bleed, don't they Sunny? Of course, since you are a nurse, you would already know that hypothermia and blood loss are a dangerous combination."

With that, Gretchen strode out of the cave, leaving Sunny alone in the darkness.

Jeremy moved cautiously from his hiding place. Dodging his abuser for most of his life greatly improved his hiding skills. He had hidden behind a bush, waiting for the tall woman to leave. He knew she was the security chief and would take him back to the school. Now that he knew Crank was his father and Sunny was his aunt, he needed to be free to help. He had overheard Leonard and Rambo saying the island was in danger. That's why they were locking kids into the school. Sunny entered the cave after Gretchen; he wondered why his aunt had not left. Using the penlight Crank had given him, Jeremy crept to the cave entrance. Slowly moving the light around the interior, he saw a small pool of crystal-clear water. Startled by the light, several tiny transparent frogs hopped in the pool. He crept further into the cavern. Rounding a corner, he spotted a still form lying in the darkness.

"Uh...Aunt Sunny?" he whispered, shaking her gently, jerking his hand back when he felt the sticky substance pooling around her. Blood. And lots of it.

❖

"We located Jeremy!" Rambo tore into the room, skidding to a halt, taking in the group huddled around a digital screen listening to Crank.

"Where?" barked Crank.

"We picked up his location from the cell you gave him. He's on the south end of the island! He's not moving from that location. We sent some men that way with medical supplies in case he is injured and radioed Captain Mike for possible transport."

Turning back to the group, Crank said, "Matt! You and—"

A distant sound cut through his words, low and thunderous, causing the building to shake. Crank froze mid-sentence, jerking his head toward the sound. "That's the ANAM station! We disarmed those! Jax or Gretchen must have been watching! The building should be empty. Those men are guarding the school, but Chief? Take some men there and check for any injuries! Matt? You are at the school protecting the kids." Seeing Matt's nod, he continued. "Ken? You're at the most likely landing beach,

Playa Hermosa. The boats will try to unload the Mestizos there, and Gretchen and Jax will head there to get off the island. Take men with you."

Not waiting for responses, Crank moved to the door.

"We're on the same channel, so let's keep everyone in the loop. I am sure Gretchen and Jax have been given orders to leave no one alive who has information about Bolo's involvement. That's everyone in this room. I'm just glad we got Sunny off the island in time."

"Crank?" asked Ken. "Where the hell are you going? You're a walking target. You know how lethal those two are. Take some backup."

Turning to the group, Crank grimly said, "I'm going alone. After I get my kid to safety, I will let them find me."

CHAPTER 20

Cursing the dense foliage, the sweat running into his eyes blurring his vision, Crank swung the machete. Focused on reaching Jeremy, he barely heard the soft popping followed by a staccato burst of gunfire at the ANAM station and Playa Hermosa. Ahead, he heard men's urgent voices and radio static. Crouching low, he watched the foliage part and his men carrying a litter with a small still form. Jeremy! Knowing better, he stood abruptly to find four guns pointed his way, then slowly lowered.

"Sir? You startled us! That's a dan...!"

Ignoring them, he turned to the stretcher, demanding, "How is he? Jeremy!"

"I'm ok, Mister—I mean dad. It's Sunny! She's really bad!"

Two things registered at once. Jeremy, holding onto the litter, was safe, and the bloodless face lying deathly still was Sunny. Grasping her cold hand, he barely noticed the IVs running in both arms and the bloody bandage around her head. Leaning closer, he whispered in her ear.

"I thought you were safe! You were supposed to be in Santa Catalina. My love, I should have locked you up somewhere. You have to hang on! Hang on for Sam, Jeremy, and me!"

"Sir, we have to get her out of here. Her vitals are stable now, but it's a long way to the hospital."

"Okay," replied Crank. "Jeremy, you need to go with Sunny. She will need you. Where the hell is he? Son of a bitch!"

Looking wildly around, Crank shouted, "Jeremy, I know you want to stay with me, but this is an order! You are to stay with your aunt. Show yourself, now!"

Frustrated, he turned to the team leader.

"Go ahead! I will find him. Her mother and son are staying at the Santa Catalina Hotel. Get them to the hospital."

Still holding Sunny's hand, he was surprised to feel a weak squeeze. Her beautiful blue eyes stared at him, and her voice was hoarse and faint, her words slurred.

"Crank, I love you. I will be fine. Save the kids!"

Approaching the cave where Sunny was found, Crank noticed movement in a bush near the entrance.

"Jeremy," said Crank, looking down at the small crouching form. "What the hell?"

Jeremy put his finger to his lips and motioned for Crank to crouch.

"There's a man in there. I've never seen him before. I was going to hide in there until you quit looking. This is where

Gretchen hurt Sunny! I want to stay with you, Dad. I'm sorry, but—"

"First of all, son, I would have never stopped looking—" began Crank when Jeremy was suddenly jerked from the bush. Turning around, Crank saw Gretchen tightly gripping his struggling son.

"Well, we meet again, Jeremy. Crank? What are you two up to?" asked Gretchen coldly

"C'mon, Gretch," said Crank, smiling easily. "I know you're involved with Bolo, but we're professionals. We don't use kids to get things done. Let him go, and we'll talk. I can get you off the island quickly. Get you away from Bolo's people. Give you enough money you can go anywhere. Think about it."

"That does sound interesting, alter Freund," said Gretchen, matching Crank's smile. "But I have no interest in running from Bolo for the rest of my life. Let's go inside and talk. I have a surprise for you. An old friend of yours."

Holding tightly to Jeremy, she motioned for Crank to enter the cave. Trained to gather data quickly, Crank noted the scattered provisions, the pool of water, and the large, dark red stain on the floor. A fierce anger flashed through his body, leaving behind a deadly calm. That large stain was Sunny's blood.

As Gretchen entered the cave, Crank noticed Jeremy clamped tightly to her side, no longer struggling. Looking down almost fondly at Jeremy, Gretchen said, "He is not a bad boy. He does not want to see his father get hurt." Her eyebrow arched at the word "father."

"I thought we had a deal," Crank said. "You let the boy go, and we talk."

"Is Gretchen reneging on a deal?" A whispery voice echoed off the cave walls. Recognizing the voice, Crank whirled around as a figure emerged from the cave's deep shadows.

Jax's bulked-up, muscular body moved silently forward.

"Let the boy go, Jax. Is this how far you've sunk? Terrorizing children? You were a great agent once. What the hell happened to you?"

"You might have been happy to exist on an agent's pay, Crank, is it now?" Jax continued, receiving no answer. Anyway, I have bigger plans, but we had some good times, and I respect you. This isn't personal. It's just business."

"Just business?" Crank snarled. "Let the kid go, and we'll settle this between us."

"I don't think so," interrupted Gretchen, glancing at Jax. "He is our insurance policy."

"Gretchen shut the hell up," Jax said coldly.

Crank remembered the coldness Jax displayed during their missions. It didn't bode well for Gretchen. It seemed Jax was in charge, which might work to Crank's advantage.

Ignoring Gretchen, Crank focused on Jax. "Okay, now that we've established who's in charge. Jax? What about it? Release the kid, send Gretchen out to play, and let's settle this. I'm the one Bolo wants dead. We were equal sparring partners at the agency. Don't you want to see if you can beat me?"

Crank watched in silence as the big man considered his offer, the only sound being the drips of water echoing in the chamber. Hearing a strangled gasp behind him, he turned to see Gretchen holding a knife against Jeremy's throat.

"You hurt him, Gretch, and you will never be able to run far enough or fast enough. I will find you." Turning his back on her deliberately, he watched as Jax slowly raised his Glock 17 and fired.

Crank dropped and swiveled around to see Gretchen on the floor, her body jerking in a rapidly growing pool of blood. Jeremy ran to him. Relief flooded his body as he enfolded his trembling son in his arms.

"What the hell, Jax? You could have got him killed! Of all the stupid stunts..."

"Relax," drawled the ex-agent. "That was an easy shot. To stay alive, I had to agree to terminate her. She'd become an inconvenience to Bolo's organization. I guess they don't have a retirement plan."

Crank began edging Jeremy closer to the cave entrance while Jax talked. Silent messages flashed between him and Jeremy.

"The thing is, Crank, my contract with Bolo only included you and Gretchen. Bolo never cared about the kids. If I could get them, fine, but it was secondary to eliminating you."

"Because I know the location of the embryo farm?"

Jax shrugged as he slowly took off his tactical gear. "That's part of it, but not the main reason," Jax answered, bending down to place his gun on a rock.

Moving quickly, Crank shoved Jeremy through the cave entrance.

Jax straightened up, smiling. "I would've been a little disappointed in you if you had let that opportunity go. Now it's just us. Shooting you down like a dog won't work for me. As I said, I always respected you. Sorry it had to come to this, but the money this job will bring in is my retirement plan."

Shifting into a fighting stance, Crank said, "You didn't finish. Why me? If not the embryo farm, then why?"

Jax flexed his muscles, shifting his balance. "Your father. We know he's dying. We know you're his only heir and will run the organization after he kicks the bucket. They're working on huge expansions all over the world. Due to governmental contributors, legislation will be passed regarding the handling of fertilized embryos. The impact on Bolo's business will cost her billions."

Crank smiled coldly. "And you think that will stop because I die?"

Jax smirked, advancing slowly on Crank. "The organization has always had just one leader. With your dad and you gone, it'll take years for it to recover and advance. The infighting alone while a new leader emerges will be damaging. Bolo has already infiltrated the high ranks, and in the chaos, she'll step in as the new leader."

Moving closer, a cold smile stretched across Jax's face as he advanced toward Crank. "You're the only obstacle, but I fix that today."

CHAPTER 21

The intermittent flashes of lightning briefly illuminated the cave, casting stark shadows on the jagged walls as the two men faced off. Jax moved first, delivering a precise, brutal kick aimed at Crank's ribs. The impact drove Crank back against the cave wall, his breath escaping in a sharp cry. He stumbled, struggling to stay upright as the pain surged through him.

Crank fought through the haze of pain, forcing himself to focus. He couldn't afford to falter. Jax advanced with vicious blows, his fists and elbows striking ruthlessly. Crank managed to block and deflect some attacks while delivering brutal hits to Jax's face. The relentless assaults made their movements grow slower and more labored.

A powerful uppercut from Jax caught Crank off guard, sending him sprawling to the cave floor. Blood trickled from a gash on his forehead, mingling with the rainwater that seeped into the cavern.

Despite the overwhelming pain, Crank's resolve remained unbroken. He rolled onto his back with a pained groan, then pushed himself up with fierce determination. His body trembled with the effort as he launched himself at Jax, their bloodied bodies crashing into the cave wall with a bone-jarring impact.

Crank, driven by sheer willpower, unleashed a series of precise strikes. He maneuvered Jax into a vulnerable position, delivering a brutal elbow strike to his opponent's ribs. Jax staggered, a flash of pain crossing his face. The cave seemed to vibrate with the intensity of their fight, the fading storm outside now a distant, muted roar.

In a final, desperate move, Crank seized Jax's arm, twisting it into a painful lock. Jax roared in frustration, struggling against the hold. Crank's muscles screamed with effort, but he grimly maintained the lock. Silence prevailed, interrupted only by the men's grunts as the fight neared its conclusion.

Crank maneuvered Jax into position and delivered a decisive, devastating blow to his temple. The force of the strike was overwhelming. Jax's body crumpled to the cave floor. The sound of his fall, a final echo of their brutal struggle. Crank stood over Jax's lifeless form, his body trembling with exhaustion. The cave was illuminated by the soft, intermittent light of the moon filtering through the entrance. Crank's breaths were heavy and ragged, each inhalation a struggle against the pain that wracked his body as something soft and small barreled into him.

"Dad! I brought help! You're bleeding, Dad," said Jeremy, hugging him tightly.

Wincing, Crank gently broke his son's hold. Looking at two backlit figures standing in the cave entrance.

"We figured we would show up when the fighting was over," said Ken as he moved into the cave and over to Gretchen. Finding no pulse, he stood up. "She's gone. Who did her? You or Jax?"

Chief quickly checked Jax before coming to Crank, who still seemed dazed.

"You ok, son? You look pretty rough. Sit down and let me stop that bleeding." Leading him to a rock, he gently pushed him down, taking bandages from his kit.

"You had your bell rung, didn't you? We need to get you to the hospital. You likely have a concussion."

Pressing the bandage to his forehead, Crank moved away from the Chief. "I'm all right. Just a little fuzzy. Jax killed Gretchen. How's Sunny? Are the kids safe? What about…"

"Whoa!" said Ken. "Slow down. I'll fill you in. First, the kids are safe. We were able to keep the Mestizos from even landing. Matt is with Sunny. She's unconscious but stable. The doctors say there is every reason to feel optimistic. You have Jeremy to thank for us finding you even if we were a little late. You have a brave boy there."

Smiling at his boy, Crank said. "Thanks, son. Let's go and meet your brother and check on your aunt. "

CHAPTER 22

Squeezing her eyes shut against the bright sun, Sunny stretched languidly. Muted voices surrounded her, lulling her back to sleep. Turning on her side, she felt something pull on her arm. Irritably, she jerked only to have one of the voices whisper in her ear to be still. Coldness crawled up her arm, soon followed by darkness.

"Sunny? Are you in pain?" the voice asked later. Her forehead wrinkled with the effort it took to concentrate. She had heard that voice before.

"Mom?" she asked, eyes shut, still afraid of the light that sent piercing pain through her head.

"Yes, baby. It's me! We've been so worried about you!" said her mom. "Open your eyes, Sunny!"

She said softly, "I can't, Mom. It's the light. It hurts. Turn it off."

Waiting for an answer, she heard a door softly shut. Exhausted, the darkness that had become an old friend came for her. Drifting off, she wondered if she was dead, and then she remembered the cave, the fight with Gretchen, and hitting her head.

Where is everyone?" Ms. Day? Ms. Day?" said an unidentified male voice. "You need to open your eyes. It's okay. We have darkened the room."

Unwilling to risk the pain, she lightly shook her head, tears running down her cheeks. Suddenly, held in strong arms, a familiar husky voice whispered in her ears.

"C'mon Red, don't be so stubborn. I want to see those beautiful eyes! The room is dark now."

Carefully opening one eye slightly, she saw her hero's bruised and bandaged face. Carefully holding his face, she groaned.

"Oh my God, what happened to you? Your poor face," she said softly, eyes filled with tears. Crank smiled softly, saying.

"Honey, have you looked in a mirror yet? You look worse than I do."

Seeing her horror, he amended quickly.

"Though nothing could mar your beauty."

"I don't care about me, Crank. Where's my family? How are the island people? Is everyone safe?"

Gently drawing her back into his arms he arms, he said,

"Yes, everyone is ok. I will go into the details later; you must rest and know everything is fine."

She searched his eyes for any hint of untruth, then relaxed and smiled. Releasing her grip on Crank, she looked over his shoulder to see her mother with tears in her eyes. Crank moved off the bed, so her mother could approach.

Tears flowing, Sunny hugged her mom. Babbling, almost incoherent, she told her mom about the fight with Gretchen. How afraid she was of dying and never seeing her family again. The tears eventually ceased in the circle of her mom's comforting arms.

After meeting with Matt, Chief, and Ken to recap the events of the last twenty-four hours, Crank walked back into Sunny's room to a beautiful sight. She was sitting up, her hair brushed, and the big smile on her bruised face assured him she was better. She fairly radiated curiosity and excitement. Settling comfortably in the chair, he awaited the inevitable questions. He didn't have long to wait.

Later, all questions asked and answered, Crank's voice low and husky said, "When I saw you lying on that litter... not moving and white as a sheet, I wanted to kill her. I'm just glad it was Jax instead. I never saw myself as having to kill a woman."

Seeing the haunted look in her protector's eyes, she slowly drew his head to her chest and gently stroked his back and shoulders. Growing up, she had read many romances. She was familiar with their talk of "becoming one" and "exchanging love" between the hero and heroine. She always had secretly hoped to experience this. Still, as she grew older and more disillusioned, she felt it might never happen. Today, she knew she and Crank loved each other and had "become one." They were partners and would love long and always protect their family.

Looking into his eyes, she knew he had realized this also. "Ahem…. don't mean to intrude, but…hell…we're going to," her brother's voice boomed from the doorway. Jeremy and Sam squeezed past their uncle and ran to Sunny's bedside. Her mom followed at a more sedate pace.

Seeing Sam and Jeremy together was quite an experience. They were identical boys, one a little taller. They searched her face for any pain as they gently pressed against her mattress.

Seeing tears forming in her eyes, they looked frantically at Crank. Most twins tend to finish each other's sentences, but there is nothing usual about her guys. She watched as they looked at each other for a few seconds, and then one or the other would say something. She realized they were sharing thoughts and smiled as she leaned up to hug them both.

"It is so neat to see you both together at last," she said happily. "I'm doing fine. The doctor said I could get out tomorrow. I can't wait to spend time with you both exploring this island."

Seeing Crank nod and smile, the boys relaxed. Grinning from ear to ear, they hugged her and told her about today's exploits, including snorkeling, swimming, and a school tour. Halting the boy's storytelling, Crank gently pulled them from Sunny's bedside. "Okay, chatterboxes. Let's give the rest of the family a chance to talk." Smiling, he steered the boys toward the door and the waiting guard. "It's time for your school field trip; since it's whale watching, I don't think you want to miss it."

After the door closed on the excited boys, the rest of Sunny's family hugged her and sat down. They were all talking excitedly when Sunny suddenly exclaimed, "I forgot about Ken!" She looked at Matt and missed Crank's narrowed eyes.

"He's fine. He's debriefing the staff right now but said he will be down to see you after supper," said Matt. "He's decided to retire here and won't be going back to the FBI. Says he's worked hard and deserves paradise."

Smiling gently, she said, "So he won't tell anyone about the island. I knew he was a good man right from the first. He worked with us when anyone else would have thought we were crazy. He's right. He deserves paradise, and I'm so glad he will stay."

Matt smiled at Crank's sour look and clapped him on the shoulder. "We all are, honey. Aren't we, Crank?" His smile widened at the look he got from Crank.

Later that day, she awoke from a nap and saw Ken sitting quietly and looking out the window. With the sheets rustling, she sat up slowly. She still had a slight headache and was subject to dizziness if she moved too quickly.

"What are you thinking about?" she said, smiling at the agent.

Shaking his head, he approached the bed.

"Just going over the whole story from start to finish. It's such an incredible story. Someone ought to write about it... have to be a fiction novel. No one would believe it."

"I want to thank you, Ken, for not telling the FBI about our island and for believing Matt and me when we first met you on Tybee Island. The story was farfetched, to say the least, but you kept an open mind."

Sitting down in the bedside chair, he leaned forward and smiled gently.

"No. Thank you! Because you were determined to locate your sister's child, the FBI knows much more about Bolo's organization. Chief is with Crank's dad now. They will be weeding out her plants in the organization. Someone will talk. It's only a matter of time before we break up the whole ring."

Gently taking her hand, he said, "You've helped not only your sister's child but possibly a thousand others and…"

"Is there a particular reason you are holding my fiancée's hand, Ables?" came a growl from the doorway.

Startled, she looked at the doorway and saw a whole different Crank, not a happy-looking one. A hand-tailored silver-grey suit lovingly clung to every muscle. Shiny Italian shoes completed the look.

Chuckling, Ken stood up and shook hands with his old friend.

"Fiancée…? Now that's news to me. When did that happen?"

"Yes, Crank," interjected Sunny, "when did that happen? I know I had a concussion and might have forgotten you asked me, but I doubt…"

Crank jerked his thumb toward the door, indicating that Ken should leave. Ken looked down at Sunny, smiling.

"Have you noticed the man has no sense of humor? The whole agency used to talk about it. All this time in paradise should have sweetened him up some."

Hearing the growl behind him, he smiled and stepped around a glowering Crank to the doorway, throwing "Congratulations" over his shoulder.

Seeing her love's discomfort, she smiled and patted the side of the bed.

"Do you have something to ask me?" she said softly.

Looking into her eyes, he saw the depth of her feelings and smiled, drawing a small box out of his pocket. Taking a deep breath, he started to speak. "Sunny, I know we haven't known each other long...and for a lot of it, we were yelling at each other..."

"Or you were bossing me around," she interrupted.

"Yeah," he agreed, looking uncomfortable. "I want to say that won't happen again, but if it comes to your safety or the kids..."

Gently covering his large hand with her much smaller one, she said, "I know that. I depend on that. I dreamed of a silver haired man riding a white horse along the beach. I instinctively knew he would care for me and our family."

"I have to be honest," he said. "I never saw myself as a married man, much less a father. FBI agents have a hard time with relationships. We're gone for long periods. It's rough on the family. But that part of my life is over. Of course, when a child needs saving, I will be away for a few days. You would need to know that upfront..." Seeing Sunny's smiling nod, he continued. "I want the boys and you with me...here on the island. You would have to get out a story of relocating to another country since no one can know about the island. I know it's a lot to ask, but it must be done."

Looking at his strong, handsome face filled with character and integrity, she again nodded.

Slowly opening the little black box lid, he pulled out a gorgeous three-carat emerald and gently pushed it onto her ring finger.

Sunny gasped at the shining beauty of the jewel. It was perfect.

Still holding her hand, Crank looked searchingly into her eyes.

"I love you, Sunny. I don't know how to explain it. I have never felt this before, but I know what I feel for you has always been there waiting for us to meet. Let me be your protector on the white horse."

Speechless at the beauty of his offering and with tears streaming down her face, Sunny nodded and went into his arms. There was absolute quiet in the room for a long time.

Two weeks later, Sunny strolled down the path to the beach. The full moon shone, making her white sundress glow in the dark. Silky hair gently brushed her shoulders. Ahead, she could see the glow of the torches and hear the laughter of the people gathered by the sea, awaiting the happy couple. Tonight was to be Sunny and Crank's engagement party.

She stopped when she saw Crank standing on the path, resplendent in a white tropical suit. In two weeks, they would marry and begin their life on the island, working together to protect children worldwide. Chief was retiring and would live on the island, fishing and enjoying life. He and Sunny's mother had been spending a lot of time together. Ken had been appointed as the security officer, and Matt would make the island his home base. Her friend, Jackie, promised to consider joining the school as a nurse and health educator.

Crank watched her for a long moment, seemingly without words. Then, he strode to her in a few quick steps and wrapped his arms around her. Their kiss was long and sensual, and momentarily, she thought of their wedding night. Finally, they pulled apart and, hand in hand, padded barefoot toward the sound of native drums. On the beach, tiki torches illuminated the faces of their family and island friends. The Embera natives wore beautifully beaded clothing usually reserved for feast days. Huge tables laden with food and drink indicated this was a VIP party.

Moving in for one last kiss, Crank nuzzled her ear and said teasingly, "We have inherited a large family from your sister, my love. Counting the ones you and I will have, we might need our own island."

Sunny smiled, squeezed his hand, and led her hero toward their family and friends.

Thank You to My Readers

I want to express my heartfelt gratitude to everyone who has taken the time to leave a review of this book on Amazon. Your words not only mean the world to me but also help other readers discover my work. Reviews are a powerful way to support authors, and I'm so thankful for every thoughtful comment, star rating, and recommendation you share. You make this journey possible, and for that, I am forever grateful.

With appreciation, Wren.